POPULAR PUBLICATIONS · FACSIMILE EDITIONS

Terror Tales #4 (December 1934)

Starting in 1934, editor (and publisher) Harry Steeger unveiled *Terror Tales*: perhaps the flagship magazine in Popular Publications' so-called "Weird Menace" lineup of titles. Running for almost 50 issues, *Terror Tales* showcased some of the best suspense, mystery and terror stories to see print in the pulps. This facsimile of the December 1934 issue contains stories by Arthur Leo Zagat, G.T. Fleming-Roberts, Wyatt Blassingame, John H. Knox, and Laurence Donovan, among others.

Authors:

Arthur Leo Zagat, G.T. Fleming-Roberts, Wyatt Blassingame, Frances Bragg Middleton, Laurence Donovan, John H. Knox, H.M. Appel

Illustrators:

John Newton Howitt, Amos Sewell

TERROR TALES

Volume One   December, 1934   Number Four

Cover Painting by John Howitt
Story Illustrations by Amos Sewell

Published every month by Popular Publications, Inc., 2256 Grove Street, Chicago, Illinois. Editorial and executive offices, 205 East Forty-second Street, New York City. Harry Steeger, President and Secretary, Harold S. Goldsmith, Vice President and Treasurer. Entry as second-class matter pending at the post office at Chicago, Ill., under the Act of March 3, 1879. Title registration pending at U. S. Patent Office. Copyright, 1934, by Popular Publications, Inc. Single copy price 15c. Yearly subscriptions in U. S. A. $1.50. For advertising rates address Sam J. Perry, 205 E. 42nd St., New York, N. Y. When submitting manuscripts kindly enclose stamped self-addressed envelope for their return if found unavailable. The publishers cannot accept responsibility for return of unsolicited manuscripts, although care will be exercised in handling them.

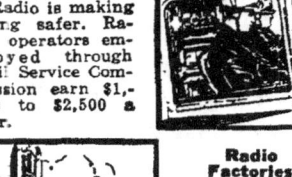

3

5

6

WHAT *will you be doing* ONE YEAR *from today?*

THREE hundred and sixty-five days from now — what?

Will you still be struggling along in the same old job at the same old salary — worried about the future — never quite able to make both ends meet?

One year from today will you still be putting off your start toward success — thrilled with ambition one moment and then cold the next — delaying, waiting, fiddling away the precious hours that will never come again?

Don't do it, man — don't do it.

There is no greater tragedy in the world than that of a man who stays in the rut all his life, when with just a little effort he could advance.

Make up your mind today that you're going to train yourself to do some one thing well. Choose the work you like best in the list below, mark an X beside it, and without cost or obligation, at least get the full story of what the I. C. S. can do for you.

Swamp Madness

By
Laurence Donovan

Complete Mystery-Terror Novel

The Thing that came out of the swamp had once been a man—until it took the death walk. . . . Now it shrieked madly, its skeleton body jumping from colored pavement square to pavement square, its hollow eyes seeing only things that were not there.

HIGH noon in Miami. Cloudless sun flooding the city street. Hundreds of happy, hurrying feet. Oblong, colored squares of pavement resounding to the thudding tramp and patter. Traffic with the hissing of tires. The carved facade of the Arcade Building bathed in sunlight above.

Girl office-workers hurrying to lunch.

Gay greetings. Musical and carefree laughter. Men's hearty, "Hiya, Bill!" " 'Lo, Joe!" Important shrill of a corner traffic whistle. Cool, caressing breeze off Biscayne Bay and the ocean beyond.

A girl's merry laugh froze in her constricted throat. It took on the high, terror-filled note of a scream. Seeing the thing that she had seen, the crowd paused.

Another woman shrieked and fell, pitching forward on her face. The hands of an automobile driver went stiff with horror and his car ploughed into the back of a truck.

A big green sedan with the curtains closely drawn purred swiftly past the crash-jam. A girl of slender, lithesome grace, the exquisitely lovely features of a patrician family and jeweled white hands, swayed on the curb at the edge of the

9

sidewalk. Her vivid lips moved soundlessly and her white hands fluttered upward to shut out the Thing from her wide, horror-filled eyes.

Then the crowd screamed! Screamed with the mingling discordance of men's shocked, strangled curses and women's awful shrieks of fear! They rolled back against the white-tiled front of the Arcade Building—to make way for the leaping, gibbering, horrible Thing. Only the women whose blood-drained brains gave them the respite of unconsciousnesss remained in its path, but they were only huddled figures in brightly dressed lumps, lying on the colored squares of the sidewalk paving.

The Thing gave them no heed. It leaped over them from paving square to paving square, its gaunt, toothless, skulllike face twisted on a neck so thin and long it seemed mummified. Eyes in the sunken, bony sockets were rolling in white-balled terror. Thus the Thing went leaping, always looking back, always looking down, but never touching a line which separated one colored square of paving from another.

The crowd scream rose to a madness of inharmonious sound. Then it died for a moment on drying tongues. A little girl on the edge of the throng pulled with her small, futile hands at the clothes of a woman who had fainted and lay directly in the pathway of the leaping Thing.

"Mama! Mama! Get up, Mama! Betty's scared!"

As if the child's piping voice had aroused her from a trancelike stupor, the lovely girl with the fluttering white hands moved after the leaping monstrosity on the sidewalk squares.

"Arthur! Arthur? Oh, my God! It can't be! Arthur!"

In the cleared space through which the Thing was passing, the girl walked, groping with her slim hands as if she must reach this fantastic apparition that must once have been a man, yet shuddering as if she dared not touch, dared not believe this could be true.

"Arthur! Wait! Oh, I'm coming to you! I must!"

The frenzied cry was wrung from her soul. Men with bloodless faces heard it and forgot to curse, watching. Women, shrinking, beginning to scurry away as the paralysis of terror slowly left their limbs, halted again to see this sweet-faced girl walking thus toward the Thing.

"Zona Van Zandt!" breathed a man in a hoarse guttural. "Good God, Bill! You hear? It's the Van Zandt twin! She said, 'Arthur!' You don't think it could be him—her brother?"

Zona Van Zandt moved forward on legs as stiff and cold as icicles. Now the leaping Thing apparently saw her coming. Before its drawn slash of a mouth had only slobbered and gibbered; now a rasping, unearthly scream tore from the mummied throat.

"Go back—go back! They're there—on that square—they'll strike. Damn you! Go back! You're one of them! You've got a woman's face, but your tongue is red and long! Go back! Go back! Go Back! . . ."

The warning of the hideous voice wailed then to nothingness.

"Oh, God! It's you—Arthur!"

THE girl sprang forward, sought to overtake the slatted, knobby figure. And it struck at her—struck with the awful stub of an arm that had been sheered off at the elbow—struck at her again with the stub of the other arm.

It struck at the girl again and again. Yet always it looked down, always it leaped from one colored square to another as if they were red-hot under the bare feet. Yet the girl's white hand reached to the Thing's shoulder, pulling the figure around, unheeding the stub of an arm that bloodied her lips.

Across the breast of the naked skeleton of a man were two crossed swords, a small tattooed design in red and blue. And seeing this Zona Van Zandt screamed for the first time. Screamed and screamed again. For she knew now without doubt that the hideous figure that had been a man was indeed her brother.

Sportsman, polo player, yachtsman, idol of an exclusive social set because of his cleverness, his wit and his clean handsomeness. Son of the multi-millionaire oil man, Howard Van Zandt. That was the Arthur Van Zandt of yesterday, of a month ago.

Zona Van Zandt's fluttering hands tore at the flimsy, silken garment which formed a summer cape for her frock. It came away, ripping with it the upper part of her dress, exposing the lovely white shoulders. She tried to cover with it the nude, skeleton-like figure of the Thing that was her brother.

He leaped away from her, burning insanity in the sunken eyes.

"You're one of 'em!" he screamed. The crowd shivered and recoiled from the cackling horror of his voice. "You've a woman's face, but your tongue is long and red! Go back! Go back! They're on that square! No! The next square!"

"Oh, somebody help me! Somebody help!"

The girl's plea was a whisper, but the hushed, awe-filled crowd heard it. A dozen men started forward. In their hearts was fear and sickness, though they knew now that this naked, leaping monstrosity had been the idolized Arthur Van Zandt who but weeks before had led his polo team to victory over the Army.

The nude skeleton gibbered and screamed and struck at the men who surrounded him. Struck as best he could with his handless elbows. The crowd

rolled away in a wave, and another wave surged forward, then turned away shivering when it had seen. The traffic policeman's whistle shrilled closer and the cop's white-shirted shoulders pushed through the crowd.

"Whatisit? Whatisit?" he demanded. "Hey! Yuh can't be runnin' around the likes o' that!"

Now Arthur Van Zandt was in the hands of men who held him firmly. He strained and tried to push himself to another sidewalk square with his bony feet, screaming again and again, "They're there! They're comin! Don't let a woman's face fool you if she's got a long red tongue!"

Zona Van Zandt's slender white hands lifted as if in supplication, twisting above her bright blonde hair, forming a pattern of despair. She did not know her white shoulders and breasts had been bared by her frantic effort to shield her brother from the gaze of the crowd.

The traffic policeman shrilled on his whistle. He caught Arthur Van Zandt, easing him to the burning sidewalk. Merciful weakness had come at last to this carved remnant of a man. Blind unconsciousness shut out whatever horror had sent him leaping from pavement square to pavement square.

A tall, red-haired young man pushed through the throng to the policeman's side. He was Pete Carson from the New York *Blade,* and he had come flying down to Miami when the first word of the Van Zandt kidnaping had leaked out. Until this minute he had gotten nowhere on the story. He had not even been lucky enough to get a word with Zona Van Zandt, though he knew her from the dozens of published photographs.

"What the hell's it about?" he growled to the traffic officer. Then he saw the girl.

THE men had thrown coats over Arthur Van Zandt's shriveled, mutilated body as it lay on the sidewalk. Pete ruthlessly pulled a coat aside. Hard-boiled as he was, he shuddered and wished he hadn't.

A police siren was wailing clearance into the Arcade Building Square. Pete looked into the eyes of Zona Van Zandt.

Abruptly he pushed forward and got one lanky arm around her shoulders, flipping his raincoat across her arms. The fixity of the pupils in her wide eyes had told him that unless someone provided swift diversion, gave the girl some sudden relaxation, she too in a moment would be running and screaming.

Already she was murmuring, and it sounded as if her mind had snapped. She was seeing no one, nothing. Pete could tell that. The spell that held her must be broken or this flash of temporary insanity might well become permanent.

A police car pulled up to the curb. The traffic officer was issuing a profane order to the crowd.

"Come away," said Pete, holding the girl's arm, propelling her gently forward. "They'll do all that can be done. Come inside here. You've got to talk. You tell me what has happened."

His voice was kind. This was a story, a big story, but just now he wasn't seeking that. The dam holding back Zona Van Zandt's tortured, agonized emotions must be broken or there would be insanity.

She did not resist as he led her across the sidewalk, through an open doorway. They were in a real estate office. The owner, half comprehending, pushed back the curious and closed the door.

"You've got to talk, to help yourself—to help him, your brother," Pete Carson said quickly. "Tell me what happened."

Gently he wiped blood from the girl's lips. His hand passed close before her face, but her eyes did not flicker.

"My baby brother," she murmured dully. "Arthur! Oh, God! Now I remember. They said to bring the money in front of the Arcade Building at noon.

"I brought the hundred thousand in a package. I didn't tell anyone. I was afraid. They've got Zola, my sister—my father—God! Who are you? Are you one of them?"

Zona Van Zandt seemed to see Pete Carson for the first time. She uttered a little scream and choked it with the back of her hand. Her eyes closed and her body grew cold and rigid. Pete caught her before she fell.

"Thank God for that," he said. "Call a doctor. This'll save her mind."

The real estate man called a doctor. He came back then to the front of the office. He was a little gray man and now his face was ashen.

"It was the most awful thing I ever saw," he said. "I noticed the girl here standing at the edge of the walk. A big green sedan drove up. A man's hand pulled back the curtain. She gave him a package.

"Then the car started so suddenly it almost knocked her down. This—well!—the naked man—her brother, they say—he'd been pushed out of the other side of the car. He jumped to the sidewalk and started leaping and looking back.

"God, man! It was terrible!"

Pete Carson had a duty to his newspaper, but just now he saw another duty. He got on the telephone, but he kept his eyes on the girl's face.

The doctor came in. Under a hypodermic the girl revived, opened her eyes.

Pete breathed with relief. Deep pain was there, but not madness.

CHAPTER TWO

Into the Swamp

FROGS croaked a guttural chorus in the swamps hedging in the little river. The stream was hardly more than a twisting line of ink under the red Everglades moon. The chugging launch brushed the thick-growing mangrove bushes and palmetto fronds in the dark, narrow bends.

From where he stood at the boat's pilot wheel, Pete Carson could see down into the small cabin. His strong hands itched suddenly to be at the throat of the hunched, angular figure in the long black coat, that occupied a bench in the cabin.

More than itched, for the ghostly oppressiveness of the Big Cypress swamp filled Pete with dire foreboding. Now that he had succeeded in making this strange contact with Homer Severn, the noted criminal lawyer, and was acting as his guide in the Big Cypress, Pete Carson felt that he was going straight into a trap.

Severn hadn't been friendly, and his small eyes were baleful. They seemed smaller now beside his hatchet-like nose; and the whole face was made more malevolent by the rat-trap mouth with its thin lips. Yet Zona Van Zandt had been compelled to thrust the lawyer as her go-between. Notorious as he was for his criminal clientele, there had been no other way.

Draping Spanish moss vaulted the Stygian river into a tomblike tunnel. Pete looked closely at the crude map under the binnacle light beside the wheel. Without it he never would have attempted to pilot this boat into the heart of the big swamp, that afford only hunting and fishing grounds for the last of the Seminoles.

On a short straight stretch of the little river, Pete glanced again at his passenger, at the black satchel he held between his feet. He knew the satchel contained $500,-000 in currency. The ratlike lawyer had somehow established contact with the monstrous kidnapers who had sent Arthur Van Zandt back to Miami mutilated and insane. Now he was carrying the ransom for Howard Van Zandt and his daughter, Zola.

Pete smiled grimly as he wondered what Severn would do if he discovered his supposed guide to be Pete Carson, newspaper sleuth, instead of Porter, the stupid fisherman he had appeared to be when hired at Estero. And what would happen when he discovered that this Arturo Cabana, who called himself a foreign nobleman, a suitor for the hand of Zona Van Zandt, had obtained possession of the mapped route to the kidnapers' lair long enough to make a copy?

Half consciously, Pete fingered the automatic concealed beneath the waistband of his dirty cotton slacks. . . .

A high, weird cry rang over the swamp. Deep, chugging noises sounded above the *put-put* of the boat's exhaust. Carson shivered involuntarily. The plunge of alligators into the black ooze of the swamp brought back the picture of Arthur Van Zandt and his mutilated arms. . . .

The launch left the winding river and seemed abruptly to be suspended over a black, bottomless void, with only the ghostly palmettoes of the Everglade swamp against the sky. A squawling, unearthly cry floated over the water. Pete had been warned that the big swamp was alive with wildcat and panther. It was said that the inky depths of its waters concealed even worse than the huge alligators and the poisonous moccasins. Old fishermen at Estero, where Pete had made his contact with the go-between lawyer, hinted at scaly antediluvian monsters still living in Big Cypress.

Under the glare of the Florida sun, as he had plotted with Cabana and Zona Van Zandt to become the fishermen guide for Severn into the kidnapers' hideout, these stories had seemed fantastic. Tonight, with the eerie cries of big swamp birds around him and the ink of the water an impenetrable refuge for slimy, mysterious reptile life, the yarns were not so unconvincing.

Severn stuck his head out of the cabin. His snaggy teeth made his rat-trap mouth almost a disfigurement. He spoke with a whining inflection.

"You sure you can follow that map, Porter?"

"I've been fishin' the water of this big ol' swamp nigh ten years," Pete drawled. "If you-all just make yo'self easy, I reckon we'll be comin' to the place that's marked along midnight. You-all can make it back to Estero before daylight."

Severn came out and looked around. He nodded, apparently satisfied that Pete was a fisherman who knew his business. Seemingly he did not suspect that Pete had made but two trips into Big Cypress, and was having great difficulty now in picking out the channels and hummocks plainly marked on the map.

ONE thing alone cheered the newshound. Cabana was somewhere not far behind. Zona Van Zandt's friend had said he would form a sheriff's posse and follow his own map in, close behind Pete and Severn.

Pete glanced along the wake of the launch as the boat again entered a tunnellike channel roofed by knotted, snakelike vines. No light of any kind was showing. He shrugged his shoulders. Hell! Cabana and the sheriff's men naturally would have sense enough to remain out of Severn's sight. They would want him to make a direct contact with the kidnapers before they descended on the hideout.

Zona Van Zandt had been against even this. The girl was worth several millions by her mother's will, and would have parted with her last dollar to insure the safety of her twin sister Zola and her father.

As the launch glided over the murky depths of the Big Cypress and the mangrove growth of the last salt water was replaced by the giant cypress with the crooked knees, Pete's worries increased. He began to believe he was lost. Worst of all, Cabana would have hired a real fishing guide and would be following his copy of the map faithfully. Pete Carson was truly embarked on a mad adventure, with scant hope of success.

Zona Van Zandt had done that to him. She had accompanied him and Cabana as far as Sarasota on the upper side of the Everglades. Cabana had insisted she remain there. It was Cabana's idea that Pete Carson play the role of a fisherman, procure a launch and transport the ratty Severn to his rendezvous with the Big Cypress snatchers.

What was that on the water ahead? The huge knees of the cypress projected into the swamp channel like the limbs of once human mammoths. A long log lay across the narrow channel. Pete slowed the motor, threw the propeller into reverse.

The log seemed to slit open from one end, to almost half its length. A horrible fanged aperture, red and white, appeared. The thing that had seemed to be a log rolled over and sunk with a gurgling sound. The old alligator must have been all of fifteen feet long. A thousand years old.

Severn poked out his hatchet face from below. "What're you stopping for?" he rasped. "You said it'd take four hours. We've only been gone two."

"Just runin' round a big ol' mud bank," Pete drawled.

He had quit consulting the map. In that tangle of cypress knees and serpentine vines which seemed to sway with sinister life, he had lost all sense of direction. He knew he must have lost the following Cabana and the sheriff's men.

But Pete would not tell Severn they were lost. Not yet. For somewhere in

Big Cypress was the torture house. Somehow tonight's rendezvous must be kept. The kidnapers would be looking for them. They should hear the launch or see its lights. After that, if Cabana and his posse failed to arrive—well, at least he could find out a few things.

Severn was looking up at him with beady eyes. The lawyer couldn't tell Pete was observing him. Severn's tongue licked his thin lips. He reached inside his coat and a small tube gleamed for an instant in his hand. He was looking at Pete's legs, all he could see by the cabin lights.

The newspaperman's muscles tensed. He read the truth in that look. It was in the crooked smile across the rat-trap mouth. Howard Van Zandt and his daughter, Zola, might be returned in exchange for that half million, but it was clearly intended that one supposed fisherman from Estero should disappear.

Who would know? The launch would be burned or sunk. What was a fisherman more or less?

Was it only dope, or some deadly poison in the syringe Severn had returned to his pocket?

Pete slowed the motor and listened. Not the faintest sound of a following boat could be heard. A whippoorwill whistled its death note. Another log gaped cavernously at one end, and slowly sank into the oozy depths. What a hell of a place this would be for a sudden dive.

Common sense suggested to Pete that he crack down right now on this crook lawyer and turn around. Get out of the Big Cypress. . . . He thought of the maimed Arthur Van Zandt with the light of reason forever gone from his burning, sunken eyes. There had been queer blue perforations on the mutilated maniac's legs. That syringe Severn carried . . . Had it been something like that?

Yet Zona Van Zandt had said, "I'll be waiting right here, Pete Carson. Waiting for my sister and my father. You're the best friend I've ever had."

The girl's word had brought a brief scowl on Cabana's dark face, but at once he had smiled goodnaturedly.

He had said, "Certainly, Pete Carson is one fine chap."

No, he couldn't let them down. Zona Van Zandt's own sanity might depend upon the success of this venture. Her reason hung on the slender thread of a crooked lawyer's doubtful promise. Pete had to see that Severn kept his pledge. . . .

Pete started. The boat containing three men was so flat on the dark water that it had come from between the big cypress knees and bumped the slowly moving launch before he saw it. Pete sprang from the pilot wheel, shutting off the motor. The automatic whipped into his hand. He hardly realized he was fully revealed in the light from the oil lamp in the cabin.

"Drop the rod!" snarled one of the men in the boat. "Don't be so damn sudden or you'll get blasted! You got a passenger, mug?"

The hollow twin tubes of a sawed-off shotgun was punched over the rail of the launch into Pete's belly. The man holding it had a scarred chin and a nose so flat that his face seemed only glittering eyes and the slant of a snarling mouth.

"Talk up, guy! Severn 'long with yuh?"

"Hello, Smiler!" came the lawyer's voice. "Who've you got with you? I was thinking maybe this dumb cracker couldn't follow the map! Everything's okeh! Come on up!"

SMILER RAWLINGS! He had been out of New York more than a year, Pete remembered. The Smiler had laid too wide a path with a chopping-gun and killed several bystanders. He had been reported in South America, then in Europe. Up the river at home they were keeping a chair hot for him.

One of the other men Severn addressed as Weasel. His pinched face and dilated pupils gave the reason. Severn called the other squat, hook-nosed hoodlum by the name of Joe. They tied the flatboat they had been poling and clumped onto the deck of the launch.

Pete had dropped his automatic. He was standing barefooted and unarmed. Smiler's gash of a mouth leered at him.

"Think you'd know us again if you saw us somewhere, huh? Don't let it worry you, mug! You won't be talkin'! Run this boat where Joe says!"

Joe pushed the shotgun with vicious emphasis into Pete's back. Smiler stooped his way into the little cabin and Weasel followed.

"Swing it to the right round that next bunch of cypress," Joe growled. "An' don't move sudden or nothin'. I got the shakes an' this blaster might go off."

Peter strained his ears vainly to catch the sound of some following boat. The whippoorwill's death whistle was all he heard. A swamp mist was fogging the moon. He turned the launch into the black water of the channel Joe indicated.

"You brought all the dough, huh?" rasped Smiler's voice in the cabin. "What a take!"

Severn's rat-trap mouth was a-grin.

"It's all there, more'n you ever saw before, Smiler! I held out my fifty grand."

Smiler's teeth clicked ominously.

"You held out—say! You was to bring the whole take here an' get your split! Who's runnin' this show?"

Pete's eyes, unknown to the guard, were following the tableau. Severn seemed unperturbed. His mouth sneered thinly.

"You aren't, Smiler. There's $450,000 and it isn't marked! You're still taking orders from the boss!"

Smiler's smile was deadly with hate.

"Four hundred an' fifty grand! Chee! An' you think you know all about the chief's orders, huh? Okeh, Weasel!"

The Weasel's eyes were round and green as a cat's. His slender hands were quick and strong as steel. Abruptly his fingers imprisoned Severn's wrists.

The lawyer's angular figure writhed with pain. He rapped out a curse and then—"You damn fools! What d'you think you're doing? The boss'll—"

Smiler's big head gave a jerking nod. Severn saw it and screamed.

"No! No! Smiler, for God's sake! You gone crazy? You can't do this to me—you can't—"

Smiler slashed the back of his hand across the lawyer's mouth. The thin lips split and blood trickled over his chin.

Severn gurgled. "The chief'll get you for—"

"Chief's orders!" snapped the Smiler. "We'd figured maybe he'd let us give y' the death walk, but he said no. See what y' missed! With you it'll all be over quick, only—Weasel!"

Pete's eyes bulged. He dropped one hand from the pilot wheel.

"Hold it!" Joe growled. The shotgun scraped the skin from Pete's ribs. "Y'll see what's comin' to yuh, guy!"

One of the Weasel's hand slipped from Severn's wrist. The lawyer's beady eyes popped as if on strings. He screamed another plea, but it was cut short as the Weasel's hand went up and snapped down. Pete could hear the sickening thud of the blow. Severn gasped and went limp.

"The works!" said Smiler. "It'd be better maybe if he was found hangin' onto one of them cypress roots an' the boat was sunk where it'd be found. Neat an' natural! That's me!"

From the Weasel's pocket came a shining tube of silver glass. He sank the needle at its end deep into Severn's neck.

The lawyer's body twitched, though he was but half conscious.

As the syringe was jerked out, the lawyer reared upon his skinny legs. His little eyes seemed to bug past the ridge of his hatchet nose. With an animal scream he sprang toward the little door of the cabin.

The horror Pete saw spreading over the man's face tore his hands from the wheel. With a spring he jerked himself to one side. The shotgun in Joe's hands belched. The shock and heat of the charge seared the flesh over Pete's thigh, but he came up with one knee and a flying fist. Joe streached out, the other barrel of the shotgun roaring into the sky.

Severn plunged out onto the deck.

"Get 'em, Weasel!" Smiler rapped.

But the lawyer had dived blindly for the rail. His angular figure went flying over the inky water. Pete had a glimpse of the body striking across two bent knees of cypress, hanging there.

The screams coming from Severn's throat were as hoarse and animal-like as those of a pig in which the knife has been stuck. The lawyer was lying with his face turned up to the Everglades moon. The pilotless launch was swinging. Its bow rammed into a palmetto hummock.

Before Pete's horrified eyes two apparent logs floated suddenly to the surface. The strong, deathly odor of animal musk assailed his nostrils.

Joe scrambled to his feet. The Weasel had whipped out a gun and was aiming it. But Smiler struck up his arm.

"You damn fool!" he roared. "They all get the same dose! Give 'im the swamp poison!"

Pete hurled himself forward, striking at Smiler's flat face. The blow registered. But a blackjack in the Weasel's fast hand smacked across his ear. Pete felt himself sinking, going to his knees.

The tube of silver glass flashed toward his neck. The rodent eyes of the Weasel bored into him. Pete came up with a headlong rush that caught the Weasel in the pit of the stomach. The syringe needle grazed his neck as he went over the rail of the launch.

CHAPTER THREE

The Swamp Poison

WEEDY muck clogged Pete Carson's mouth and nose. Trailing water tendrils with the slimy feel of snakes' bodies enwrapped his neck. Something slithered along his side and his arm was rasped as if by a rough file.

He strangled with the sudden impulse to cry out. He was in the bottom ooze of Big Cypress with feet of inky water of his head. Again his arm and shoulder were rasped by that scaly, file-like body. Above him he could feel the whirling suck of the disturbed water as a long body passed him.

Though his lungs threatened to crack his ribs and his throat was a constricted tube through which it seemed breath never again would be drawn, Pete fought his way along the bottom, feeling the best he could toward where he judged the knees of the cypress trees projected. God! That scaly, rough skin rubbing again, this time with the whip of a tail that drove with cruel force across his back.

The blow brought a gasp. Filthy ooze poured into his throat. Choking, strangling, he struck out blindly with his fists, though he realized the senselessness of the action. A flame danced in his brain. Queer thoughts raced through his mind as the certainty came to him that this was the finish.

Why had they given the needle to Severn? Swamp poison? Why put him on the cypress knees where the dying crook lawyer had put himself? Why sink the launch?

This Smiler wanted his body found, poisoned. Poisoned with swamp poison! What was that?

Had Cabana been able to follow his copy of the map? Would the sheriff's men arrive before Smiler and his killers again vanished in the depth of Big Cypress?

Most important of all, would Zona Van Zandt think he had failed her?

A vision of the tortured eyes of the girl, as the Thing that had been her brother leaped the colored squares of a Miami street, came into Pete's mind. It spurred him to a last despairing access of strength. With hands and feet he fought the clinging, slimy weeds, struck out futilely with his fists at the long scaly body which seemed continually to be circling around him.

His senses all but failed him. He had reached the point where power of the will could no longer fight the tearing impulse of his agonized lungs to draw in deeply, to gulp for air—and fill his body with the mucky water. Knife-like pains darted through his stomach, writhed with burning torture around his laboring heart.

His fist struck something solid. Drowning, he laughed, and the ooze and water gagged his mouth shut once more. This time it was not the sinister, scaly log with its whipping tail and gaping mouth. It was the substantial, knuckle-bruising bend of a cypress knee.

Somehow he managed to pull himself under it, and then on up.

His body was shielded by a tangle of the roots. The swamp's miasmic air was the sweetest breath he had ever had. Though he retched with illness from the foulness of the weeds and muck he had swallowed, he forced himself to remain motionless, listening.

His vision cleared. Men's voices came faintly, swelled to growls, arose to ribald oaths.

"They say they never come up." It was Smiler talking. "That's one smart mug'll decorate the inside of a 'gator's belly! We're sinking the damned launch right here alongside these cypress knees, see. Maybe you'd better pull the plug an' then set 'er on fire! Neat an' natural! That's me! They'll find the mouthpiece drapin' the roots over there an' the burned boat over here! Swell idea!"

Pete clutched at the slippery bends of the cypress. He scarcely dared to breathe. His straining ears could not catch the sound of any other boat. What happened to Cabana?

Hell! Unless he had a guide who knew every twist of the devious channels, Cabana by this time would be hopelessly lost. And when he went out, Zona Van Zandt's admirer could only carry to her the word that they had failed.

That Pete Carson had failed. . . .

MISERABLY sick, Pete got a grip on himself. This whole thing had been some sort of ghastly trick. Severn, the thieving go-between lawyer, had been tricked as well as the others, and done horribly to his death. Clearly Smiler had no intention of accepting the fortune in his hands as a ransom.

The former big city hoodlum had become a slimy killer—worse, a torturer. It struck Pete with sickening force that Smiler and his mob probably never could be smoked out of Big Cypress. They would get all of the Van Zandt fortune before they quit, and then . . .

Smiler's sudden loud ribaldry was demoniac in its implication.

"Neat an' natural!" he shouted. "That's me! Next we'll have the little dame take the death walk, eh Weasel! Won't that be sweet? Walkin' an' walkin'! Tearin' off her clothes! Squealin' an' laughin' like her brother laughed! Only you won't cut off her arms, Weasel! Uh-uh . . . After she's walked an' walked, I've got other ideas! Can't you see her now when we turn on the juice! We'll—listen! What's that?"

Through the swamp water came the evenly spaced thudding of little blows. The thumping fell into a steady rhythm. Smiler cursed loudly.

"Hey!" he shouted. "It's some trick! That's another boat sure as hell! Severn was being followed! The dirty, lowdown double-crosser, if I had him here—Joe! Pull that plug! Here, wait! Get into the flatboat. Spill that can of gas. Got that plug? Okeh, Joe! Touch 'er off! The fire'll pull 'em over here! We'll go back across the south bayou!"

Pete restrained the impulse to climb on the roots and hurl himself upon the foul-mouthed Smiler. Unharmed and sick, he was helpless. But the boats were coming. Cabana and the sheriff's men would soon be here. If he could only discover some way to follow the killers' boat, or to make certain the direction it took. . . .

A whiffing explosion was followed by a flare of light. The upper works of the launch stood out gauntly in a wreathing blast of flame. The boat was half hull down in the water. With a roar the fuel tank let go and spread the blazing fluid for yards around. The liquid fire poured over the cypress roots where Pete was holding on, only his mouth and nose above the surface.

Taking a long breath, Pete went under, but not quickly enough to avoid the searing sting of the flaming gasoline. When he tried to come up, he was forced to let go of the roots and swim under water to escape the floating blaze.

When he emerged at last, he was too far away to determine the direction taken by Smiler and his men. Their voices sounded faintly in the distance, but Pete had lost all sense of the compass points.

Smiler's malelovent laughter came again, was moving away. Pete's teeth gritted. The death walk? The little dame would be next? God! Did they mean like Arthur Van Zandt? Would she be brought back to Miami to become a leaping Thing in a horror-stricken noonday crowd?

The launch was sinking, the flame dying quickly. Pete pulled himself around the cypress roots. The exhaust of the approaching boat sounded closer. He saw a man's legs hanging down, draped over one of the big cypress knees close beside him. They moved slowly back and forth, as if the man were walking.

The head and face of Severn, the lawyer, swayed on a swinging vine. The head seemed swollen to twice its normal size. The beady eyes, even the hatchet nose, had disappeared in what now was only a great purple and black balloon-like bulb.

The humid heat of the swamp mist bathed the naked upper half of Pete's torso with beaded perspiration. As he stared at the bloated, discolored ball that had been Severn's head and face, the sweat enswathed him with a film of ice. His nerves for a moment seemed stricken with shuddering paralysis.

The mournful cry of a whippoorwill sounded to his tortured senses like the shriek of damned souls. Only by tremendous force of will, by remembrance of the horror he had helped to shake from the brain of Zona Van Zandt, did he succeed in moving. Severn's head was an enormity. That crafty, cruel brain must now be distended in his death to the bursting point.

Pete dragged himself upon the cypress knees. The faint harsh oaths and foul laughter of Smiler Rawlings had died away. The thumping rhythm along the black water was coming closer. Pete diverted his own brain from madness by a frenzy of action.

Severn's body was slowly slipping from the cypress knees, moved horribly by its own swelling. Pete recalled the moment in the cabin when Severn had taken the gleaming syringe from his pocket. Averting his eyes from the awful face, he thrust his hand into the dead lawyer's inside pocket.

THE syringe was enclosed in a little box. The pasteboard had been soaked away. The plunger was set and the silvery tube was filled with a colorless liquid he could see in the moonlight. Pete wrapped the leathal needle in half a dozen folds of his soggy handkerchief. This he stuffed into his leather billfold before pushing it into a rear pocket of his cotton slacks.

Couldn't take chances on the needle pricking through the cloth. God! To look like that! Better be stripped flesh and crunched bones in an alligator's belly, as Smiler Rawlings believed him to be.

He knew now the contents of the syringe. The swamp poison! . . . But what was it? . . .

From among the cypress roots came a slithering movement. The water seemed to hiss as if a red-hot iron had been thrust into it. Pete instinctively scrambled higher on the cypress knees. The hissing was repeated.

Against the inky surface something moved slowly—a thing as white as flaked snow. From it darted a tiny red tongue. Pete kicked out at it, threw himself past Severn's body into a more secure crook of the cypress roots.

The thing writhed around the tree and vanished. It was a cotton-mouth moccasin. Pete stared again at Severn's face. The swamp poison? Now he knew what it must be. Smiler had boasted of the walk of death. "The little dame," Zola Van Zandt, was to be the next.

Squealing and laughing! Tearing off her clothing! Her beauty becoming a hideous thing—when they turned on the juice!

Along the twisting channel he could see, dimly, a launch approaching. It was within a few hundred yards now. Pete's automatic was gone. He had no means of signaling, save to cry out. The motor would probably drawn his cries. Cabana's boat might pass within a few yards without his plight being discovered.

The thudding of the motor's exhaust was a single rhythm. The sheriff's boat must be following, then. Or perhaps Cabana had collected his posse on the one launch. . . .

The Everglades moon washed itself out in the mist. Its ball went blood-red and it was gone.

The mist above the wavering palmettoes was sliced abruptly by the sizzle of an aerial serpent. Its long, wiggling tail zig-zagged with blue fire into the sky. Its head burst with a shower of flaming blue rain.

Cabana had said that in an emergency he would send up a rocket, when he believed his launch was coming close. Pete was to have replied to the signal with three shots. He could not reply. He could only wait for them to come closer, swearing through chattering teeth to hold his brain steady.

There it came. The searchlight of a launch bored between the cypress. Smiler and his men must have seen the flare of the rocket. Not that it mattered, for they had fled at the approach of the launch. They were already aware of the trick, of the pursuit. Pete would have to do his best to remember the direction taken by flatboat toward the south bayou.

The low black launch swung into the narrow channel. Its pencil searchlight flicked along the cypress knees, passed over and missed Pete and the body of Severn. Pete tried to call out. But his throat was constricted and his voice only a rasping hoarseness.

God! If the boat passed and he remained unseen. . . .

The boat was moving slowly, the pilot feeling his way. It was yet some yards distant. The hoarse mutter of men's voices sounded in the steady pounding of the propeller and the motor. Two figures were revealed by the light coming from the cabin door.

Then there was another, a woman's voice—or was Pete's imagination playing him a trick? In the madness of this night a man's senses could hardly be depended upon. The launch was about to pass and Pete's hoarse cry had gone unheard.

In another minute he would be left alone on the cypress knees. Alone with what had been Severn.

Pete looked once at the inky spread of water between him and the launch. Then, with clenched teeth, he plunged from the roots, flailing with a frenzied overhand stroke toward the boat.

Between him and the launch, a loglike thing floated up. He beat the water with his flat hands. The surface swirled and the log disappeared. Then his hands were clutching a trailing rope bumper.

He heaved his body upward to the rail, rolled over it and splatted on the boat's small rear deck with his bare feet.

A fisherman pilot turned, mouth dropping open, staring at him with scared, stupid eyes. Cabana's slender figure turned, outlined by the cabin light. His face held incredulous amazement. But he moved quickly.

With a short oath he hurled himself upon Pete, striking at him with an automatic pistol!

"Wait!" Pete gasped. He dodged the blow. "It's me, Cabana! Pete Carson!"

THE swinging pistol had struck his shoulder, numbing it. Pete stumbled

and fell to the deck. He realized he must have presented a horrific sight, coming like some creature of the swamp up from the black water. His matted red hair was streaming over his eyes and his face was bruised and swollen. Slimy weeds clung to his body and muck oozed along his neck and shoulders.

"Good God!" Cabana exclaimed. There was instant concern in his handsome face. "Carson? Lord, man, I'm sorry!"

He was pulling Pete to his feet, pushing the hair back from his forehead.

"What happened? Where've you been? Where's Severn? Did you meet 'em?"

"They've got Severn," Pete mumbled brokenly. "He's over there. We'll have to get him. Is the other boat coming? I can start you after them."

"Severn? Over there? They got him? For God's sake, Carson! Your boat? The ransom money?"

"They've got the money, Cabana. They killed Severn. Swamp poison. Hell, Cabana! You know what swamp poison is?"

Cabana's dark countenance looked suddenly strained and white.

"This is awful, Carson! You say Severn is over there? Well, we'll have to get him then!"

"No! No, Cabana! Leave him there! Never mind it! No! Turn that light off! Turn it off, damn you! D'you hear?"

Pete had recovered his voice with a hoarse shout. He sprang upon the fisherman who was slowly swinging the searchlight beam along the cypress knees. In another instant it would have picked out that awful balloon head of the crook lawyer.

His fist lashed out, hitting the fisherman's shoulder. His hand caught the wires leading to the small searchlight. With a frenzied pull he yanked them loose. The pencil beam vanished.

Then Pete turned with wide eyes to the cabin door. He was looking at the flowerlike white face of Zona Van Zandt. The girl's wide, terrified eyes were fixed upon him and her bloodless lips were moving.

"Pete Carson," she was murmuring. "Pete Carson. Then it failed? They didn't bring Zola and my father? Oh, God! My little sister!"

Cabana was supporting Zona, telling her she must get back into the cabin, helping her.

"Couldn't avoid it, Carson," he said regretfully. "She found the boat and hid in one of the bunks. She wouldn't go back. I was afraid we'd lose our chance if we didn't come on in. Then we lost the sheriff's boat. Haven't seen it for more than an hour."

The fisherman stood in bewilderment. He hadn't resented Pete's interference with the spotlight. He seemed to be wholly dumb.

Cabana had gotten Zona Van Zandt seated again in the cabin. Her face was in her hands and she was moaning. "My little sister! You didn't find her!"

Cabana's dark face was grim-lipped. He softly patted the girl's shoulder, attempting to quiet her. The launch was moving slowly ahead. Pete looked into the blackness of Big Cypress, slowly realizing the utter futility of their position. Nothing to do now but go back.

Even if he could guide them in the direction Smiler Rawlings had taken, it would be sheer madness. He was unarmed. Cabana apparently had only the automatic. Doubtless Smiler had others in his Big Cypress gang. The sheriff's boat was missing.

"We'll have to go back, Cabana," he said. "There's nothing we can do. We'll have to get Miss Van Zandt out of here and come in with a posse big enough to clean out this gang."

"My little sister! My father!"

Zona sobbed bitterly. Pete was glad of that. Tears would save her tortured mind. Cabana nodded grimly.

"I think you're right, Carson," he said. "We'll have to go back. Jim, better turn around and—"

He broke off as wood scraped against wood. The small launch jolted against another boat. Smiler Rawlings' flat face reared up over the rail. Behind came the Weasel, an automatic in his hand, and back of him the hawk-nosed Joe swung his deadly sawed-off shotgun.

CHAPTER FOUR

The Hissing Moat

"NOW ain't this somethin' sweet!" rapped Smiler. "Walked right into it! Neat an' natural! Why you—"

Pete had lunged at him wildly, recklessly. One fist squashed with a crunching thump on Smiler's already flat nose.

But the valiantly intended attack was overcome by Carson's own exhausted condition. A flailing blow from Smiler Rawlings' huge fist crumpled him to the launch deck.

Pete rolled over with a groan, consciousness fading. Through a red haze of pain Smiler's bulk showed in the cabin door.

"Well, I'll be damned!" roared Smiler. "Wouldja look at this! It's the little dame's twin sister an' she's—"

Pete heard a bitter curse from Cabana. In his hands the automatic crackled and red spurts of flame leaped straight at Smiler. The gang leader swung back from the cabin door. Cabana plunged out.

Pete's vision was a mixture of distorted figures. The Weasel and Joe crossed the deck. The Weasel's clumping feet tramped on Pete's face. Though the automatic pistol had been fired pointblank at Smiler, the mobster was still on his feet and Cabana was down. The automatic had slipped from his hand; it slid near Pete's leg.

Pete was unable to move to seize the weapon, but he got one leg over it, concealing it from the others. Smiler loomed in the cabin door, vanished inside. Joe and the Weasel were bending over Cabana. Now they were heaving him over the rail into the flatboat.

Inside the cabin Zona Van Zandt screamed.

"Don't! Oh, please! Oh, my God!"

Smiler's harsh, obscene laugh rang out. "Neat an' natural!" he bawled. "That's me! C'mon, baby! Your boy friend's waitin' for yuh! Hey, Weasel! Think of a *couple* of dames takin' the death walk!"

The ribald speech, the terror in Zona Van Zandt's voice wrenched Pete back to active consciousness. He twisted, reaching for the automatic under his leg. He had it in his hand now. All of his thought was centered on getting the Smiler. After that, well, they would get him.

He could see Smiler's broad shoulders through the cabin door. His hands were on the girl's white shoulders, pulling her with him. After that first cry she had been silent. Pete saw only her despairing eyes, luminous, beautiful, tortured.

His weakened fingers gripped the automatic. As nearly as he could aim, the weapon was pointed at Smiler's spine. He squeezed desperately.

The pistol exploded, jumped in his hand. Smiler swung the girl around, an evil, lecherous sneer on his mouth. But that was all. The mobster's hands were gripped in the smooth lovely flesh of Zona's shoulders.

Before Pete could squeeze the weapon again, a sickening blow caught him under one ear. The Weasel's booted toe had swung viciously. The square of the cabin door went black before his eyes.

IT WAS as if the light in the cabin door had abruptly been flashed on again. Pete had no means of knowing the interval of time that had passed. His aching, numb senses told him only that he was still lying on the deck of the launch and that consciousness was returning.

Exerting every nerve, he moved. Then he realized he was alone. The light in the cabin door was more than just a light. Licking tongues of red darted through a white glare. The heat of it was blistering.

With a groan he rolled to escape it. After sometime he was able to pull himself to a sitting posture. Torturing pains shot through his bruised body. The launch was burning swiftly. Above him the branches of the cypress tree interlocked, imprisoning him in the inferno of flame.

Striving to recall all that had happened, he fell again, sprawling on the small deck. The searing heat of the fire in the cabin scorched his shoulders.

Abruptly, then, his face was in cool water. It lapped at his nose and lips. Instinctively he sipped at it, easing the parching dryness of his throat.

The water deepened on the deck. In the cabin the blaze hissed and steam rolled up in thick white vapor. The launch was sinking.

Pete got to his knees. The boat had drifted from under the trees into a clear lagoon. Pete blinked at what he saw. For a few seconds the swamp mist lifted over the flaming boat. An eerie thread of strange blue light ran across the blackness.

The black water rose to his knees. His bare feet slipped on the deck and he plunged headlong, in the direction of the trees and the slice of blue light. That he had been left for dead, or alive, to be cremated on the boat before it sunk, he realized now.

The dive into the water revived his dizzied brain. A good swimmer, his arms and legs moved mechanically. A hard lump in one hand seemed to hamper him. He discovered he was still clutching the automatic pistol that had been knocked from Cabana's hand. He thrust it into the holster.

Behind him the launch went down with a final sizzling hiss. Small waves slapped the back of his neck. His arms moved wearily, as if his hands carried leaden weight. He went under and the water sucked into his nostrils. He floundered back to the surface.

His knees struck oozy mud. Breath coming in great sobs, he rested for a moment. Then he started crawling weakly onto the shore under the live-oak trees. This was the highest land he had seen.

The slice of weird blue light was still there. He saw now that it came from what appeared to be a continuous row of small round windows. The bulk above the windows told him this must be some kind of a house.

Then, as he dragged his aching body onto drier land, every nerve tensed. A harsh, croaking, obscene laugh had floated out on the night. It came from the row of windows. It was the ribald voice of Smiler Rawlings!

Pete staggered to his feet. Desperately he strove to pierce the darkness surrounding him. Undoubtedly this live-oak island was the hideout of the Big Cypress monsters. Up there were the snatchers and their prisoners.

Now they had Zona Van Zandt. And they had Cabana. What was it the Smiler had boasted?

"Neat an' natural! The death walk!"

Pete Carson shuddered. His brain protested against the monstrous thought, refused to accept the fantasy the night had become. But his strength was returning and his fingers touched the lump of the pistol under his waistband.

It was real. Damnably so. He was here only by a freakish miracle. For the second time Smiler Rawlings believed him dead.

Except for the light, Pete could see nothing. Again he felt as if he were in another world, suspended in the black void of Big Cypress.

The sheriff's boat? What had become of that posse?

No sound out there in the blackness. No movement. He was here alone.

But something had moved, out there on the water. A flash of phosphorescence as if a paddle had been silently dipped. A gliding shape almost merged with the other shadows. As if a stiff figure were riding in a canoe over a soundless river of death.

"God! I'll be crazy, too!" Pete muttered. "And I've got to go on!"

His bare feet sucked in the mud. He climbed noiselessly to higher ground, in the direction of the blue light. His groping hand touched something in the darkness. Metal. Wires.

It was a fence of finely netted wire, but it was not more than three feet high. It topped the shore rise of the hummocked island.

Pete halted and listened. A hoarse mumbling was borne to him, the mingled harshness of men's voices at a distance, in the direction of the luried blue light. The building seemed less than fifty yards away.

Pete's hand ran along the edge of the meshed wire. It was like the side of a chicken pen, but the mesh was much finer. He walked along it a few feet, crouching, trying to prevent the suck of his feet in the mud from being heard. Again he had the automatic in his hand. Each instant he expected a hail, a challenge from some guard.

HE CAME to a corner of the wire, but discovered it was only a cross-wall of the same height. He could step over it easily. Pete wondered if it might be some sort of electrical trap.

Strange. he had encountered no one. . . .

But then, Smiler and his gangster would believe themselves perfectly safe. Probably they had watched the burning boat dive to the bottom.

That phosphorescent gleam on the water again. Had it been a dipping paddle, or only some movement of the scaly denizens of Big Cypress? Pete's aching eyeballs seemed to pick out the silhouette of a figure in a canoe, but he couldn't trust his bewildered senses.

There must be some way through the wire. He was chary of touching it. Perhaps if he attempted to cross, it would set up an electrical connection.

He paused, listening intently. A coarse laugh shuddered in the blackness. It came from the middle of the little island. Pete was half-way around the lighted building now.

Another cross-wall of the same finely-meshed wire. Should he risk stepping over and creep toward the building?

Moving along, barely touching the wire fence to guide him, Pete struck his toe against a yielding hump. His skin prickled and he sank to his knees, breathlessly feeling with his hands. For an instant the blood ceased to pump from his heart.

His hand was touching smooth skin. It was a man's shoulder. Though his stomach muscles shrank with revulsion, he forced his fingers to continue their exploration. He touched what had been an ear, but was now only a solid lump of distorted gristle imbedded in the side of an enormous head.

"Good God!" he mumbled. "Who—?"

His first thought had been of Severn, for the head and face were like that—ballooned to shapelessness. Then he knew it couldn't be, for Severn had been fully dressed. His hand ran over the upper portion of the dead man's torso until it came to the belted cotton slacks.

The fisherman pilot!

Pete pulled away, weak and sick again.

He pulled himself erect, holding onto the tightly stretched wire mesh of the fence. So they had given the fisherman the swamp poison. Then only by the sheer luck of being unconscious and fuel for the fire of the launch, had Pete escaped this same horrible fate. . . .

The body and the cotton slacks were soaking wet. The man had been washed ashore. Pete shuddered again, moved on, ploughing his way along the wire. Surely there must be an opening. Probably a guard would be there. He made sure the safety catch of the automatic was open.

Another cross-wall of wire. Now Pete realized he had nearly circled the small island. The row of blue-lighted windows were on the other side. He faced a wall of the building that was in darkness. Only the shine of the lights could be seen against the live oaks.

The wire fence, only three feet high. He could step over it. And it might mean his death.

A woman's voice screamed.

"Oh, God! You can't do that—you can't! Oh, don't do that—to me!"

The words were cut off as if a hand had throttled a white throat.

IT MIGHT have been Zona Van Zandt, or it might have been her sister. It did not matter; the pleading cry broke the last thread of caution in Pete Carson. Leaping the low wire mesh, he sprang in the direction of the building.

From all about him sounded vicious hissing! Along with it came the high-pitched burring of deadly rattles A slimy body slid across Pete's arm. The touch of it brought him heaving to his feet.

He whirled on his toes, back toward the wire he had crossed. His cotton slacks dribbled around his legs, soggy with swamp water. He jumped for the death-fence.

Then he cried out with the pain of

fangs that sunk into the flesh of his legs.

They had the tearing feel of double fishhooks sunk to their barbs in the living meat, then ruthlessly torn out. The strike of the snakes turned to agonizing burns.

With the fangs of one big diamond-back still sunk in the tendons of his ankle, Pete struck the low wire mesh and rolled over. The hooks tore out.

From the building in the middle of the island floated a raucous, obscene laugh.

Again the cry, "Oh, please! Don't do that to me! Don't—oh God!"

But Peter Carson did not hear that cry. He had stumbled and fallen face down in the oozing mud at the edge of the bayou.

He squirmed in the mud; with the desperation of a man making his last stand against horrible death, he pulled the belt from his slacks.

He got it around one leg above the knee. He twisted it ruthlessly into the flesh, checking the flow of poisoned blood through his veins. He knew now that he had but minutes to live. For him there could be no miracle of rescue, even respite. His one shuddering thought was of the bloated, bulbous heads of Severn and the dead fisherman.

He did not realize he had been uttering the whimpering moan of a hurt animal. That his agony had become a voice floating across the water.

Into his poison-filled brain came the vision of what might be happening to the lovely Zona Van Zandt. He could picture the girl's beautiful, delicate body under the hands of the brutal Rawlings. Her will being broken by torture. The death walk?

Pete struggled up, made one last attempt to crawl back up the muddy bank —to crawl toward that hideous trap. Now he knew why no guards had been placed around the little island. The meshed wire with its fenced-off squares was a moat.

Yes, a moat—like those dug around medieval castles. Only this moat was not filled with water—its stream ran with poison. The swamp poison. Diamond-backed rattlesnakes and cotton-mouthed moccasins.

Pete's hand clawed futilely into the mud. He slid back, his body plopping into the black water. One glimpse he had of the floating gray mist above the live-oak trees, of what seemed a taloned hand reaching for his throat.

The hand closed with a grip of steel on the side of his neck. Barely conscious of it, he lashed out feebly with a fist. His arm had no strength. Dimly he thought he must be drowning—and that was much to be preferred to this other, slower death by poison torture.

But he wasn't drowning. Hands seemed to be lifting him. He knew it must be only a fantasy of his dying imagination.

CHAPTER FIVE

The Double-Cross

PETE CARSON awoke to a strange and pleasant lethargy. Memory returned with the sharp vividness of a lash across his brain. He struggled to sit up.

Eyes black and deep looked down at him. A thin-nosed face with a rugged chin, the whole carved in bronze, was smiling slightly. Straight black hair ridged back from a high forehead. The Seminole Indian's shoulders had the smoothness of rubbed copper.

Pete remembered and shuddered. His limbs were beginning to tremble. He moved one hand, looking at it.

"Then I'm alive?" he said suddenly. "You? Who are you?"

The Seminole nodded slowly, with satisfaction, but did not speak. In the wonder of being alive, Pete said, "You speak English? You saved me?"

The Seminole's smile broadened. It was glowing in the light of a wood fire.

"Hell, yes!" said the Seminole. "On both counts!"

"But if I hadn't had the luck to come on you in the first few minutes, you'd have been cold turkey, brother. You had enough snake poison in you to have killed an elephant."

"What the hell?" said Pete. He looked down at his bared legs where half a dozen blue punctures showed. "You an Indian or just made up for the part? I thought the last of the Seminoles were wild."

"But I'm not the last of the Seminoles," smiled the Indian. "I've three sons of my own. I couldn't be as wild as you looked when I found you."

"Yes," said Pete slowly. Terrible memory burned again in his brain. "By that damnable island trap. Listen! You saved me! I've got to get back there!"

"I know," said the Seminole quietly. "Sure. You've got to get in. We've both got to get in. I've been watching the island since last night. This is another night."

Pete groaned.

"Then we're too late. God! But I almost forgot. You're a wonder to have pulled me through. I suppose you Seminoles have roots and herbs and things like that to cure snake poison. What's your name?"

The Seminole shrugged and smiled.

"You couldn't wrap your tongue around my name. Call me John, say John Smith. You think it was roots and herbs? That's ancient hooey. What saved you was triple injections of the latest serum for snakebite that medical science has produced."

"Maybe we're not too late," he said. "Two women are still alive on that island. I was close, listening. Something's due to

happen tonight. We've got to cross that snake fence. They have a bridge over it they let down from the inside, but I've got another way in. It's there in that basket."

Pete looked with wonderment from John Smith to the lidded wicker basket near the fire. From inside the basket came a slithering, scraping sound.

"More snakes?" said Pete. "Hell, I don't want to ever see another one!"

"Kings," said the Seminole. "Good snakes. Black ones. Get up and see if you think you're fit to travel."

Pete rose shakily. He was weak and sick. He trembled.

"Wait. Sit down," commanded the Seminole.

He poured a tin cup of steaming liquid from a pot on the fire. It was bitter, pungent, but it seemed to leap through Pete's veins like fire. Strength coursed through his muscles.

"And that's some of the hooey," said the Seminole. "Some swamp roots and herbs, only it's been distilled. It will help you."

JOHN SMITH'S cypress canoe glided silently as a shadow over the black bayou. Propelled by his bronzed arms, the craft slid past the knees of the huge trees. A blue light gleamed faintly over the water.

"We land here," said the Seminole. "We'll wade through these palmettoes and be on the island. You'd better take your pistol. I had some thirty-eight cartridges and I've loaded the magazine. Here are the two shells I took out."

He dropped two unfired cartridges into Pete's hand. Pete stared at them, then back at John Smith.

"You took these out of that automatic?"

"Yeah. It seemed funny to me you should have them like that."

It seemed funny to Pete. He slipped the shells into the pocket of his tattered cotton slacks. They rested with the leather billfold enclosing the syringe taken from the body of Severn.

Pete was thinking hard. Thinking of how Smiler Rawlings had stood up to the pointblank fire of Cabana's pistol, and afterward when he himself had aimed directly at the Smiler's spine. Somebody must have slipped something over on Cabana. The shells were blanks. . . .

With the wicker basket over his head, John Smith waded toward the dense shadows under the oaks. Pete's bare feet sunk in the ooze, then they climbed to the slippery but more solid mudbank. Only by force of will could he reach out to touch the meshed wire fence.

"This way," the Seminole whispered. "The snake-pen is built in a circle. It's divided into small squares which keep a certain number of diamond-backs and moccasins to each few yards of fence. Now watch—be ready in a minute to follow me."

With noiseless hands the Seminole lifted the wicker basket to the edge of the wire. He opened the lid. Pete shivered as he heard the sliding of sinuous bodies over the edge. The black kings, most deadly enemy of the rattlesnake, were being freed in the hissing moat.

Diamond-backs burred more rapidly. *Thump-thump-thump.* The striking of tails. The flailing of bodies.

A rattle slowly died out. Another was silenced. A striking head imbedded itself in the wire close to Pete's hand, sending him back, sliding down the mudbank. The Seminole was beside him.

"In a minute it'll be all over," he whispered. "The black kings are fast. They nail the diamond-backs just behind the head. They twist around them. They're quick stranglers. The rattlers and the moccasins haven't a chance. . . ."

Five minutes later Pete, with John Smith beside him, drove his reluctant body over the wire. The flesh of his legs drew into knots, but he kept going. There was a slithering movement underfoot, but that was only the black kings scurrying away. No rattles sounded. . . .

Then they were over the inside fence, crouching, stealing toward the end of the long low building farthest from the blue lights. The Seminole laid a hand on Pete's shoulder.

"The door in front is over there," he whispered. "I'll go to the tree beyond it. You have your gun. I have one. I'll stick this flashlight in a fork of the bushes, make a noise to draw them out, then flash it on. They'll rush, maybe shooting at the light. You can see them and—"

Pete said, "No! Wait! The Van Zandts! We've got to make sure they'll be safe. You wait and I'll crawl close enough to see or hear what's going on."

The Seminole demurred, but he quickly realized the wisdom of this precaution. Pete started on his way.

"If trouble, call or shoot," said John.

THE slice of blue light was a knifelike beam in the night mist. Beyond its illumination the darkness was almost opaque. Pete reached the corner of the building, constructed of rough-hewn cypress logs. The silence was ominous, filling him with foreboding. Despite the Seminole's assurance that the Van Zandt girls were still unharmed, Pete was filled with a chill foreboding of what he might see if he succeeded in reaching the small windows studded into the logs.

The stimulation of the liquor John Smith had administered was beginning to fade. Pete felt sick and weak.

He was almost under one of the blue-lighted windows when the sudden harsh murmur of men's voices froze him motionless. The words as much as the voice marked the ruthless, fiendish Smiler.

"Neat an' natural!" he was croaking. "Listen, Weasel! It's the chief's idea an' it adds a clean hundred grand to our end of the take, see? Too bad about that dumbhead Joe, but the boss is smart!"

The Weasel's ratty laugh proved his agreement.

"You an' me, huh Smiler? Just you an' me to split three hundred grand?"

"It's somethin', you're right," grunted Smiler's voice. "We go through, see? Joe, he's down at the end of the walk all alone. You're standin' up here with me holdin' the chopper kinda careless. When the boss jumps an' socks at you, you throw up your hands an' let go the gun.

"The boss grabs it. He cuts loose an' gives Joe the works. As soon as he's rubbed out, he swings the chopper back on you an' me. All the time I'm clawin' for my rod, an I'll be doin' some shootin', but it won't mean anything, see?

"We back up into the wall. The boss finishes off by grabbin' the girl. He's nuts over her, see? Well, maybe. Anyway, that's after the other little dame takes the death walk and goes screwy. We couldn't miss that, could we, Weasel? Neat an' natural! That's me! She'll be bugs as her brother, but you ain't choppin' off no arms this time, Weasel! I got other ideas—an' the boss says okeh, just so her or the old man don't come back!"

"Too bad for poor old Joe!" chuckled the Weasel.

"Poor old Joe!" mocked the voice of Smiler Rawlings. "An' a neat hundred grand more for us to split. You got it, Weasel?"

"I got it, Smiler!"

Pete arose with shaking hands. If he could only find an opening in the logs.

Severn, the lawyer, the go-between and procurer of the half million ransom, had been double-crossed and horribly slain.

Cabana himself must have been double-crossed or tricked. His automatic had been loaded only with blanks, possibly a substituted rod. Perhaps his fisherman pilot was in with the mob of fiendish kidnapers and torturers.

But the fisherman had been killed. Had he, too, been double-crossed? Whether or no, he had died with the swamp poison turning his veins to distorted channels.

And now the man Joe. . . .

For some unexplained reason, perhaps for no more than to add to the bloody profit of the foul crimes, he was to be put on the spot. And by the boss. . . .

Then Smiler Rawlings was not the brains of this outfit. Severn had mentioned it, and twice the chief had been spoken of by Smiler himself. The boss himself was about to put on a show, rub out the unsuspecting Joe without a chance, aided and abetted by Smiler and the Weasel. Who was this boss?

PETE had a troubling thought. This island hideout had been prepared by somebody familiar with the swamp. None but a native could have devised that hideous hissing moat, have trapped the deadly diamond-backs and the moccasins alive. There was in this whole island of torture evidence of superior understanding of the tropical swamp and also of acquaintance with modern devices.

No doubt but that humming motor and generator inside supplied the electricity for the lights, perhaps for something else as well. This Seminole who called himself John Smith had proved himself a remarkable Indian. Equipped with the latest serum produced by medical science. Prepared to loose king blacksnakes in a section of the hissing moat to gain undetected entrance.

Could the Seminole have saved him merely for some sinister purpose of his own? How did John Smith happen to be watching this island, be so familiar with its operation?

Where was John Smith now?

Pete called out cautiously, hissing the words. No reply came to him. With noiseless haste he slipped along the building to the first blue-lighted window. He sought vainly for some sign that John Smith, the Seminole, was nearby. But the Indian had vanished.

From inside the window above Pete's head, issued a strangled cry.

"Oh, please! Please! Please! Not again! Oh God, not that again!"

The frantic appeal was a wail of weakness, as if the woman were forcing the words from a long-wearied throat. Then another voice rang out, clearer, stronger.

"Don't! Oh, don't do it! I'll give you anything, everything! Put me into the pit, but spare my sister!"

Pete's body burned with a raging fire. That second voice belonged to Zona Van Zandt. Then the first had been her twin sister Zola.

Pete clutched at the logs. He drew himself up to the window.

He was looking into a queerly shaped oblong room. At the farther end was a raised narrow platform, six feet above the floor. On this platform three persons sat stiffly bound to a wooden bench, the bodies of two upright and rigid with strain. The hands of the three were twisted behind them and their ankles were crossed with cords.

Pete's fingernails dug into the log under the window until blood welled from under them. The middle figure was that of Zona Van Zandt. Her face was white as the carved clean marble of a statue with congealed and bloodless lips. She was leaning a little forward, staring into the pitted room below.

The Smiler stood at one end of the platform, the Weasel at the other. Rawling's lecherous eyes were upon the rounded figure of the girl on the bench, whose intent agony seemed to make her heedless of her torn dress. Three red welts crossed her white bosom.

Pete dragged the automatic into his hand. He raised it, to thrust it through the glass of the window. But his purpose was stayed.

The other two figures on the bench were Cabana and a gray-haired man with sunken cheeks and lifeless eyes. A ragged stubble of dirty beard made Van Zandt, the multi-millionaire, almost unrecognizable. His upper body was bared and gaunted to the thinness of a skeleton man.

Cabana was erect, staring down. His eyes glowed like coals of hate beneath the mop of black hair that fell over his forehead. Pete saw that his slender hands were working, working at the twist of the cords on his wrists.

"Neat an' natural!" said the bullfrog voice of the Smiler. "Okeh, Joe!"

The weak scream of Zona's sister came again, almost at Pete's feet. Straining, he looked down into the oblong room. His whole body chilled with revulsion.

CHAPTER SIX

The Death-Walk

INTO Pete Carson's range of vision had come the figure of a girl. The weird blue light turned her white skin to the color of mottled gray chalk. Its illumination etched every flowing curve of her slender figure, revealing hollows and outlined bones where the flesh had all but shriveled away.

Arms that undoubtedly had been rounded and perfect, were thin and knobby as those of a scarecrow. Her neck showed in corded ridges. When her head was turned suddenly toward Pete, blazing eyes of terror glowed in a masklike face.

Yet the girl was still pretty, had without doubt been as lovely as her twin sister who strained against the binding cords, on the platform bench. Pete's breath sucked in with horror. For his mind flashed back to the Thing that had leaped from colored pavement square to pavement square on a noonday Miami street.

The girl had leaped. Looking back. Looking down. Lips writhing. A scream.

Pete saw the colored squares of the floor. Each was about three feet across. They were arranged in a pattern. Through the middle of the room ran a smooth wall to the roof. But the squares circled this at each end, in the form of a small track which might have been devised for sprinters.

A door inside, under the window, slammed shut. Pete could not see this, but the hawknosed mobster, Joe, climbed into view just beneath the window.

"Please!" she wailed. "Oh, please!"

Smiler's hand flashed up. It closed an electrical switch. Pete saw the mechanism of an intermittent contact begin turning on the wall near the platform. Wires ran from this to the floor of the oblong room.

Zola Van Zandt leaped again, her bare feet pattering on another of the colored squares. She was clad only in the clinging silk of her underwear. It no longer fitted, hanging on the bony shoulders like a bright rag. The Smiler's eyes had turned from Zona Van Zandt now, looking down, gloating at each revealing movement.

With spine-pricking penetration, the rattles of a huge diamond-back burred. The snake seemed to coil and strike his way into Pete's line of vision. Like the girl, he had jumped from one colored square to another. Then his venomous

tongue darted and his sleek triangular head slid across to the square on which the girl stood.

Pete could then see that the girl's legs were trembling, as if from some vibration beneath the soles of her feet. The rattlesnake's head hit the square near her heels and she leaped again, her cry silenced. She was twisted halfway around, looking back, looking down.

But the snake's head retreated as if the slimy reptile had been thrown back by a physical blow. The rattler coiled, rattles again burring loudly. High on the wall the electrical mechanism slowly turned. The snake struck straight up, as if galvanized into action, then slithered to the square on which the girl had just been standing.

"Neat an' natural!" croaked the Smiler.

"Oh, you filthy beast!" Zona Van Zandt screamed. "You foul thing of hell!" Then as quickly she was pleading, forgetful of her words, of her action. Offering herself, her millions, her body, everything, to save her sister from further torture.

Cabana stared down, muscles rippling along his shoulders. The ratty eyes of the Weasel devoured the figure of the girl in the pit, swung back to the more lovely form of her sister.

Old man Van Zandt's lips moved. Pete could hear his words. Suddenly he reared horribly against his corded bonds, then fell back, sagging in the middle as if life had been cut out of him. His shoulder fell and the gray head rolled on a limp neck.

Pete knew the torture for the multimillionaire, the proud father of these girls, of the mutilated maniac in Miami, was ended.

Pete's hand went up again, holding the automatic. Yet he hesitated. If he attacked now, before the Indian came to his aid, it might mean Zona's death.

Perhaps only a minute had passed since the girl's first scream. Pete understood now this walk of death. The colored plates of the floor were charged with a light current of electricity. The mechanism swung it along from plate to plate. The huge diamond-back, six feet of sinuous, terrible venom, was being driven ahead. Its body reacted to the electrical current and it kept seeking the plate from which the juice had passed.

And always just ahead was the girl. Pete's immediate wonderment was why she had not fled farther away, then rested. All at once he found the reason. Two plates ahead of her was another diamond-back! The death walk. God!

HOW many hours had Zona Van Zandt been forced to endure this torture? How many hours and days had her insane brother been kept leaping from plate to plate, so that when he returned to Miami he was only a pitiful bundle of armless skin and bones, without reason or hope?

Pete shook himself free from the stupor of horror drugging his senses. He tore his gaze away from the leaping, almost naked girl. He tried to close his ears to her repeated shrieks and sobs. Now he knew why her brother's arms had been sheered off. Doubtless he had fallen, been bitten.

The arms had been amputated to save his life, to make him into the Thing they could send back.

Pete turned, straining into the darkness, calling, "John Smith!"

No answer came. Pete's mind was now possessed with almost insane suspicion. Who was the boss? The chief who was to chop down the unsuspecting Joe?

Zola Van Zandt's cries were mouthings now. Soon she would be as mindless as her brother.

The Smiler's eyes gloated.

Cabana was twisting in his cords. It seemed to Pete he had one arm nearly free. The Weasel was lounging against the wall, slitted orbs on the nearly nude girl undergoing the leaping madness. He held a machine-gun carelessly in his hand.

Was that another door at the far side of the building?

The blue lights were deceptive. Pete pressed his rigid face to the cold glass of the window. He saw he was very close to the mobster, Joe.

Yes, across the building a door was slowly opening. A carved bronzed face and coppery shoulders gleamed for an instant in the light. The Seminole!

Pete's suspicion turned now to sickening certainty. He had been tricked and double-tricked. The Indian who had saved him must be the chief of whom Smiler and the Weasel had talked.

The Smiler was looking across at the unsuspecting Joe. The Seminole's figure came in through the opposite door, was merged with the shadows. The sobbing scream of Zola Van Zandt became a steady wailing cry. Pete saw her fall to her knees, stagger up again, leap ahead. Looking back. Looking down.

Cabana seemed to have one arm almost free. The machine-gun hung carelessly in the Weasel's loose hands. John Smith, the Seminole, must be in the shadows very close to him.

Pete gripped his automatic tightly, raised to his toes and smashed it into the window. Broken glass sliced into his arm as he pointed the weapon straight at Smiler Rawlings, shouting a warning.

"Look out, Joe! They're going to chop you down! You're being double-crossed! Kill the Weasel!"

It was only a wild thought that the sudden words might arouse the stupid Joe to some action, stop this walk of death. And Pete's automatic was pointed straight at the Smiler. He squeezed and the pistol's mechanism caught. It only clicked

The Smiler yelled an oath. Pete saw Cabana surge to his feet, make a headlong dive toward the Weasel. He had a glimpse of another coppery figure, swift and sudden as one of the diamond-backs, flashing from the shadows.

Then the Smiler's hand had flicked a switch. All the lights at the platform end of the oblong room winked out. Only one blue tube was burning. Its weird light shone luridly on the end of the snake-pit nearest Pete.

Pete dared not shoot then, though the automatic mechanism seemed ready to work. The five figures on the platform, or perhaps it was six, were confused in the darkness. There was a writhing struggle, the sound of a crunching blow.

From the darkness came the hammering explosions of the machine-gun. The mobster Joe screamed with agony, but the scream cut short. He was pitching down into the snake-pit now with his head all but torn from his shoulders by the ripping line of slugs. Almost in Pete's face, the bullets spattered into the windows, showering him with splintered glass.

Cut and bleeding from a dozen minor wounds, Pete slid to the ground, running on his toes. His bare shoulder thumped the door on the window side of the building. It was solidly barred.

Inside the building more shots cracked. Curses and shouts made pandemonium. The Smiler's voice was roaring.

Zona Van Zandt's voice cried, "Oh, take me! Anything! Let my sister go! Oh, don't—"

THE machine-gun chopped again. Other shots crackled inside the darkened building. Curses and groans mingled with the crying of the two girls. Pete's thought was of the horror of Zola Van Zandt's abandonment in the death-walk pit with the huge rattlesnakes, with the protecting electrical current switched off.

A heavy body thumped. It seemed to have fallen some distance. Pete visioned someone hurtling down, lifeless, into the snake-pit. He was at the back of the building now. The door which the Seminole had entered was merged with the blank shadow of the wall. Pete groped along the logs.

"Oh, help me! Help me! Pete Carson!"

The strange appeal came from Zona Van Zandt. Yet surely the girl must believe him to be dead. He tore the skin from his knuckles, striking at the logs, looking for the door. Then a panel swung outward.

Against the mist showed the outline of a tall figure. The man had the machine-gun in his hand. The girl, Zona, was beside him. She was pulling at the sagging, nearly nude body of her sister. The man holding the machine-gun under his arm was gripping Zona's wrist. Pete tried to aim his automatic in the darkness, but couldn't be sure. He dared not shoot.

With a spring he was on the man with the chopper. His fist lashed out weakly, slapping ineffectively into the man's face. The darkness enabled him to see only a dark countenance topping browned shoulders. The man snarled in his throat, let go of Zona Van Zandt and attempted to swing the machine-gun around.

Pete set himself on his toes and dived into him, his head burying into the other man's stomach. Zona's scream of terror, the falling of her sister face foremost to the ground and a hissed curse from the man were all in the confusion of the following second. Pete was hurled to his back.

"You! Pete Carson!"

The voice grated on his ear. Then he had been correct in his conjecture of the Seminole's role of torture boss. Strong, talon-like fingers were fastened on his throat, grinding his head into the mud.

Pete brought up his knees; it only brought an obscene oath. The hands tightened until his windpipe seemed to collapse.

Weakened by the events of the past hours, and sick, Pete felt himself going out. His hands flailed about, but as he struck at the other man's smooth body he realized the blows were mere taps. His lungs swelled with a desperate attempt to breathe. Half conscious, he saw the white face of Zona Van Zandt.

He heard her whisper, "Pete Carson?"

Her small hands were tearing at the man's black hair. With a brutal thrust of his foot the fellow sent her sprawling to the ground. His hot breath was on Pete's face. The ground surged, whirled. Pete was sinking into blackness. One hand twisted under his body.

His fingers struck the pocket of his torn cotton slacks, came out clutching his leather billfold. A soggy handkerchief was in his hand and in it a silvery tube. Pete's action was hardly a conscious intention. He writhed in his struggle against the throttling hands, a spasmodic twist in his effort to tear the fingers from his throat. The other man's body slid to one side, rolled off him.

From the mouth pressed close to his face came a fearful scream, an oath of agony. The man's whole body twitched, pulling his hands from Pete's throat.

One of Pete's hands was jammed down into the soft ground. It was the hand holding the soggy handkerchief and the silvery glass tube with a hypodermic needle that had been broken, but was still jagged and sharp.

The splintered silver had sunk deeply into the other man's stomach. His weight had closed the plunger. He was rolling over and over now, his freed hands clawing for some hold on the ground where there was none. His face was burrowing into the dirt, a cry of agony mumbling from a mouth filled with island muck.

Pete was on his hands and knees. He was aware that Zona Van Zandt had crawled to her sister's side, was trying to lift the other girl's head to her lap. The man who had attacked him was a stiffening mass of flesh. Pete knew he would be the third victim to become a swollen horror of Big Cypress.

The pencil beam of a flashlight struck his eyes and blinded them. It swung to the man dying in the mud. Pete's eyes followed. Shuddering question came from his lips.

The man who had throttled him, who had fallen on the syringe filled with the deadly venom, was Arturo Cabana!

Above the swinging flashlight loomed the carved bronze features of the Siminole who called himself John Smith. In one hand he held an automatic pistol, from the muzzle of which a little wisp of gray smoke still floated.

"Machoka!" exclaimed the Seminole. "You hurt much, Pete Carson?"

Pete attempted to reply, to bring his muddled brain to a grasp of the amazing situation, but he was falling. His senses were fading. He only dimly realized that the Seminole had dropped his pistol and was lifting Zona Van Zandt to her feet.

From the building of the death-walk torture came a blasting burst of flame. It flared against the moss-draped live-oaks, a funeral pyre. In its light John Smith, the Seminole, strode to the body of Cabana. "Machoka!" he said again. "It is good this way!"

He swung Cabana's body into his coppery arms. His tall bronze figure stood out for a moment in the glare of the flames. His shoulders heaved and Cabana's poisoned body went through the doorway of the blazing building.

As Pete fell senseless, he was aware that Zona Van Zandt's hands were pressed over her eyes. Her bloodless lips moved without sound.

JOHN SMITH was talking. "This Cabana posed as a Spanish nobleman," the Seminole said. "He was Machoka, my half-brother, a breed! We were educated together, and I came back to Big Cypress. Machoka said he would have a fortune. It was the white man's blood talking."

They were on a launch moving slowly out of Big Cypress into the little river leading to Estero. Pete lay on the deck in the shade of the cabin. One of John Smith's reviving drinks was sending new life through his body. Inside the cabin were the sisters.

"Me?" said the Seminole. "For months I have watched. Machoka, he came back to Big Cypress. He had the building of snake torture built on the island. He trapped the diamond-backs and moccasins. Somehow he became friendly with the Van Zandt's. He was on their yacht when this man, Smiler Rawlings, carried out the kidnaping.

"It was Machoka's purpose to seize all of the Van Zandt fortune. He devised the method of driving Arthur Van Zandt insane. The girl Zola was to be next, then her father.

"The ransom money taken from Zona Van Zandt was to pay off his hired killers. Then he plotted to play the hero to win Zona Van Zandt. You, Pete Carson, were too smart. You might have found out too much. So he plotted to get you out of the way.

"He had not called a sheriff's posse or any other boat. A fisherman persuaded Zona Van Zandt to hide on the launch that followed you; it was Machoka's plan. It looked good to you, to Zona Van Zandt, when he attacked Rawlings; but he was shooting blanks in his automatic and it looked as if he had been knocked out.

"The blue rocket that night was a signal to Smiler, not to you. Then the killing of the gangster Joe was to be the final act this Cabana thought would make him solid with Zona Van Zandt. In the confusion he was to escape with the girl, leaving her twin sister and her father in the hands of Smiler Rawlings and the man called the Weasel. They were to disappear.

"Smiler Rawlings was to have the girl and the father was to have been killed. But he died."

"So Cabana was the boss who engineered the whole thing?" murmured Pete. "Robbed Van Zandt of his life and made Arthur Van Zandt an insane cripple. Stole the reason from Zona's sister."

A low sob came from the cabin.

"No," said the Seminole. "Zola Van Zandt is still sane. After many weeks she will be all right."

"Thank God for that much," Pete said.

"This girl, Zona, you love her, Pete Carson?" smiled the Seminole.

Pete shook his head.

"It may be," he said slowly. "But she's an heiress. She'll have millions. Me? I'm just a wandering newspaperman."

Zona Van Zandt was standing in the door of the launch cabin. Her lips were touched with a sad, wistful smile.

"Without you, Pete Carson," she said softly, "I have nothing."

She bent swiftly over and kissed his swollen, battered lips.

The Seminole's black eyes were impassive. He looked along the inky water.

"Machoka has paid," he said. "You are a good man, Pete Carson."

THE END

IN THE NEXT ISSUE!
A Spine-Tingling Complete Mystery Novel
By Arthur Leo Zagat
The January Issue Will Be Out November 23rd

MANIAC'S MASTERPIECE

*Danger—tiger-cunning and rep-
tile-vicious—had lived with Guy
Fraser almost every hour of his
life. But the crafty trail of a love-
wild man-beast led him to over-
whelming terror while his fiancée
faced death as a madman's masterpiece. . . .*

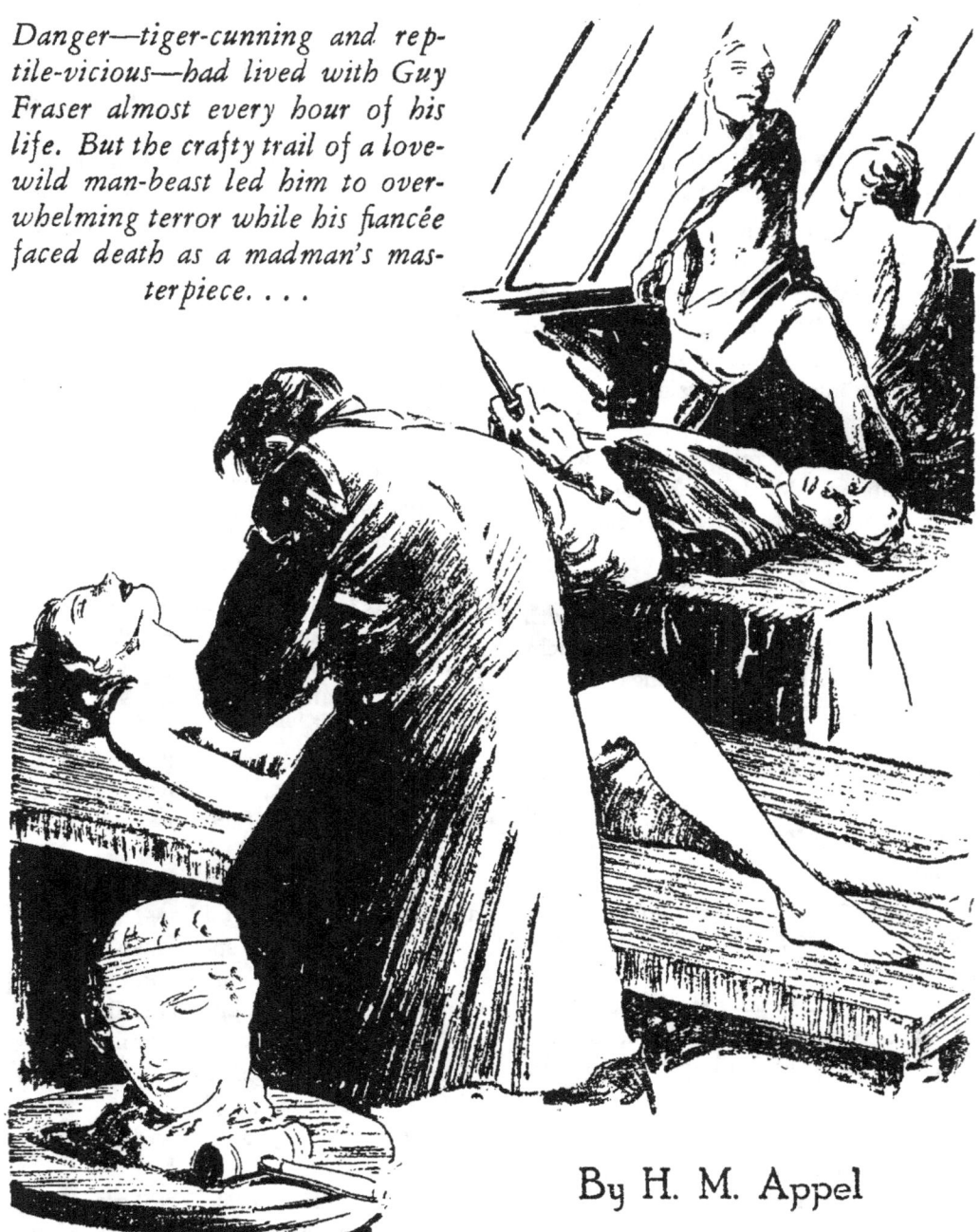

By H. M. Appel

ANXIETY ridged Guy Fraser's brow deeply. *"Why* doesn't she come?" The question hammered in his head. Vagrant fears swarmed like rats across his brain and he was haunted by the same whispered threats that had

tinged Clare Cornell's days and nights with terror.

Loungers in the lobby of the St. Francis eyed the tall, tanned man in dinner clothes as he paced the tiles so fretfully. There was friendliness amounting to

36

hero-worship in their eager glances, for Guy Fraser's adventurous exploits appealed to popular fancy. The Los Angeles public had taken to its heart this far-traveller who invaded oriental jungles and brought back dangerous beasts alive.

"If Hinton dares harm her," he muttered through clenched teeth, "I'll kill him if I hang for it! This can't go on—"

Heartbreaking things had happened during his two-year sojourn in Burma and Ceylon. Now, on every tongue, there was kindly gossip concerning his affair with lovely Clare Cornell, whose meteoric rise to stardom in the motion picture world had occurred during his absence. With hot eyes riveted upon his lithe wiry figure, one darkly beautiful woman drawled to her companion:

"After being married and divorced while he was away, Clare is a fool to keep him dangling now. I wouldn't—"

Halting in his nervous march, Fraser frowned up at the lobby clock. How slowly the hands moved! For the hundredth time he asked himself: "What *can* be keeping her? Something is wrong, *wrong* —" Clare was an hour overdue. Tonight was the première of her latest picture, *Winner Take All.*

And it wasn't like her to be late.

He crunched a cigar savagely, threw it away. Upon hurrying back to the hotel, expecting to dress and call for Clare, he had found a telephoned message requesting him to wait in the lobby. He had waited . . . too long. A sixth sense clamored of danger. . . .

With an impatient exclamation he swung toward the telephone-booths. Before calling Clare, he phoned the garage to ask for his car—the new white roadster delivered only a few days before. An attendant exclaimed: "Why, your friend drove it away, Mr. Fraser—after you sent him with the note!"

Fraser's eyes went sick, his lips tightened to a bloodless line. He dialed another number hurriedly.

"Gretchen? Your mistress—" his voice was vibrant with alarm, "where is she? This is Mr. Fraser. She was to come."

Fright twanged in the quick cry: "What do you mean? Why, *you came for her*— in your car. . . ."

"Listen, Gretchen." He controlled his voice with difficulty. "Tell me carefully. Clare drove off with someone, in a car like mine?"

"Yes, yes! It *was* yours. White, with your initials on the door—oh, God, sir!"

"Keep your head, girl! Tell me—she did *not* telephone, asking me to wait here?"

"No, no! Oh, he's got her. He has threatened such horrid things—"

"Don't go to pieces!" Fraser's voice sharpened sternly. "I'll be out soon. First, I must notify the police."

SO it had happened—the worst! His cheeks were ashen. The strong hands, which could hold a rifle so steadily in the face of charging death, trembled a little now. Blindly he fumbled for a number on the dial, and reported the abduction to Police Headquarters, finishing: "I'll come right over."

Lieutenant Herzog, of the Detective Bureau, exhibited a nonchalance that raised a red fog in Fraser's brain. "We've broadcast an alarm," he drawled. "We'll send out a detail. That's all we can do until we get something to work on."

Fraser hated the careless air, the dangling cigarette, the bored drumming of thin fingers on the desk. "You take this outrage rather lightly! Everything must be done—everything you can do!"

"Now, don't get ants in your pants, Mister!" The detective shrugged. "If it's a snatch, we'll handle it fast enough. But I've got a hunch it's the same old gag."

Herzog leaned forward with a sudden show of friendliness. "Say, I just recognized you, Fraser. You're the animal catcher! You've been out of the country a long time, see? You're not on to the latest rackets. The cockeyed press agents in this burg have abduction on the brain. Easy publicity!"

"You mean—?" Slowly, Fraser shook his head, eyes fixed upon Herzog's face. "No, this is real. I'm afraid it may be . . . murder." The dread word burned in his throat and his lips twitched involuntary. "There's a lot behind it that you'd better know—"

It hurt him—remembering! But he steadied himself, and outlined the situation in short, bitter phrases: "For years I've loved her—long before she became a star. She's younger than I am; too young, maybe. Anyway, we agreed to wait until I returned from this last voyage. Of course, she knew Mark Hinton. He was the taxidermist at the museum—handled all my specimens before I began bringing them back alive. A wizard in his work, his skill never equalled. A big, blond chap with a handsome face and manners, but —I know it now!—the heart of a fiend."

Herzog nodded languidly. "I remember —the mug she married and divorced. It was all in the papers."

Fraser looked away, the salt taste of rage in his teeth, staring into a future peopled with creatures who would never understand that act of madness born of a woman's pique. "It wasn't the way you think. Clare was true to me, but Hinton was vile. He lied, telling her I'd taken another woman along. Showed her pictures snapped aboard my ship, although they didn't mean a thing. Well—she married him. . . ."

"Then, what you're driving at is that this Hinton—" Herzog straightened.

"Of course. He has been writing and telephoning queer vague threats ever since

the announcement of our engagement. Clare was almost sick with fear. She hasn't seen Hinton in a year—he disappeared—but she knows his voice, his handwriting."

A MAN bustled in, interrupting: "Look, Lieutenant! Ain't this nuts? From a dozen different directions, all at once—"

Herzog snatched the sheaf of tissue reports, reading aloud: "Clare Cornell recognized as passenger in black touring car driving through Redondo Beach. Another: Clare Cornell seen in small sedan, speeding toward Monrovia. And this one —what the hell? Clare Cornell spotted in car headed for Oxnard! How many Clare Cornells got snatched, anyway? I'll say it's nuts!"

"Couldn't they have switched from one car to another?" Fraser's eyes were puckered questioningly. "Oh, no! I see—"

"Of course you do. It would take three or four hours for one person to appear in all these places." Herzog shuffled additional reports through his fingers, mystification growing in his face.

Another officer rushed in, mouth spread in a grin, laughter rumbling in his chest. "Now comes the answer! Same old stuff—"

Herzog swore roundly, passing the first sheet to Fraser. It read:

Overhauled sedan. Clare Cornell a wax dummy. Driver for Lifelike Form Company delivering model to outlying store.

"Three more," snapped Herzog, "all say the same. I told you it was a publicity stunt. Your sweetie is hiding at home, snickering in her sleeve."

Fraser sprang up angrily. "You can't put it off like that! She's gone! Her maid told me—"

"Ah, hell. Her maid would be in on the gag. She'll turn up as soon as the newspapers smear enough free ink on front pages."

A man spoke from the doorway. "You're Mr. Fraser? Your roadster was just found, deserted in a back street. Neighbors said some one got out of it, and into another car parked near, helping a woman who seemed ill. They said she acted sort of stiff—couldn't hardly move—and the man almost had to carry her."

"You see?" Fraser whirled on Herzog.

"Stiff!" snorted the detective. "I'll say she was stiff. Another wax model."

Fraser raged: "If anything happens to her—if you don't turn every stone—the papers will 'smear enough ink' to make you squirm all right!"

He went out. A squad car took him to his abandoned roadster. With a clash of gears he sent it hurtling toward the heights of Hollywoodland.

GRETCHEN, a pretty flaxen-haired maid of twenty, quavered tearfully: "I was sure *you* came. It was your car. She was waiting when it drove up and honked. I stood at the door when she ran out."

"Did you see the driver?"

"Not clearly—it was dusk. When she stopped to speak to him, I remember that she stiffened suddenly—just dropped into the seat. Then the car moved away, with the man singing—"

Fraser stared. "Singing?"

"Y-yes, sir. I thought nothing of it then, not knowing you very well, sir. He was singing, deep and low, that old tune, *Among My Souvenirs*. Oh, I'm so afraid it was *him*. After all his threats . . ."

"Hinton?" Fraser's face was gray and worn. "Of course, he did it."

Gretchen nodded wretchedly.

"Did Clare model for the Lifelike Form Company—for some wax figures?"

"Oh, yes, sir! Nearly all the stars do that. It brings in a bit of pin money. Many of the exclusive shops like to display their most expensive gowns on figures of the leading lady when each big picture breaks."

Fraser bowed his head wearily. Had the appearance of the forms on all the highways at the hour of Clare's abduction been mere coincidence?

"Keep your chin up, Gretchen. I'll see what I can do. Phone the police, and my hotel, if you hear anything."

Wheeling down out of the hills toward city lights spread over the vast valley below, he flogged his brain for any idea that would serve as a starting point. Hinton, of course—but to find the man! The efforts of two detective agencies employed by Clare Cornell ten days before had not disclosed any clue.

Down in the town, swinging with traffic around the corner of a large department store, he jerked his roadster to the curbing and stared into a display window. Anguish gushed up in his throat and a hoarse exclamation slid across his dry lips, at sight of Clare Cornell, posed there in all her dusky beauty, eyes alight in the broad, sweet face, dainty hands lifted in a graceful gesture.

He sank in the seat with half a groan, realizing that the apparition was only another waxen form from the mold which so recently had clasped her dear body. Fascinated, his glance was drawn back to the figure. Mentally he cringed before a likeness so perfect that he found himself listening for the sound of her lilting voice.

ABRUPTLY, he sent the car surging away; only to encounter the same vision in no less than five establishments. The last window had halted a crowd of excited passersby; for now the raucous shouts of newsboys heralded Clare Cornell's disappearance.

Fraser beat his fists upon the wheel in a spasm of despair. The police would act, of course. But not in time! Hinton was smart—too smart to be caught in the ordinary dragnet they would throw out. There would be artistry in his crime, as superbly efficient as in his work.

Again came the recurring question of a possible connection between the appearance of those disturbing replicas of Clare Cornell, and her physical disappearance from the house. Could the deliveries have been timed with intent to tangle the trail?

Fraser parked in front of a drug store. A glance at a city directory, then a swift ride through crowded streets and into the deserted warehouse district, brought him to a big building which housed the Lifelike Form Company. There was a light in an office window.

Following his imperative knock at the locked door, a young man appeared. As Fraser's quick scrutiny encompassed the well-tailored clothes, the clean-cut face and untroubled eyes, a sense of futility seized him.

"I wish to get in touch with the manager. A matter of urgent importance—"

"I'm the manager—Johnston. Will you come in?"

Fraser glanced about the office. Reason told him that this substantial business place was not the home of deceit and treachery. He said frankly:

"I'm afraid I've followed a blind hunch. Clare Cornell has disappeared. She was carried off from her door by force. Highway patrolmen reported her presence in car at widely scattered points shortly afterward. In each automobile they found one of your wax models."

"Good Lord!" The young man gaped. "Clare Cornell? Why, that's terrible! You're from the police, I suppose. About the models—nothing unusual in that. We have contracts for quick service to quite a number of stores. Each première of a big production means rush work for us,

for the wax figures are not released until the last moment."

Fraser turned to go, but hesitated. A deep-seated hunting sense with which few men are blessed—an instinct for the trail that had led him safely through a thousand miles of Burmese jungle in search of dangerous prey—now urged within him insistently. Fraser asked:

"Who molds your forms? Have you a fellow named Hinton working here?"

"Never heard of such a man. All the figures of stars are made under the personal supervision of Vronsky, our technician. You can talk to him if you wish, but he's a queer case. Seldom leaves the works. A Russian refugee."

THROUGH long, dark corridors which reeked with chemical odors, Fraser followed the manager. Here and there Johnston paused to snap on a light, but these did little to lift obscurity from the gloomy chambers. In the finishing room they passed between rows of weirdly human shapes. It seemed a dark world of phantasms. Some were naked, others clothed. Some strikingly beautiful, others lacking arms or legs or heads. Fraser's raw imagination pictured the lovely body of Clare Cornell as broken and dismembered.

He shuddered, dreading the revolting brutalities to which Hinton's jealousy might lead, for there was in the man a bestial lust that he had never guessed. In her brief experience with him, Clare had discovered a perverted, sadistic streak of character that disgusted and appalled her. Filled with loathing she had severed their bonds as quickly as she could.

Johnston opened an inner door and a bell clanged somewhere beyond. A voice demanded harshly: "Who's there? What do you want?"

"Vronsky! A gentleman to see you."

They waited. Down darkened aisles

sounded the clump of approaching footsteps. Into the dim circle of light walked the wide, ponderous bulk of a man made huger still by bulging features above a flowing black beard. Fraser observed with distaste the blue-vained beak of a nose, the dark-circled eyes which glinted queerly. Beneath a shabby coat the man's shoulders seemed hunched. Big, splay-fingered hands dangled at his sides.

"Who wants to see Boris Vronsky? I want to see nobody. I am busy—"

Fraser said: "I came to ask if you have employed—or if you happen to know —a man called Hinton. About your size, but not stooped. Younger, and blond—"

"For this foolishness you call me from my studies?" Vronsky snorted violently, turned on his heel, started off. "Ask such questions at the office, and don't bother me."

"You see?" Johnston, the manager, chuckled tolerantly. "Crazy—but all artists are crazy, and he's one of the best. Worth ten times what I pay him. Why, he won't let me enter certain parts of my own plant! Jealous of his secret process." He led Fraser away, flicking off lights, evidently eager to be rid of his visitor.

Fraser's mind caught up the thought of secret things and worried it. How easily, for instance, this gloomy building could conceal the body of Clare Cornell. How possible that a queer character like Vronsky could have fallen in with Hinton and lent his aid to the scheme for vengeance.

Something about Vronsky definitely disturbed him. He could not put his finger on the cause. But his mind, trained to super-sensitivity in quaking jungles, felt the impact of mysterious, menacing forces. Hinton and Vronsky! With a faint similarity in their respective arts, mutual interest might have brought them together. The certainty grew in him, that the Russian was, somehow, involved.

THOUGHTFULLY, Fraser went out to his car. The idea was fantastic, reasonless, a blind groping for a clue. He thought that his imagination was building suspicion out of nothing—or had some strange aura of evil about the man registered in an alert cell of his brain? He had experienced stranger phenomona. Almost involuntarily he pulled in to the curb when his car approached the end of the factory.

A taxi passed, and halted at the office door. Johnston came out, departed. Fraser tarried, he knew not why. Minutes later, across the silence of the street, a faintly heard sound floated through an open factory window. Face drawn taut, he listened, scarcely breathing. Music! Accompanied by a voice. The words were indistinguishable but he recognized the air. *Among My Souvenirs.*

Leaping down, Fraser crossed the sidewalk and sought means of reaching the opening ten feet overhead. With the aid of a drain pipe he scrambled to a ledge of stone, wriggled broad shoulders beneath a tilted square of glass and steel, and dragged his body through the aperture. Headlong he dropped, outspread hands striking a work bench.

The music was louder now. A woman's contralto voice raised in song. He hurried across the floor, aided by light filtering in from a corner street-lamp, finding himself in the finishing room where waxen figures stood like rows of pale ghosts. Opening a door at the end he swore softly when a bell clanged. He had forgotten that. But the song continued, undisturbed. Cautiously he made his way along a black corridor. The singer's voice died away on the final note of the score. Fraser paused, hugging the wall, alert eyes boring into the darkness. Then, to his surprise, the song began again, the same refrain. Obviously a phonograph.

He came to another door. What lay beyond? Vronsky, he was sure. But intuition hinted at something more—something fashioned from the stuff of horror. With infinite care he turned a knob. The portal moved noiselessly. He stared through a narrow crack, eyes wide.

Buried in the depths of the grimy factory was this studio, richly furnished. Weird paintings, depicting naked bodies in grotesque positions, hung the walls. Fur-draped divans were scattered about the floor. Lights in amber globes threw a golden sheen over all the scene, and the singing voice swelled into sweet harmony. Four listeners reclined in attitudes of wrapt attention. Beautiful girls, all nude, warm flesh glowing against the skins of animals upon which they lay. But Fraser saw no man.

Without warning a needle-point bit into his side. He gasped, whirled, peered into the impenetrable darkness. Vronsky! Hoarse breathing sounded close at hand. He tried to raise clenched fists defensively. What had the man done to him? His arms seemed weighted down. He could not move. Cold perspiration broke forth upon his brow. Spreading over his muscular system like a frigid tide crept a hideous paralysis.

A despairing cry started up in his throat; his frozen lips and thickened tongue moved once, convulsively; but no breath issued from the congealed lungs. The blackness of eternal night slid down across his mind like a drawn shade. Only the sense of hearing lingered—long enough to register a burst of deep, malignant laughter.

FRASER was awakened by the tumultuous motion of his own heart. Its beating sounded like a drum in his ears. Barely conscious, he lay inert, burdened with torpid uneasiness that he could not, at first, comprehend. So far, he had not opened his eyes, but a sensation of light made him blink; and he stared up at the ceiling, wondering where he was. Then came remembrance—and blighting fear. A wild desperation seized upon him as an inkling of the truth sank home. He struggled to rise, but it was a mental struggle, for his body did not stir upon the couch. Still imprisoned in the grip of that strange paralysis which had vanquished him, he could only roll his head a little.

Memories surged over him. Hinton—and a promise made two years before. The man, after listening to dangerous details concerning the capture of a clouded leopard, had said:

"I'm working on something, not yet perfected, that will make child's play of your work. A chemical agent which, when injected into a beast by arrow, hypodermic, or even a low-powered bullet, will paralyze it instantly and leave it so for hours. It will take all romance out of your new profession." Hinton had laughed enviously.

With intolerable certainty came the thought that Vronsky had hidden Hinton in these secret quarters. Which meant that Clare Cornell, or her dead body, was somewhere near at hand. Fraser's mind reeled with fear for the girl, then steadied into the collected calmness of despair. His eyes swept the length of his outstretched frame. Unfettered he lay, rigid as a log, but each muscle seemed manacled by the drug more effectively than with bands of steel. No, not each one—for he could move his head! Hope sprang into being. Yes, he could clench his fingers, too; and within his boots could wriggle his toes. Since the paralysis had withdrawn from his extremities, would it leave his body?

His eyes focused upon a girl reclining on the nearest couch. Another was visible beyond. The bare leg and foot of a third was within range of his vision, but he could not raise his head to see more. His mouth extended in a red circle as he tried to speak, to shout; but though the lips moved, his tongue felt like a woolen gag and he could utter no sound. Why didn't the women look his way—why didn't they move? Why did they lie in such utter passivity? Realization dawned. They were not girls! Wax models!

Fraser's sense of hearing had grown more acute and he heard some one walking across bare boards. A door opened, the Russian strode into the room, bearing in his arms the slender shape of Clare Cornell. Fraser's heart leaped within him. Waxen or real? Vronsky laid the dainty figure upon a table top, bent over it mouthing cynical endearments. his ugly hands caressing the lovely curves. The girl moaned and stirred. Vronsky threw back his head and laughed—the same guttural bellow which Fraser had heard in the hall. Then the bearded man came toward the couch. Fraser's eyes flicked shut. Vronsky looked down, prodded him with a finger. and muttered:

"You'll be the same as dead for hours."

WALKING over to a small piano in a corner of the room, Vronsky sat down and began to play. Exultantly, victoriously, he sang the song: *Among My Souvenirs.*

Through slitted eyelids Fraser saw that Clare Cornell was regaining consciousness. Feebly she writhed upon the tabletop, a pitiful whimpering in her throat. Vronsky heard, and got up.

"My pretty dear!" He examined her closely. "So you're coming out of it? Maybe I can help." From a drawer he produced a wooden rack which held two hypodermic syringes. Holding them to the light, one in each hand, he checked their contents. "In this one—" he leered down at Clare, "is paralysis or death, according to the dose. And in the other, restoration. You shall taste of both."

Into her tender breast he drove a needle and pressed the plunger with meticulous care. "So! That is enough. Now, for a little while, you shall be normal again."

The girl struggled, sat up. Speechless with insufferable terror, she gazed at her tormentor. And Vronsky—while her eyes distended—removed his coat, displaying square, straight shoulders. He began peeling off patches of black beard, removing plugs and lumps of wax from his nose, rubbing off copious make-up. Finally tossing aside the black wig, he disclosed close-cropped blond hair.

"Mark Hinton!" she gasped.

"Mark Hinton it is. Your beloved ex-husband. The man who cherishes your beauty so highly that he cannot share it with another, nor let it ever fade!"

Slowly but inevitably, Guy Fraser felt himself growing mad. Helpless upon the couch he lay, while a purple frenzy hazed his brain. Then, suddenly, he fell calm when intelligence began to fabricate a thought. He *could* fight off the drug

Clearly across the void of Time came memories of a day in Rangoon. A native riot had threatened desecration of the hallowed precincts of the Shwe Dagon Pagoda until, with fist and pistol, he had driven marauders from its steps. A venerable priest, wishing to reward him, had imparted an ancient Buddhist secret. The wise man called it, "Control of Superlative Strength." The simple truth he preached was domination of mind over matter. Confidence flooded Fraser's senses. Therein lay the strength of the soul! He could— by God, he *would!*—find power to fight.

Hinton was dragging Clare Cornell from the table. "Scream if you must," he sneered. "In the dead of night no one will hear. Come! See the lovely fate I have planned for you." He pulled her toward a feminine figure on the nearest divan; reached down to stroke its hair and face. Seizing Clare's trembling hand he laid it against the pink cheek. She shrank back, eyes riveted upon the lifelike visage.

"She's dead! Oh, God—it is a corpse! The skin . . . is soft . . . not wax."

"Quite dead," Hinton agreed, "all save her beauty. That is Alda—an extra girl who might have been a star. This one —" he pointed, "is Helen Dare. Meet Gloria—" he bowed toward another figure, "and Shirley, too. Are they not as beautiful as when alive?"

WITH a moan, Clare Cornell sank in a quivering heap, face buried in her hands. "Shirley Blaine! I knew her. Oh, you murdered them all . . ."

"All but their beauty," he persisted, smiling crookedly. "Since that is only skin deep, it is easily saved. Just as with the hundreds of animals I've mounted for that fool—" he gestured toward Fraser, "so with these girls—and next with you! It is merely a matter of care and skill to spread the skin over molded forms of wax and preserve it permanently."

Clare's bloodless cheek blenched whiter. "You intend . . . to flay me?"

Hinton nodded. "Alive! But you'll never know. One injection of the liquid I discovered, and you'll feel no pain while I prepare you for perpetual beauty."

"My body," she moaned. "What will become of that?"

"Fraser shall have it!" Harsh laughter crackled on Hinton's lips. "A clever thought. That much he shall have, since I'll bury you together. Down there—" Kicking aside a rug near the table's end, he lifted a wooden trap, pulled out a large, round metal lid. "The acid vats run under this room. It is there that I disposed of the other cadavers, where all trace will soon be lost."

Excitement grew in Hinton's feverish brain. "Now, to work! To remove your beautiful skin—oh, so carefully, so skillfully! You shall be my masterpiece."

Clare Cornell pleaded: "Mark! You can't! Have pity. Oh, you're insane—you'll regret this monstrous thing—"

"You're my wife! I'll do anything I please. Every man to his hobby, and this is mine." Mirth rattled in his throat. "Fraser collected animals from all over the world. Souvenirs of the chase. But I shall collect souvenirs of Love—because they are more beautiful. You'll be queen of the collection." Grasping the second and more deadly syringe, he made an injection that seemed to turn the girl to stone.

Guy Fraser's straining, tortured mind caught up the phrase, twisted it. "Souvenirs of Death!" That was Hinton's dream. The words rang in his head like the tolling of a bell, rousing him to fiercer fighting against the drug. His face streamed with the cold sweat of enormous inward struggle. The dormant muscles *must* respond—the deadened strength must be made to flow.

Wide, staring eyes centered upon one hand, he commanded it to lift, the fist to clench, the arm to move. Mind must prevail! The brute flesh *must* move! Hesitantly, almost imperceptibly, the member rose and dropped again. Broken by the unspeakable exertion, he paused briefly— tried again—focused every spark of his life force upon the awful struggle.

MARK HINTON had brought forth a case of knives. He whetted the gleaming blades with care, gloating as he tested the keen edges upon his thumb, laying them side by side near Clare Cornell's shoulder. Glancing across at the rigid figure of Guy Fraser, he taunted: "Too bad that you can't watch and enjoy this. See, now, how her ivory skin curls away from the steel!"

With point pressed against the girl's arm he made a slight, delicate incision. The gush of crimson seemed to explode a spark in Fraser's brain, and his torpid muscles lashed into life. Staggering up from the couch he launched himself head-long at Hinton. The big man started back, cursing in surprise, blundering against the table jarringly. Knives clattered upon the floor. Hinton drove his heavy fist squarely into Fraser's face.

Fraser's fleeting burst of energy had flared but to die. His tongue lolled between parted lips, his eyes were closed, and he scarcely breathed. Hinton studied him curiously, muttering: "Tough as hell, but you're finished now."

Standing astride the fallen man, callously turning to the task at hand, he regarded the stricken girl upon the table, eyeing the gash in her arm.

"A moment more, and her blood will coagulate enough so that I can finish the job without a mess."

Fraser's half-opened eyes were fixed upon a number of gleaming objects near his head. Knives. Two syringes. His lips curled back from dry teeth in a grimace.

Which one? *Two* syringes! One, Hinton had used to revive Clare. The other contained complete paralysis, if not instant death. Which one?

Slowly, painfully, his right hand crept toward the shining instruments. Which one, ah, God! *which one?* His wild eyes could note no difference in their contents. His fingers clutched the nearer hypodermic spasmodically. Stake all, now, on an even chance? Jab it into Hinton's leg, as he towered there? If the paralyzing fluid froze the man's muscles it would spell deliverance. But if it were the energizing drug—what then?

Fraser's senses wavered. Feebly he fastened his thumb upon the plunger. For life or death! Horror or peace! At one last command of his tottering reason, he sank the needle into his own wrist.

The arm tingled. Over his prone body rushed an exhilarating tide of strength.

With a fierce, roaring cry Fraser reared up, seized Hinton in a crushing embrace. They rocked and strained beside the table, two evenly matched human animals, each burning with the lust to kill.

FRASER caught the upraised hand which grasped a knife. He butted his head into Hinton's chin. But the man was clever—tripped him neatly—and they crashed to the floor. Fraser locked one forearm across the beard-flecked throat. Remembering that the slashing claws of beasts he had captured are more cruel than their fangs, slowly, inexorably, he began to twist the man's knife-arm to the back. Under pressure of a hammerlock the fingers opened, the weapon fell clear.

But Hinton broke the hold, sprang up and away. He drew back his heavy boot for a killing kick. Fraser dodged, caught the swinging foot. Hinton pitched forward, arms and head plunging squarely into the open trap above the vats where he stuck. A slithering rush. Fraser grabbed the flailing legs and heaved with all his strength. A weird, wailing cry as Hinton slid down out of sight. A splash, the gurgle of liquid in a tank.

"Into . . . the acid!" He choked with exhaustion. "Where he destroyed . . . the girls. . . ."

Feverishly he searched about the floor for the two hypodermic syringes, found them unbroken. No question now, as to which was safe. That which held the reviving dose was almost empty. Breathing a prayer that the drug might do its work, he injected the last remaining drops into Clare Cornell's thigh.

Soon her dark eyes opened. Fear went out of them when she saw Guy Fraser standing there. With a glad cry she lifted up her hands to him, and he gathered her into his hungry arms.

The Unholy

By
Wyatt
Blassingame

*(Author of "River of Pain,"
etc.)*

I SAW her first there in the moonlight. It was just a bare stirring of something which I could not see, but I must have known, even then, that it was she. I felt the need and the terror of her, and I went toward her as a spider goes to his death, knowing that it means destruction—unable to resist.

That's the way it started, Doctor. You have asked me to tell the whole story to you. Well, here it is . . .

You won't believe, because it does not agree with the slender thread of knowledge you and your profession use to sew

Goddess

**Novelette
of
Fear and
Dread**

*They have hidden my face, they have masked me;
They have locked me into a cell.
For my face is the face of a demon,
And my soul is a spirit from hell.*

body and soul together. But how much do you actually know, you and your profession? You'll *say* it was the dope, but when you look at my face—which you are afraid to do now—and at the thick, black hairs on the back of my hands, *you'll know!*

I had to finish my designs for the Jefferson Davis bridge. There were only two weeks before the contest closed. Winning that contest meant everything to me. There was the big prize, the fame, and the big contracts it would bring. I could have married Nita then. God! How I loved that girl. And she loved me, too. She wanted me to win as much as I did. She was the one who suggested that I take Mike's cabin in the mountains and work. I had to work day and night if I were going to finish on time. She and her brother Mike would drive up and see me Friday night.

I went up on Sunday. It was lonely there, not another house in miles. Just that flat, grassy shelf high up on the mountain where the cabin sat, and the long, black-green sweep of trees downward and the short, steep rise to the top. On the far side of the clearing was a tangle of big rocks and out of them the little spring bubbled. Lobo, my airedale, used to lie there and watch the little green lizard in the water.

The plans didn't work out as rapidly as I'd hoped. After two days, I started working nearly all night.

At first I took just a little dope to keep me awake. It made my head feel clear and bubbling like the spring and I worked better. After that I kept taking it. But the dope didn't have anything to do with what happened. You don't believe me, but I know! Look at the marks on my chest. How could I bite myself there? No. That was Arlisa . . .

IT BEGAN on Wednesday, at late twilight. I was working before a great open window that looked out across the grassy clearing. I could see the dark blur of the rocks about the spring and the black wall of trees that reached straight up—the way trees look at twilight, as if they didn't have any limbs but were one solid, black mass reaching up to touch the gray-blue sky. There were a lot of crickets keeping up a shrill, sleepy chirping and very suddenly a mocking-bird began to sing.

The moon, almost new, was like a curled feather just above the tree tops straight across the clearing. It was giving a lot of light for such a small moon. There were pale silver beams floating down. I sat there staring out into the moon-light without knowing what I was watching. At first I didn't see anything abnormal, but for some reason I couldn't take my eyes from that almost new moon, and I marveled at the way it came streaming into the yard like sunlight through a curtained window.

Then I saw something else.

The blood went very cold in my veins. It was warm weather and I was working without a coat, but I shuddered. The pencil slipped from my fingers, thudded on the drawing-board, and rolled downward with a brittle sound.

Some deep, hidden recess of my brain must have known even then that horror and agony and death were to come, for there was nothing out there in the moonlight that first time to make a man feel as I did. Yet it *was* strange. The light from that slender moon flooding into the yard and those tiny, dancing motes, like the motes in a sunbeam. There was just one group of them, and they all seemed to move together, swaying back and forth. There was something sinister, something horribly lovely about the way they moved. I thought vaguely of a woman and the soft undulations of her hips. And I thought, too, of a panther, or a snake.

Abruptly, then, I was conscious that all sound had ceased. The crickets' chirping had faded into the dusk. The mocking-bird had hushed. The very wind seemed to hang motionless.

Lobo growled. I moved my head slowly until I saw him. He was less than five feet away, standing stiff-legged, head thrust toward the window, eyes glowing. I said, "What is it, old fellow?"

He looked at me and took one step forward. I could see that the hairs along his neck were stiff and erect. He stood there, looking up for a long moment. Abruptly he began to back away.

"What the hell!" I said. Lobo had belonged to me since he was six weeks old. I'd shared my last can of potted ham with him on bad-luck hunting trips. I loved him and talked to him like a human being. He backed away until he reached the wall.

Then, in the utter silence that crept like an animal through the cabin, I *felt* her calling me. I can't say I heard her, for there was no sound. But suddenly I was thinking of a woman, of some half wild, primitive, savage woman. A hot ball seemed to rise from my stomach and lodge high in my chest. I caught one long breath and turned toward the open window, staring out through it, expecting—I don't know what . . .

There was the moon just above the wall of trees, the soft stream of light falling into the clearing. And in the moonlight the motes moved vaguely. Once **again** I thought of a woman—and of a beast.

I don't remember getting up from my chair, but I remember the way Lobo edged away as I went toward the door. I almost stopped then; my mouth was open to speak to him, but no sound came. For deep in my stomach I could hear the voice calling me again, though I didn't know then that it was a voice. I didn't even know why I went on through the door and across the porch.

The roof cut the moonlight off the top step and I stood there looking out to where the motes showed like some half-forgotten dream. I wondered why they were just in that one place. Perhaps some little wind devil had tossed up a bit of dust. But there was no wind.

Then I stepped out into the moonlight.

COLD spray seemed to strike *inside* my body. There was no feeling of anything touching my skin, and yet I was conscious of the savage coldness stirring within me. I stood there, mouth half open, sucking quick, deep breaths. My

eyes felt wide and staring, yet I was looking at nothing.

Abruptly I noticed that my breathing sounded like Lobo's growls. I shut my lips and began to breathe more slowly through my nose. My muscles were taut and again I found myself thinking of some creature that was almost as much beast as woman—a girl with the grace and beauty of a tiger, uninhibited, flaming emotions, who took love . . .

I shook my head. "That's a hell of a thing to be thinking," I said aloud. "Better get back and go to work." Looking up, I saw that the moon had sunk below the trees and I was standing in deep shadows. Down the mountainside a mocking-bird whistled a few broken notes. A cricket chirped shrilly.

I went back into the house, clicked on the light and sat down at the desk. My work didn't go well, though I stuck at it until long after midnight.

Three hours sleep did little **to refresh** me, and all the next morning my work continued slowly. I was too restless to stay at my drawing-board. I knew I had to work, but I kept getting out of my chair and pacing around the room like a caged bear. Then I would force myself back to the drawing-board.

I tried to think of Nita and of how much it meant to her that I should finish these plans. But somehow the thought of her wouldn't come clearly.

At eleven that morning I stopped work to eat lunch. It was a full hour earlier than usual, but I was hungry. Always I had eaten only a salad at lunch, but now I took a steak from the icebox. The meat felt good to my fingers and I gripped it tightly until blood oozed up across my nails. I dropped the steak into a frying-pan and licked the blood from my fingers. It tasted good. I didn't realize then that I was acting strangely.

I walked back into my room and looked

out of the big window. Lobo was lying in the shadows near the spring, but he wasn't watching the water lizard now. He had his head raised a few inches above his paws and his eyes were fastened on the house.

I stuck my head out of the window and called to him. "Hey! Come on in. Lunch's ready."

He got to his feet slowly. His head was thrust stiff and straight in front of him, eyes glaring at me. Then he all but cringed backward. He vanished behind one of the rocks.

I stood staring after him, saying "What the hell?" I had seen him meet a mountain cat once, but I had never seen him afraid. He had looked at me as if he were afraid, but why . . .? I half turned toward the door to go after him, stopped. "I'll eat first," I said aloud.

The frying-pan was hot through now, and the steak was just beginning to sizzle.

Usually I like my meat well done, but as I stood there staring down at the steak, smelling the thick odor, I wanted to eat this one rare. I took it up with my fingers, set my teeth in it, and tore loose a piece. I tried to chew it, but I felt too hungry and swallowed the whole thing. I began to gnaw at the steak, swallowing it in chunks.

Perhaps I ate half of it this way before I realized what I was doing. It made a chill shiver along my spine, and I stood motionless, staring at the meat. It was almost raw and my fingers were smeared with blood. I put the steak on a plate, took out silverware and sat down. But I kept dropping my knife and fork to pick up the meat with my hands without knowing that I did so. When I caught myself, I felt ashamed.

I felt a little terrified, too, without knowing why. Somewhere back in my brain I must have known what was hap-pening, but it was only a dim, restless feeling that frightened me.

When I had finished the first steak I ate another. And it, too, I ate almost raw. I knew I ought not eat that much, but I didn't seem able to stop. My fingers were clumsy with the knife and fork and I had to fight myself to keep from devouring the meat like a dog.

THE afternoon passed slowly. About four o'clock I took another capsule. After that my head was a little clearer and I worked better. Now and then when I looked up from the drawing-board I could see Lobo in the shadows near the spring. He wasn't sleeping, but kept wide eyes fastened on me. And even at that distance I thought I could see something in his eyes which had never been there before. I shivered as if the water lizard had crawled along my spine.

Perhaps I became absorbed in my work. Perhaps I dozed without knowing it. All I can be certain of is that suddenly I was fully conscious of myself hunched over the desk, a pencil in my hand. But I wasn't drawing. My hand was very still and the fingers gripped the pencil until my knuckles bulged. Even my breath was high in my chest, and motionless. My eyes were staring down at the drawing-board.

It was very dark in the room and I knew that twilight had come again. Far out on the mountain a cricket chirped, and ceased. Stillness came flooding like a great river through the cabin—an intense, straining silence that hurt my ears like thunder.

Inside my body I was cold and still and listening. I knew that moonlight was streaming into the little clearing outside the window, but I had not raised my eyes from the board. And once again I began to think of some savage, half-wild woman. Of how her naked arms would feel about my shoulders, red lips curled fiercely back from white teeth.

Slowly my eyes moved along the paper-covered drawing-board, across the black gap between the desk's edge and the window-sill, and beyond the window into the night.

The trees at the edge of the clearing were a black, serrated wall towering into the sky, leaning toward the cabin, ready to crash down upon it. And above the trees was the broken edge of the moon, just a little larger than the night before. Over the tree tops, silver-gray light came drifting down into the clearing.

In the center of the grassy yard was the little cluster of motes that floated and swayed in the moonlight. My eyes got bigger as I stared at them and the muscles at the hinges of my jaw began to ache.

For the motes were thicker tonight. Their shape was hazy and indistinct, broken now and then by the low wind out of the dusk. I couldn't say, "That is a woman." The moonlight was not as bright as the night before, and staring with bulging eyes I felt sure the figure was only moonmist. But a woman with long, blowing hair seen dimly through a weaving fog might . . .

I felt her call again. I didn't think there was one sound in that vast world of silence. Nature hung paused, waiting. But perhaps there was some sound, perhaps it was the wind.

A wild and terrible longing gripped me. I staggered to my feet and the chair crashed over. The noise boomed about the room, ending abruptly.

It was then that I began to fight against the feeling. I can't tell how I knew that to surrender would bring death or a terrible, wild and unbelievable horror worse than any pit of hell. But I knew.

My body was a furious torment of desire. It was as if I had always been in love with some woman whose love was

fire and muscle and tearing passion and now that woman was just outside the window, almost within reach. I couldn't quite see her there in the moonlight, but those motes, moving with the lithe, sensual grace of a panther, might be her shadow. I turned and took one lunging step toward the door.

With my back to the window the thought of Nita came to me and I stopped. "I'm going crazy," I said aloud. "I can't give in to this thing. It's—it's death if I do!"

But even as I could foresee the vague shadow of horror, so I knew that it was unavoidable. I knew then that I was damned and that fight as I might, I could not win. But God! I didn't know the things that were ahead. I didn't know the horror and agony and bestial lust which was to follow.

The porch was gloomy under its overhanging roof. I walked to the end of it and stopped just within the shadow. Somehow I was desperately afraid of the moonlight and I tried to cringe back from it as a candle-fly might fight back from an open flame.

A low wind came out of the dark trees and slid across the clearing. It caught the motes in the moonlight, blew them closer to me, made them writhe and twist like a woman racked by passion. It touched on my face where sweat stood in large beads—and again I thought I heard the mewing, sobbing catch of a woman's voice.

My shoulders swung forward. Fear jumped in my chest and tried to stop me. Then I went off the porch into the moonlight.

CHAPTER TWO

Man Into Beast

LATER that night I tried to tell myself that the dope I had taken played some part in the thing which followed.

I tried to say that my nerves were cracking under the strain of working day and night.

I stood there in the moonlight shaking the way a sapling quivers when an ax strikes it. Deep down in my soul something was stirring, changing, growing into horror. My brain was a torrent of fear and I wanted to turn and run, dive back into the cabin, slam the door and lock the windows. But I could not move.

The wind came again, as soft as the touch of a woman's hair. I was sure now that I heard a voice, but there were no words. It was only sound, a purring, passionate sound, such as a black panther might make.

Fear went out of me then. I was conscious of nothing except desire—a savage, blood-hungry desire. I started toward those floating shadows in the moonlight. Now they were more definitely like a woman half hidden by mist. I thought I could see the furious sweep of tawny hair about naked shoulders, hear the heavy, panting breath. There was a harsh, feral noise in my throat as I moved.

Without warning there was another sound. Ferocious, horrible, it came from behind me and slightly to the right. I whirled, hands clawlike. Bestial anger whipped through my body.

Lobo was coming full tilt across the grassy lawn. His lips had curled back showing long teeth. Saliva drooled from his mouth.

He was trying to save me by attacking the thing he feared. Unconsciously I knew it even then. But it made no difference.

I went berserk. I flung myself headlong between him and those eerie, swaying motes.

He tried to dodge me, but he was running too fast. His feet skidded and he went over on his side. I crashed down on top of him.

I don't remember the minutes or two that followed. I must have been mad. I could feel my fingers sink into his throat, feel the rough brush of the hair against my hands, his feet clawing at my chest. I heard the choked sound that he made, and another sound. It was a blood-hungry growling, a sickening, insane noise, but I scarcely knew that it came from my own mouth.

We rolled over and over, fighting. My fingers never lost their grip on his throat, and never once did he try to bite me, though it was only later I thought of that. At last the writhing of his body grew fainter and stopped. I stood up then, holding the dead dog by the throat.

I was laughing. It wasn't like any laughter that ever came from the mouth of a human being, but it didn't sound strange to me then. Joy flooded up through my body like hot breaths of air.

We were near the right edge of the clearing where the ground dropped almost perpendicularly for twenty feet to a tangle of rocks and bushes. Whirling the dog, I flung him out over the edge. A moment later the body plunged through the bushes and made a soft, crunching sound on the rocks.

I KEPT laughing, but I was becoming conscious of the sound. The flame of anger and desire was going out of me as I turned, expecting to see the vague, half definite shape in the moonlight. I expected to go toward it and find—I don't know exactly when I expected.

I took three steps and stopped. I felt dazed, puzzled, like a man awaking from a nightmare and uncertain whether it were dream or reality. My gaze moved slowly across the clearing.

The grass showed black and the house was a dark blot against the mountainside.

My head turned slowly toward the west, and up. The moon had slid from sight.

Remembering the thing I had done to Lobo there was a part of me that became physically sick. I had loved that dog, and had killed him. Why? Terror swept over me like a great wave striking. The toughness went out of my muscles and I dropped on my knees, my hands clutching at my face. "Oh God!" I said. "I must be going crazy. I couldn't have done that! I couldn't!"

But somewhere in me there was a thing that wasn't sorry. Like a crawling worm inside me I could feel a tiny spot of savage, animal joy. And when I felt that, I *was* afraid.

What was happening to me? What sort of hellish change was coming over me? Why did I see this thing in the moonlight, feel this way inside me? I knelt there holding my face, muscles ridged with cold, and tried to force my mind to accept the logical explanation. I was working too hard, taking too much dope. It was only a mental breakdown, madness, that was making me see this thing, feel this way.

I said these things aloud and when I heard the sound of the words I broke into demoniacal, choking laughter. Good God! What was this thing that I should prefer being crazy?

I stopped laughing, and quietness flooded the black mountainside. Down toward the valley a whippoorwill set up its lugubrious, three-noted call. A cricket chirped.

I stood up slowly. I know my mouth was open and my face must have been very white in the darkness. Twice I tried to speak.

At last the words came. "I've got to fight it. I've got to fight it. I won't give in—when *she* calls again."

For a long minute I stood listening to the sound of the words, realizing what they meant. I didn't really believe it was the dope or madness which made this thing come to me in the moonlight. I knew that *she* was real, and I think I knew that she brought death and terror with her. My knees were weak as I went toward the house and I staggered.

It was impossible to work. I forced myself to sit hunched over my drawing-board for nearly an hour, but it was no use. My eyes kept shifting furtively to the window, staring out into the darkness while my heart hung cold against my ribs. I kept thinking of a woman with savage hair blowing across naked shoulders and white teeth showing through lips curled in a snarl and a kiss.

"Maybe I better get some sleep," I said aloud. "Work better tomorrow."

It was inky dark in the cabin when I put out the light, but I found the way to my room with no trouble. It was almost as if I could see in the darkness. I didn't actually see, yet I avoided chairs and a table almost instinctively. "Must be getting to know my way around pretty well," I said. I'd developed the habit of talking to Lobo that way when we were alone and now in the deep stillness I could imagine the sound of his feet. It reminded me of the thing I had done and terror and despair and an unholy joy flooded up through me. I cursed, and reaching my room, flung myself fully dressed on the bed.

Perhaps ten minutes or more passed before I noticed the position in which I was lying. I was on my left side, body slightly curved, feet together. My arms were close against my body, bent at the elbow and my hands under my chin. It was the way a cat might curl up beside an open fire or a dog bed down in dust beside a Negro cabin. My eyes came wide open when I realized that and the bottom seemed to fall from my stomach. I sat up quickly, feeling cold. "What's happening to me?" I said aloud.

After a minute or two I stood up. "I've got to fight," I said. "I've got to fight."

IT WAS gray dawn when I awoke. It was strange the way I felt then. I must have awakened physically but not mentally and I acted as an animal might have done. I was hungry and I slid out of bed and walked straight for the kitchen. There was only one piece of meat in the icebox, and taking it out I began to knaw on it raw.

I remember doing these things, yet I did them without thought and utterly unconscious of their meaning. I had half finished the steak when I awoke mentally. It was like a somnambulist awaking to find that he had committed murder in his sleep.

Consciousness came to my mind with a jerk and I found myself standing naked in the kitchen, my hands stained with blood from the raw meat. I could feel in my belly the heavy lumps that I had swallowed without chewing.

For one long minute I stood rigid, cold. Realization went through me like sluggish blood moving slowly. Then a deep sob came out of my chest. The rest of the steak fell to the floor. I turned and stumbled back to the bed, flung myself face down, crying, "It's too late."

The hopelessness died slowly. Something hard and determined took its place. I sat up, hands clenching the bed. "I don't know just what's happening to me," I said aloud. "But I won't let it! I won't let it!" My voice rose high and shrill like the scream of a mountain cat.

This was Friday, I remembered. Nita and Mike were coming up about twilight. As soon as they came I would make them carry me back to the city. Nita had driven me up and gone back in the car. If there

had been a way to leave, perhaps I could have escaped that day.

When I thought of Nita I felt sick again. With my mind I remembered how I had loved her, and high in my chest I could still feel that love. But it wasn't like it had been. I wanted her to come and take me away from there and at the same time I didn't want to see her. There was another woman now—a woman whose love was bestial and furious. . . .

I caught at my thoughts, jerked them away from the thing I had seen in the moonlight. I carried my brain in an iron hoop of will-power and I forced myself through the rest of the day by the clock.

I dressed and went into the kitchen. Taking the meat from the floor I washed it, put it back in the icebox. It wasn't easy to do that. Hunger was like a thousand rats gnawing at my stomach. I wanted meat. My hands were shaking when I took three eggs from the refrigerator, then closed the door. I ate those eggs, toast and coffee. Nothing else. My teeth were clenched until my jaws ached when I got up from the table and forced myself into the next room.

All morning I sat before my drawing-board, but try as I might I couldn't make myself work. I kept looking out at the grassy lawn where I had seen *her,* jerking my eyes back to the desk. Now and then I would half rise from the chair and turn toward the kitchen, my nose wrinkling like a dog's. Then my hands would clench on the desk.

For lunch I cooked what was left of the steak and ate it. The odor of the meat while it was sizzling in the pan almost drove me insane. Little whimpering noises would begin deep in my chest and rise up through my throat. After I heard the sound they made I kept my lips shut and the whimpers would beat against them.

I forced myself to eat slowly. I was still hungry when I went back into the study and sat before the desk. The long afternoon dragged past.

THE SUN was still thirty minutes high when I heard the sound of a car on the narrow mountain road. I leaped to my feet and half ran toward the door. I stopped, gripping the knob.

What would I tell Nita and Mike? How could I explain that we had to leave here before sundown? It meant giving up all hope of finishing my plans, of winning the prize. We had counted on that.

Through the curtained front window I saw the roadster pull into view, puffing against the steepness of the mountain. As they pulled into the yard Nita jumped out and started toward the porch.

Mike backed the car around, headed it down hill, then he crawled out. I watched them as they came across the yard.

Nita was wearing a white sport dress and no hat. The level sun caught her brownish hair and made golden spiderwebs glitter within it. Her eyes were very level under level brows and her face was just one shade too round to be perfectly oval. The last time I had seen that face and the easy grace with which she carried her body, it had almost taken my breath away. Now I felt sullen, angry.

Behind her Mike came swinging along. He looked like his sister, but was taller, nearly as tall as I am though not as heavy in the shoulders.

Nita was at the edge of porch when I pushed open the door and stepped out. She lifted her head and little lines crinkled at the corners of her mouth as she smiled happily. "Oh Nita! I'm so—"

Her voice stopped the way a dove falls when your shot takes him head on. She stood there staring up at me, her eyes growing wider in her face, the blood falling away to leave the rouge on her lips a vicious red.

The way she looked brought me to a jerking halt. There was terror in her face, and horror.

And then anger flamed in me. It seemed to me even then, the way I acted. But I couldn't help it. I didn't want Nita. I almost hated her then. I wanted the beast-girl in the moonlight.

I said, "Well, what the hell are you standing there staring at? Come in, if you're going to."

She looked as if I had slapped her. Her mouth opened a bit, then closed. Color flowed into her face. Her voice was strange when she said, "Nate, what. . . ?"

Behind her Mike had stopped and was staring up at me. I don't think he'd heard what I said, but he'd got the tone of my voice. In the long pause my temper cooled.

Mike said, "You must have been working pretty hard."

"Yes."

Nita said, "Oh darling, that's what it is." She began to smile again. "You haven't even taken time to shave. When I first saw you, I thought. . . ." Her voice faded as though she were afraid to say the words. Suddenly she came running up the steps toward me, her arms open. I stood waiting, thinking that my face must be covered with dark stubble—almost like Lobo's.

Her body felt wooden and awkward against mine. That was odd, because God never made a more graceful, pliant woman. But I didn't want to hold her now. It wasn't a restrained, civilized embrace that I wanted. It was that woman in the moonlight with lips that snarled for a kiss.

"What did you think when you first saw me?" I asked.

She laughed softly. "It's funny, but I thought that. . . ." She had taken a step backward as she spoke and looked up into my eyes again. Her voice broke and terror leaped into her face.

She backed close against Mike. He was staring over her head at me. "What the hell," I said. "Did you buy a ticket to come stare at me?"

Mike laughed. It had a rather tinny sound. He said, "It is worth a dime to see the Old Man of the Mountain. You've got so many whiskers on your face, you'll get afraid to look in the mirror and shave."

"Well, come on in," I said, "and I'll try to cut them off." Without waiting for Nita to go ahead of me I turned and stepped through the door, went straight toward the bathroom. Behind me there was a strained silence.

I cut on the light in the bath, took out my razor and brush without once looking into the mirror. There was a cold blackness in my stomach that grew larger as I worked up a lather on my face. I began to breathe more rapidly and my eyes kept staring down at the basin.

Suddenly I knew. I was afraid to look into the mirror!

CHAPTER THREE

"Get Rid of Her!"

THE MUSCLES in my arms and back were stiff and hard as I raised my eyes. I could feel the right corner of my mouth jerking.

At last my eyes found the mirror. A harsh, feral sound jerked in my throat. My eyes began to swell, then to contract as I stared at my reflection.

There's no need to tell you how I looked. You can see that now. There was no visible change, yet there was a change. At first I tried to tell myself that it was the lather and the beard. But I knew different. I could see the animal looking at me out of my own eyes. And the way my lower lip turned back. . . . But mainly it was the eyes.

I shaved rapidly, hardly knowing that I did so. "We'll get out of here," I kept muttering. "We'll get out of here. We've got to!" But I kept feeling that thing stirring deep inside me and I kept wondering if the moon were shining yet.

And all the while I was afraid, horribly afraid. "We've *got* to leave here before the moon rises," I said aloud.

God! I tried. I tried to fight myself out of the room, leave with the lather still on my face, run screaming into the living room and tell Nita and Mike that we had to go. And I kept thinking deep inside me that they would believe me crazy. They'd want to put me to bed. There wasn't any chance of getting away in time.

I didn't look at myself any more than was necessary. When I had finished shaving I dried my face, cut off the light and went out. I could hear the sound of Nita's voice as I went toward the study where she and Mike were waiting, but before I reached the door she quit talking. They were both facing the door when I came in. Nita was in a chair to the left and I could see that her fingers made dents in the cushioned arm.

Mike tried to be natural, but there were overtones in his voice. I knew that he wasn't saying the things he thought, for he too had seen the change in my face. "How- are you getting along with your plans?" he asked.

I said shortly, "I'm not working on them much." I was staring out of the open window now. The sun had gone down, but there was still a streak of scarlet over the treetops. And in the greenish blue sky above was the moon.

Nita's sharp cry snatched my mind back to the moment. "Nathan! What do you mean, you're not working on them much? Aren't you going to finish on time?"

The anguish in her tone stirred what was left of the human within me. I turned toward her quickly and my face must have been almost natural for a moment. "Not much more than seventeen or eighteen hours a day," I lied.

MIKE asked, "Where's Lobo? I haven't seen him since I came."

The question cracked like a whip inside my chest. I was feeling almost human when he asked it, and the sudden remembrance of the thing I had done struck me like a blow. I think I staggered and I could feel my lips jerking. I was suddenly sick with shame and dread and terror. My face must have shown it for Mike said quickly, "Has anything happened?"

Nita came out of her chair with a rush. I heard the tap of her heels and turned to face her, raising my right hand as if to keep her away from me. I felt unclean and nasty.

She caught my hand in both of hers, held it close to her breasts. "What is it, Nate? What's happened?" For one moment her eyes looked into mine and I saw that look of fear and disbelief come into her face again. Her eyes wavered and she began to rub smooth fingertips across the back of my hand.

I didn't answer, and abruptly she quit rubbing her fingers over my hand. Her head lowered slightly. She said, "Why, I didn't know you had hair on the back of your hands. I—I'd never noticed it."

I said, "What are you talking about?" There wasn't any hair on the back of my hands. I knew that. Pulling my right hand away from her I looked at it.

A nerve began to twitch in my forehead and I could feel my tongue skidding between my lips like that of a dog. I held my left hand up beside the right hand, stared at them both.

Small black hairs covered the backs and extended out over the first two knuckles. The nails were dirty and rounded at the ends. The hands looked like the paws of a dog!

"Oh Christ!" I whimpered aloud.

There was no answer and a full half minute must have crawled into eternity before I realized— *Outside the window the world was a taut thread of silence where even the wind was afraid to move.*

My eyes moved with the slow inevitability of death. I didn't want to see the thing which would be just beyond the window. I was afraid once more, terribly afraid.

I saw the corner of the desk, the top of it, the drawing-board, the curtain at the window. I tried to turn then and look at Nita. God! I didn't want to look out.

It must have been a half minute that I stood there motionless—unable to turn toward Nita, not daring to look the other way. I could feel Mike and his sister staring at me with wide, dazed eyes, but neither spoke nor moved.

And then I heard the voice of the girl in the moonlight!

I heard it this time, though it was very low, and Mike and Nita may not have caught the sound. It was scarcely a whisper, but it was a husky, full-throated whisper of raging passion, and long, insatiable desire. I made a growling sound in my throat and my gaze swung to the window.

Moonlight was a stream of luminous silver pouring over the ebony grass. In the center of the yard was the point where the motes had danced, but there were no motes there tonight. *She was there!*

I COULD see the outline of her body plainly, though her back was to the moon so that her face was shadowed. She was totally naked, but with the clean, natural nakedness of a Greek statue. But there was nothing cold or marble about her. Even in the moonlight I could see her body vibrate with passion.

She was a tall woman, with long,

straight legs, a full body, and high, rounded breasts. Her hair hung in a stormy cascade about her face. Some of it fell over her left shoulder, down across one breast and almost to her hip. Even in the moonlight I knew that her hair was the tawny gold of a leopard.

Very faintly there came that throbbing, aching call again. She raised her hand and beckoned.

I turned and went stumbling to the door. Mike's wide, half-afraid eyes seemed to stare at me out of space. Behind me I heard Nita's sobbing cry, but I kept going. And fear moved with me. I knew in that moment how a spider goes to its mate, knowing that satiety is death. For it meant death for me also; I knew that, and terror was a black typhoon within me. But I couldn't stop.

Once more I felt the moonlight strike *within* me like cold spray, and once more it drove fear from my body, replacing it with a wild, animal fury and primitive desire. I went stumbling toward the girl whose naked body awaited me.

She had half turned to face me, and the moonlight fell along her profile. Her face was like her body, large and beautiful with a savage, hungry beauty. Her eyes were wide and sloping like those of a great cat and they burned like yellow fire beneath her tawny hair. Her mouth was large and eager. Against the whiteness of her skin the lips were hideously crimson as though wet with blood. They curled back in a passionate snarl.

There came a strange sound from my lips as I went toward her. It was like the screams that you hear cats make sometimes, though more guttural and not quite as loud. My hands were in front of me, reaching for her, while I was still thirty feet away.

She began to move away from me slowly, but I could see her eyes now and the desire in them.

I tried to run toward her, catch her more quickly, but my muscles were aching, jerky, and I couldn't control them. It make me angry that she was moving back toward the far edge of the clearing. I wanted to get my hands on her, sink my fingers into the milky whiteness of her flesh, gnaw at those blood red lips with my teeth.

"Damn you!" I said. The words tore from my lips. "Stay where you are! Wait!" I was within ten feet of her now and I could hear her breathing.

She stopped, almost at the shadowed edge of the yard, her face raised, lips parted, eyes glowing. The sight of her halted me for a moment and I was almost sick with desire. She spoke then, words that I understood, though they had the sound of sobbing ecstacy. "You can't—tonight. You're not yet ready for me. You're not changed enough—and there's the other woman."

At first I didn't know what she meant. I wasn't conscious of anything except the throbbing agony within me. And then slowly horror began to crawl like a slimy thing through my mind. I knew then, before I asked, what she meant, and I was afraid as no human being has ever before been afraid. There was some spark of my old self, some part of humanity left to me, and it writhed at the horror growing in my mind.

"What do you mean?" I asked.

"The woman in the cabin," she said. I could see her breasts quiver as she spoke and in her eyes there was lust and yellow jealousy.

"What—what can I do—about her?" I asked.

But I knew what this beast-woman wanted. The very thought of it made me want to run screaming into the woods, to fling myself over some high cliff.

"You must get rid of her, for me. Then come—"

Her voice stopped sharply. I saw the red lips twitch and a new look of terror and hatred come into the yellow eyes. Suddenly she vanished.

I STOOD looking after her, dazed. My body was still weak with passion, still sick at the thing which she had demanded. But the moonlight kept on sifting over me, running like some cold and effervescent poison through my veins. And as the cold light tingled through me, that change went on more rapidly within my soul. A low growl came up and pushed through my lips. It wasn't so much, after all, to kill a person. Animals did it constantly, and what were we but animals?

The steps were barely audible on the grass. I don't think I heard them, but suddenly there was a new odor in my nostrils—a human odor. I spun about, snarling.

Mike Montgomery was about thirty feet away from me. His right hand was close against his hip and I could see the moonlight glint on the automatic he held. But the sight meant no more to me than it would have to a mad dog. Mike himself had lost all personality for me. The moonlight in my body had driven out all human feeling. All I saw when I looked at him was the *thing* which had driven the woman away from me, the *thing* that must be destroyed before I could have her back.

I began to move toward him, slowly. There was a growling blood-hungry noise, and I knew that it came from my own throat. I could see my hands chest high in front of me, the dirty, hooked nails, the black coarse hair.

Sudden terror showed in Mike's face. I could see his lips twitching as he began to move backward, the gun coming more and more in front of him. "Stay where you are," he said.

I remember now that I heard those words, but at the time they meant nothing to me. There was no meaning for me except the lust for blood in my veins.

"I'll shoot!" His voice was shaking. "Have you gone crazy?"

I kept going at him, half crouched, growling. His face was as white as a ghost, and the gun quivered in the light.

"Stop!" he said again.

I plunged head first. He waited too long to pull the trigger. He didn't want to kill me. I saw him bringing up the gun slowly, saw it shaking as I dived. Then my hands were on him and we were crashing over together. The gun roared. I heard the sound, but it meant nothing to me.

Mike was no weakling, and terror put added strength into his body; but I was too big for him. I fought like a beast. I remember gouging my fingers at his eyes, searching for his throat with my teeth. His hands pounded at me, caught at my face and tore. But I hardly felt the pain.

My right thumb found his eye. He made a short choked sound and his head went back. His chin tilted up and there was his throat just below my face. I heard the snarl that came from my mouth as I ducked.

Warm blood spouted. It flowed over my face and into my mouth. I swallowed, kept my teeth grinding deeper. Under me Mike twisted like a burned snake, but I kept my hands beating at his face, my teeth in his throat. At last he grew still. . . .

I got to my hands and knees and squatted there like a wolf, staring down at him. His face was a mass of blood, his throat torn. I began to laugh softly, savagely. The moonlight felt like cold fury inside my body and I was glad—glad of what I had done to him!

Hooking my fingers in his collar, I came erect, dragged the body to the edge of the flat shelf. Here the ground fell away to the tangle of rocks and brush into which I had thrown Lobo's body. It seemed funny that I should dump the two together, and I rolled Mike down the cliff, saying aloud, "Dog and dog together. Man's an animal anyway."

I heard his body bound along the incline, crash into the brush.

The blood on my face was growing cold and sticky now. I licked as much of it as I could reach with my tongue, then I licked my hands. I was still ravenously hungry, and the blood tasted good.

I turned toward the point where the beast-woman had vanished. "I've killed for her," I thought. "She should come and thank me." Desire for her topped even the hunger that gnawed at my vitals.

But there was no sign of her where moonlight and shadow melted together. The moon was very low now.

And then again my nose wrinkled like that of a dog and I caught an odor that seemed familiar, though I didn't know at first what it was. But for some reason it sent the blood pounding through my body, made me want to kill, to rip warm flesh with my hands, and I turned about, snarling again.

Standing in the moonlight just beyond the edge of the cabin porch was Nita Montgomery. Her face was as pale as a moonflower under the brown hair, and her eyes were dark pools of shadow. Even from where I stood I could see that she was frightened.

I heard the growling sound come out of my mouth. My tongue lolled like that of a wolf across my lips, hungry for more blood. I started across the lawn half crouched, hairy hooked fingers ready for her throat.

CHAPTER FOUR

"For Each Man Kills the Thing He Loves . . ."

IN ALL the world there was utterly no sound. My feet moved as silently as those of a cat.

God knows I didn't want to kill her, not in that tiny spot of a soul I had left. But I couldn't help what I did. There was some part of a human being left to me, for I could see myself walking across the lawn, my head pushed far in front of me, lips curled back from bloody teeth.

My back was to the moonlight, so she couldn't see into my face at first. She called out, "Nate, where's Mike? He came out looking for you, and then I heard a shot. Neither of you came back, and—and. . . ." Her voice trailed away. Her body stiffened. Her mouth was slightly open and her hands came up tense and trembling toward her breasts.

I kept going forward. I could smell the delicate odor of her body as clearly as I could see her—and I could feel the cold fury of the moonlight in me, driving me. One of the scratches on my face was bleeding and blood oozed down across my chin.

Nita screamed sharply. It was a shrill, high scream, but flat with terror. She began to back away from me toward the cabin. I could hear her breathing, see myself going toward her, bloody hands ready, lips curled back.

Abruptly she spun and leaped for the house. I hurled myself after her, snarling, bestial sounds pouring from my mouth. I was still five yards from her when she reached the porch. Her shoes clattered on the floor and in the darkness her white dress was a pale blur. I raced after her.

She swung sharply to the right. Hinges creaked, a door slammed, and I smashed headlong into it. My head struck hard and the world twisted into blackness. My hands clawed at the sill as I went down.

It must have taken me several minutes to regain consciousness and stand erect again. For a moment I felt as though I had been sleepwalking and didn't know where I was. Then the past half hour came back, horribly clear. Abruptly I was sick with fear and shame. Turning my head I saw that the moon had slipped below the top of the trees.

"Every night the moon is a little older," I thought. "Every night it goes down later. Tomorrow night there will be more time, and—" I stopped myself short. God! Did I want tomorrow night to come? What would happen then?

It was strange, almost inexplicable the way I felt then, holding the door-sill, still dizzy from the blow on my head. I was conscious of the loathsome thing into which I was turning; I was conscious of the horrors which I had committed. But even more vividly the thing I had tried to do stood before me. I had tried to kill Nita, tried to rip her throat with my teeth. If I had reached her. . . . The thought made my whole body tremble.

But there was another emotion, another being within me that was not frightened. The thing that had possessed me for the last half hour was still deep in my soul, though not as strong as it had been. That thing was not ashamed of what I had done. It was glad! And it wanted more: fresh blood in my mouth, the body of the woman I had seen in the moonlight, the wild passion of her white fingers digging into my flesh.

"Nate, Nate!" It was Nita sobbing behind the door. I would never leave that place until I had obtained the moonlight woman—and I knew that having her meant death or some horror beyond the human mind. But I was still human and I had to save Nita.

I SAID, "I'm all right now. But I want to see you."

The door swung open slowly. White light streamed across the porch. Nita stood holding the doorknob with one hand, the sill with the other. Her face was raised to me and the brown hair fell in little waves about her ears. "What's been the trouble?"

I saw the fear in her eyes and the love that was in them too. It had taken courage to open that door—and it had taken great faith in me. Something snapped in my chest and I went down in a huddle at her feet, crying brokenly. I loved her, I loved her. And she was lost to me.

Then she was on her knees beside me, one arm about my shoulder. "What is it, Nate? What's the trouble?"

I fought my nerves under control and stood erect, lifting her with me.

But when her eyes looked into mine she started and drew away. I saw her lips tremble before she ducked her head and stood there, her little hands clenched. She had seen the beast looking through my eyes, the animal curve of my lips, but she had not run away.

Her voice shook slightly when she asked, "How did you hurt yourself? Your face—it's all scratched, bloody."

The word stirred that thing inside me that was hungry. The muscles jerked along my forearm and my fingers went rigid. But I kept control of myself.

I said, "There was a bobcat out there. He jumped at me, and Mike shot at him. I stumbled trying to get out of the way and fell off the little cliff. Mike missed and the cat got away."

"Where's Mike now?"

Once more the thing leaped inside me. I took a half step forward, jerked myself to a halt. "He's walked down to the next cabin, about five miles, to get some dogs and hunt."

I paused, my tongue licking my lips, my breathing heavy. "Nita."

She looked up at my face again, shuddered and looked away. "What is it?"

"You've got to leave here," I said slowly. "Tonight. You take the car and go back to the city. Mike and I'll come down later."

Once more she looked at me, and this time she held her eyes steady, though I could see the little points of fear in them. "Tell me the truth. What's happened?"

"I can't tell you!" There was a frantic note in my voice. "But you've got to go! Tonight! You can't stay here!"

The fear in her eyes grew larger, and her lips sucked in between her teeth to stop their trembling. But her voice was almost steady. "I don't know what's wrong, but I'm not leaving. You're sick. I can see it. I don't know where Mike is, but I'm staying here until he comes back. And until you are—well again."

It didn't do any good to plead with her. I shouted, stormed, but she only watched me with her hands knotted against her sides, her face erect, and the fear showing only in her eyes.

I would have picked her up and carried her forcefully to the car and driven her away, but I was afraid. If my hands were touching her and there was a struggle, that thing inside me might break loose.

"All right," I said at last. "But go to your room and lock yourself in."

There was no sleep for me that night. There was only fear and horror and a terrible, unending struggle within myself. All night I paced the house like a beast. In that black pit within my belly I could hear the beast-woman's words. "Get rid of her. Get rid of her. Get rid of her. . . ." Over and over the words sounded. Whenever I passed the door beyond which Nita Montgomery was sleeping my nose wrinkled and I could smell the soft flesh of her body.

I GOBBLED great chunks of food before awakening Nita the next morning, so that when she ate breakfast I was able to sit with her. When I told her that Mike had not come back she didn't answer, but her lips trembled. She went outside soon after, and she must have spent all morning looking for him. I made no attempt to work. I had given up all hope of completing my designs. I kept watch from the window, but Nita never came near the place where I had thrown Mike and the dog.

In the afternoon our argument began again. I tried to make her leave, but she wouldn't go. The fear was large in her brown eyes now and the right corner of her soft mouth twitched. She wouldn't look at my face and once when I reached for her with a hairy, pawlike hand she shuddered and went back a step. She must have known what was happening, yet she chose to believe I was sick.

I tried to make her go! God, I tried! I knew what would happen if she were there when night came again, when moonlight sprayed cold through my body once more. I would kill her, tear her throat out, and then turn to the beast-woman.

And as twilight came on the feeling of horror and of doom approaching like a black and inescapable storm grew stronger. I shouted at Nita until she must have thought me mad.

It was when I looked out of the window and saw that the sun had gone below the tree tops and that the colors of sunset were pale and fading, that I planned my course.

Nita was standing near the mantle. She still wore the white dress and it contrasted sharply against the golden sunburn of her arms and shoulders. But her face was pale despite her tan, and the rouge looked ghastly. I took two long steps toward her, reached for her hand with one of my hairy paws. She jerked away involuntarily; then caught a deep breath. The muscles shook along her arm and she put her hand in mine.

"Come on," I said. The words had a barking, animal note. "I'll show you where your brother is. Maybe then you'll leave here." I pulled her from the room, across the porch, started almost dragging her over the lawn.

I knew the penalty for murder. I thought dully that when she went back to the city and told them I had killed Mike, they would come after me. The electric chair. The *whirr* of the current. The body lunging forward against the straps. The smoke curling upward from burnt flesh. The mask taken away and the eyes bulging. I saw these things vaguely, but they meant nothing to me. Already the desire for the woman in the moonlight was growing into a furious obsession. But I had to send Nita back safe!

We were half across the lawn when she dug her little heels into the turf and ·stopped. "Nate, where—where are we going? I'm afraid."

I looked up and saw the moon like a broken cup high above the treetops. Already the sky was slate gray and the first, flush of brightness was coming to the moon.

"Damn it!" I shouted. "Come on! Come on before it's too late."

She held back. "Where?"

I could feel the moonlight now. The first faint drops of it were beginning to fall like dismal November rain into the clearing. I could feel them stirring up the beast within me, feel it ravening through my belly.

Furiously I caught Nita's hand, jerked her headlong and went dragging her across the lawn toward the twenty-foot cliff. "I'll show you," I shouted madly. "I'll show you your brother!"

But it was too late! I knew it even

then, but I kept trying. Oh God! I *did* try. I didn't want to kill her, and I knew that if she were there two, three minutes longer. . . .

SHE kept tugging back, wild with fear now. And I could only last a little longer! The moon-mist was in me and only part of my brain clung to the thought of Nita. Fifteen feet from the edge of the cliff I released her hand. "I'll show you," I screamed again, and leaped forward.

I was at the edge of the cliff when I heard *Her*. It was the same weird, ardent call of the night before, but now the hot flame of desire beat even more loudly in it. I stopped as though I had hit a cord along the edge of the cliff. I turned slowly.

She was to Nita's right and slightly behind her. The moonlight sifted down into the clearing with a liquescent and nebulous luster and bathed the tall and lustful body, the clean straight sweep of her legs, the high passionate rise and fall of her breasts. And it shone too on the face that was more beautiful than the face of a human being, the yellow luminous eyes and the white teeth showing.

Flames leaped through my body, a mingling of hate and scoriac desire. I started toward her on trembling legs, my lips curling.

Nita screamed, a high, flat cry of super-human terror. She turned and went racing across the clearing. In that same instant the other woman spoke. "Get rid of her. Then come to me! Quick!"

There was no bit of humanity left in me then. I turned and went after Nita the way a wounded bull charges, for my knees were still weak with desire. I staggered, but kept plunging after her.

She reached the automobile the same time that I reached the corner of the house. It was only thirty feet to go, and

I knew she couldn't get the car started in time. I began to laugh, a high, barking laugh the way a hyena howls about its food. I could almost taste her blood in my mouth and feel the flesh tearing under my fingers. But it wasn't her I wanted —it was to kill and get back to the other.

I heard the first splutter of the motor as her foot touched the starter. The motor choked. With one leap I went for the running-board.

I don't know how it happened. Perhaps my foot slipped on the running-board or it may have been a loose rock in the yard. Anyway, I missed the door with my hands and fell spinning, crashing off the fender, rolling on the grass. The world was twisting dizzily, but I came to my feet and sprang for the car again.

The motor roared; the car jumped and I missed. It raced down the road into the shadows of the trees.

THE things which followed are only a blur of ecstatic pain to my memory. My heart was a ball of fire against my ribs and passion stormed in my body.

She was waiting there in the moonlight, a dark cold shadow between her breasts. Her mouth was open and her teeth glowed between hideously red lips. I stumbled as I went toward her.

While she waited her voice came in an eerie chant of desire. "You are ready now. Half beast, half human, even as I, who am daughter of Circe and Otagern, follower of Ulysses, whom my mother changed into a panther before she

mated. Savage passion and the madness of the moon are mine, and I cannot die while I feed on the passion and madness of earth. But you—afterwards *you* must die."

Somehow I had known that and was ready. I had rather die than remain without her. I went forward, reeling.

Then my arms were around her. There was a flaming that would never end. The world sweeping back and forth in rolling waves. Muscles wriggling in frantic nothingness. The screaming of a great cat, rising, howling, tearing, sobbing. Blood streaming down my cheek from white teeth and the feeling of furious flesh under my hands. . . .

You say, Doctor, that Nita returned with three mountaineers from the first cabin and found me there in the yard, writhing in an epileptic fit, and that the three men tied me and brought me here to your asylum. It's the dope, you say, and when I have overcome that I shall be well again, and Nita still loves me. You may believe that, and you may know that I didn't kill Mike, though I thought I had. You say he was only injured falling over the cliff and that he will be out of the hospital in a few days. I believe what you tell me about Mike—and Nita. I believe I may in time recover. . . .

But why are these teeth-marks on my chest, and why is this hair on the back of my hands? And why is it that even you can't look into my face without shuddering? . . .

THE END

HIDDEN HORROR

By
Frances Bragg
Middleton

(Author of "From Out the Shad-ows," etc.)

*They warned him, with
head-shaking and dire mutterings, of the nameless peril at
the end of the trail. . . . But Hudson
Clarke, with a motive no man knew, was
grimly determined to uncover the ugly secret which Blackjack Fenton
guarded so jealously in his wilderness fortress. . . .*

WHEN the little "jerkwater" train came to a stop far up in the Kentucky hills, Hudson Clarke took up his bags and followed the other passengers outside the coach and down upon the cinders.

They were an odd lot. Clarke had been watching them throughout the trip, wondering about them. Four were unmistakably Chinese coolies, in typical attire of coarse blue blouses and trousers, and sandals without hose. The fifth man was probably Chinese also, but he had the appearance of a professional man, wearing heavy spectacles, carrying a black bag that seemed to be a cross between a doctor's bag and a lawyer's brief-case.

Clarke was puzzled over their presence here, for the town was no more than a hamlet set up in a cup-like valley whose rim rose raggedly on every hand to almost mountainous heights. There were perhaps a dozen houses, a dirty-windowed store, a red box of a station with a post-office sign hung out over a side window. As Clarke walked over to this window, he noticed that his fellow passengers had gone forward toward the baggage car. A few natives were standing about, waiting for their mail. They seemed to look at Clarke with suspicion, and at the Chinese with something deeper and darker than suspicion. It was late afternoon.

Clarke spoke through the window to the postmaster, busy just inside with a slack mail bag. "Could you direct me to the home of John Fenton?" he asked.

The postmaster's head jerked up. For a perceptible interval, a queerly frozen look lined his old face.

"Just a minute, mister," he said, "and I'll be out with you. Uncle Sam's business ain't supposed to wait."

Clarke drew aside, noting as he did so the furtive, expressionless glances the mountaineers were giving him. What little talk there had been ceased when he put his question. In total silence the men took the assorted mail that was handed them, and with a last speculative look at the stranger, went away. The postmaster locked the window and came out.

"You got business with Blackjack Fenton?" he demanded.

"Yes. I'd like to know the way to his place, if you can tell me."

"Oh, I can tell you. Nothin' easier. Only, it ain't no use. You can't see Blackjack. He ain't seeable. He might take a pot-shot at you out of ambush."

Clarke was a man of early middle age.

His face was molded along stern, even harsh lines. His eyes were gray and steady and steely-hard. His khaki clothes showed the outlines of a big, powerful, well-built frame.

"Just the same, I intend to see him," he said positively.

The postmaster shrugged. "Well, if you must, you must. It ain't safe. And it ain't no use, like I said. But if you're a mind to go in spite of warning, why, just follow those Chinks. They're goin' there."

Startled, Clarke looked down the tracks toward the Chinese. They had possession of their baggage now, consisting of Oriental-looking panniers slung from poles. As he looked, he saw the coolies lift the poles to their shoulders, two men to a load, and jog off down the flinty road. The other man, who looked like a lawyer or a doctor, followed them.

"Foller on if you want to," said the postmaster, grimly. "Tod Peele, there, will likely hire you a horse. There's two-three cars, of a sort, in town, but there ain't a car on earth could manage that road to Blackjack's place."

"And I can find Tod Peele—?"

"Right behind you," the postmaster muttered with the air of one who washed his hands of the affair.

CLARKE turned, met the level gaze of a young countryman who had just come up behind him. He was a blonde, square-jawed young man with cool blue eyes.

"Sure, I'll hire you a horse," he agreed. "But I'm tellin' you the same as Mr. Yancey. It ain't no use."

"I'd like the horse at once," Clarke told him. "I know how to take care of him. I was a good rider in my youth. I haven't forgotten how."

As young Peele started off, the postmaster called after Clarke, "Better leave your bag here, mister. Blackjack ain't goin' to ask you to spend the night. If you come back alive, I'll take you in."

Grimly Clarke turned back, handed his bags to the postmaster with a word of thanks. Then he followed Peele. They had not far to go. A sorrel stood bridled and saddled at the hitching rack by the horse trough, and Peele turned him over to Clarke.

"He's a good mount, mister, an' he'll come right home if you happen to leave him accidental-like. So if you get down on purpose, you better hitch him."

"You mean," Clarke questioned grimly, "you don't expect me to come back with him? Better take your pay now, then."

"That ain't my way o' doin' business, mister," said Peele. "Pay me when the money's earnt, an' not before."

Clarke said nothing. He swung up into the saddle, rode in the direction taken by the Chinese, with no backward look at the two men.

The road, as the postmaster had intimated, was abominable. It was washed full of gullies. Gaunt blocks of limestone, washed free, stood up nakedly, some of them in the very middle of the road. It had evidently not been repaired for many years. There was not a wheel track on it, anywhere.

Night was closing in fast. When Clarke finally overtook the Chinese, they seemed but deeper shadows in the gloom. The coolies with the panniers went on; the man with the bag came to a standstill. He flung up his right hand, spoke to Clarke in precise English which bore a trace of a foreign accent.

"I fear, sir, you have taken the wrong road."

"I am going," Clarke stated, in that grim, short way of his, "to John Fenton's house. I am told this is the road."

The dark figure stood still a moment.

Then, evenly, dispassionately, the man spoke again. "I should advise you, sir, not to go."

Clarke's temper was rising. It was his purpose, however, to learn all he could of the man he had come to see, so he kept his voice even. "I have business with John Fenton. If he is home, I mean to settle with him tonight."

Again a silence, while the man on foot seemed to reflect. Finally he spoke: "I handle Mr. Fenton's business. He lives an extremely retired life. He will not see you, I am certain. If you would tell me what your business is—"

"It's a family matter to be discussed with Fenton alone."

"Ah!" The man's breath caught. "Is your name Clarke, by any chance?"

"I am Hudson Clarke."

ANOTHER silence. "I am very sorry for you," the man on foot said at last. "I know what your business must be. But I still advise you most earnestly not to go. You can not enter Fenton's house. And even if you could, it might very well mean your death."

"Still, I am going," Hudson Clarke said flatly. "I am not altogether a fool. I am armed."

"I supposed you were. But against the peril waiting at the end of this road, no weapon would be of the slightest service to you. I beg you, do not go."

"You say that, knowing my name, and why I have come—?"

"Knowing your name and why you have come, I still say that. And I say, too, that your coming can be of no service whatever to the person you have come to serve."

"Then there is nothing more to say." Clarke's hand jerked at the bridle reins.

He passed the coolies, in a canter that was the best his horse could do over the gullied road. The darkness was so thick now that he could see nothing. Only the trees made walls of deeper blackness.

At last, a light showed ahead of him —a lantern set on a gate-post. Beyond was a house, with light showing dimly through the drawn shades at its windows.

Clarke dismounted, tied his horse to the fence, walked through the gate and up to the front door. He knocked. He heard the sound of a heavy bar sliding through its sockets. Then the door opened a little way, a chain taut across the opening. He could not, he saw, force an entrance.

Behind the foot-wide opening, a man showed suddenly—a black-haired, black-bearded giant of a man, a snub-nosed automatic ready in his hand.

"You're not the man I'm looking for," a deep, harsh voice grated. "What do you want here? Quick!"

"I'm Hudson Clarke, and you know what I want here. My mother is dying. She wants to see her daughter before she dies. If you have any humanity, any decency at all—"

"I'm sorry." The deep voice was even more harsh than before. "There is only one thing you can tell your mother—that Judith is dead—waiting for her. . . ."

The door banged shut. Clarke heard again the sound of the sliding bolt. He walked slowly back to his horse. The Chinese should be there shortly. He decided to wait for them. Perhaps he could learn from them what he wanted to know.

He waited a long time. The sky brightened as the clouds broke and a few stars came out. Somewhere a cock crowed sleepily. A whippoorwill's liquid, gurgling cry answered. A little screech owl loosed its eerie chuckles in the night.

Then silence Hudson Clarke could almost feel. The Chinese did not come. At last the light behind the window shades went out.

"Licked me—this time," he muttered grimly. "The Chinks came in another way. But there'll be another time. I'll show John Fenton that I haven't quit."

He walked his horse all the way back. It was almost dawn when he reached town. Clarke rode slowly to the postmaster's little white house behind the oaks. He waited till smoke began to rise from the kitchen flue; then he dismounted, knocked on the white door.

YANCEY opened it himself. He did not seem to be surprised.

"Come right in," he urged hospitably. "Breakfast'll be ready in two shakes, an' then you can get some sleep. The train don't leave till noon."

"I'm not going out on the train," Clarke objected grimly. "I'm going to finish my business with John Fenton."

"Well, well! That's your business, mister. Come on in an' wash up. You'll feel better after you eat, if you don't mind just takin' pot luck with us."

The breakfast was excellent—home-cured ham, soda biscuit, fried eggs, and excellent coffee. Mrs. Yancey was an even-tempered, brisk little woman with gray hair. There was no one else in the family. The little house was clean, furnished with old marred pieces of oak and walnut, with rag carpets on the floors. But Clarke was in no mood to appreciate the pleasant place.

"About Fenton, now?" he asked after breakfast.

Yancey did not answer at once. He countered with another question. "Are you with the coal company?"

"No."

"Well—I was just wonderin'. While Blackjack was gone an' nobody could locate him, the coal company sent men all aroun' in here prospectin'. They found a mighty rich vein on Blackjack's place. After he come back they wanted to see him about it. Five times they sent men in there. Five times those same men come out with bullet holes in their hats. So I thought if you come about the same thing—"

"No. My business is personal. I really haven't any choice. We— The fact is, I'm trying to find out what became of his wife. She—Mrs. John Fenton, I mean —is my sister."

"Well! Well, well. We live an' learn. Nobody aroun' here in these parts ever suspicioned Blackjack was married!"

"You mean his wife—isn't here?"

"Not so far as anybody knows, she ain't. Nobody's seen any strange white woman come in here. Now Lazarus—a nigger down on the South Fork—did tell a wild tale about a woman he saw when some quail he was huntin' led him onto Blackjack's land. But that wasn't a white woman. He said she was yeller—yeller like a mulatto—with long, sharp finger nails an' shiny black hair an' a moth-eaten face. Nobody knew what he meant. An' he's such a liar, anyhow, nobody believed him."

Clarke sat silent a long time, thinking. Then he said: "If you could only tell me something about Fenton himself—"

"Well, now, those Fentons are a tough lot," Yancey began. "Good an' tough. They come in here about the same time everybody else, along at the tail end of the Revolution. Only, they were different from the rest of the settlers. 'Most everybody else was poor folks, you see. The Fentons were—well, what they call the quality."

Yancey paused for a few draws at his pipe, went on:

"I don't know how they come to settle in here. Nobody did. They didn't act like nobody else nor have anythin' to do with nobody at all. They got a big place back there in those hills, more'n a hun-

dred acres, but they never worked it. Never cleared more'n just enough to build the house on an' raise a garden. Used to be flowers in the front yard, I remember, an' they had good horses an' cows an' pigs an' chickens. But they didn't make their own livin'."

"You mean—"

"Why, four times a year a letter come from some place in England with money in it. They cashed the check over to the bank in Garrettstown, an' after so long a time it leaked out. I did hear my grandfather say lots of times that the money was sent in here in gold back in the early days, but they stopped that long before my time. The money kept comin', though, one way or another, for more'n a hundred years. Then about twenty years ago, it stopped."

"Stopped?" Clarke prompted.

"STOPPED dead. That was when Blackjack got out of here. He was the last one. All the rest of 'em were dead. I reckon he must've been near twenty then. He never said nothin' to nobody—just left. I remember there was one foreign letter come after that, an' the postmaster—that was the one before me—laid it up to wait till Blackjack come back. Then after so long a time a letter come to the postmaster wantin' to know if Blackjack had got his letter since he hadn't sent 'em no receipt. So of course the postmaster wrote how he'd lit out for parts unknown. An' that was the last of that."

"And you think—?" Yancey's guest urged further.

"Well, in all those years, naturally there was a lot of talk. Those Fentons were queer, livin' all to themselves that way, as if they thought they were too good to have anythin' to do with the rest of us. But the boys had to marry somebody, of course, an' they'd come sparkin' roun' where it pleased 'em. Never had any trouble marryin'. The girls they married never had a great deal to do with their folks afterwards, as a general thing, still they'd drop a word here an' a word yonder, an' folks just naturally kind of put two and two together.

"They made quite a tale of it after so long a time. Accordin' to what they say, those Fentons were grand folks over in their own country, but the boy that had ought to've got the title had done somethin' outrageous, murder or somethin' an' the rest of the family agreed to pay him an' his heirs to bury themselves in a hole somewhere an' let the next of kin take the property. That's the tale anyhow, an' it's certain the money stopped comin' when Blackjack left."

"Blackjack. H'm, quite a name."

"Well, he's dark, you know, like the rest of 'em. Hot-tempered. Stubborn. Get his own way or die. Somebody called him Blackjack when he was a kid an' the name stuck. Bad blood in those Fentons. You say he married your sister?"

"Yes. I don't like to talk about it, but I've got to find out about her somehow. I was away when they married, nine or ten years ago now. She was down in Florida with relatives and he was there, too, with a bunch of scientists resting up from one expedition and getting ready for another. I don't mean he was one of the scientists himself, of course. He seems to have been no more than a guide. He'd put in a lot of time in the East, probably ten years or more, and seems to have known China and Thibet pretty well.

"He must have been rather fascinating, too, from what I heard when I got back. Anyway, they eloped. My mother used to hear from her occasionally from all sorts of outlandish places. Then six or seven years ago, the letters stopped coming. My mother—well, you can imagine how she took it. And now she's dying.

She says she can't go in peace until she can see her daughter Judith again, or at least get word from her. I managed to get this address from the scientists he worked for. However, if she's isn't here — Well, we've always feared that she had died."

"It would seem so, Mr. Clarke. She certainly didn't come with him either time. He come back here about the time you say you stopped hearin' from your sister. Looks like he might've come back here *because* she died."

"Perhaps. But I've got to know. He shut me out last night but I'm not through with him yet. I'd like a guide through the hills if I can get one."

"Well, I don't know. Nobody's goin' to *want* to go in there. Too many things have happened. Folks are scared, an' I don't know that I blame 'em.

"OF COURSE, bein' postmaster, I see everybody that comes in. So I saw Blackjack the first time an' the secon' time, too. I never had any trouble recognizin' him. You remember those Fentons once you've seen 'em good. He come back with a scad of boxes in the baggage car an' a dozen of those yeller men back in the coach with him. An' when the train stopped he never waited for nothin'. Just unloaded that junk, an' those yeller men carries it off, when he must've known any man in town would've hired him a team!"

"Queer. I thought last night this was a strange place to bring Chinese coolies."

"It looked all-fired queer to us. Then a week later here they come walkin' in an' got on the train. Must've been nearly a month when they come back, but the yeller men rode by themselves in the coach this time. Blackjack had three big boxes up in the baggage car, covered with coarse burlap, an' a funny smell about 'em. He rode up there with 'em along with that funny foreign-lookin' little man with the eyeglasses an' the shiny black bag, same as yesterday."

"Blackjack was awful particular about unloadin' those boxes, too. Those yeller men toted 'em off, four men to a box. Next day the man in eyeglasses brought the yeller men back an' boarded the train with 'em. Twice a year since then those same fellers've come in here, just like you saw yesterday. The whole thing's mighty queer. But we never saw anythin' that looked like a woman with him, even if that fool Lazarus did say—"

The old man stopped and sucked at his pipe again.

"Not a soul's laid eyes on him ever since. We saw some of his handiwork, though, a few days after he come in the secon' time. He'd come in some time durin' the night an' tacked a notice on the station door warnin' people to stay off his land if they wanted to keep their health. It ain't half fenced in, his place ain't, but he's got traps an' pitfalls set."

"Anybody ever get caught?"

"One of Jim Lane's cows did once. Had to shoot her. Made Jim awful mad. He hunted for Blackjack high an' low, went up to the house an' everythin', but he never found him. So he shot one of Blackjack's cows to get even. An' the next mornin' Jim found a live rattler seven foot long pinned to his front door with a knife. That sort of cooled folks off. Nobody's been in there since. An' as I'm sayin', it ain't likely you'll find anybody willin' to go in there with you."

"H'm. The man must be extraordinary, to bring a seven-foot rattlesnake down—alive—in the dark, and fasten him to that door. That took nerve!"

"Oh, he's got nerve, all right. The whole breed had that."

"Well," Clarke said grimly, "I've got to tackle it, anyway. Wish I could get

a guide, though. I don't know much about traps and rattlesnakes."

"You'll find plenty of the vipers on Blackjack's place. I remember a regular den of 'em when I was a boy—a cave they had for a breeding place. It fairly squirmed with 'em, an' smell! Je-e-miny Christmas! Oh, you need a guide, all right, but I don't know. Tod Peele—the young feller that hired you his horse—hunted the place over a lot while Blackjack was gone. I don't know. But I'll see what I can do."

AS IT turned out, Tod Peele proved amenable. He seemed eager and hesitant, but the pay Clarke offered was more than he could refuse.

They took Tod's wagon and team, with canvas and blankets and a week's supplies. The road by daylight proved to be even worse than it had seemed at night. It was well along in the afternoon when they turned into Fenton's land—at quite a distance from the house. Tod made camp on the lee side of a hill, hobbled the horses, and stretched the canvas from the wagon bed to the ground, tent-fashion. Under this shelter they put in a fairly comfortable night.

They explored a little, cautiously, next morning—enough for Clarke to form some idea of the place. It was all hills and valleys, with very small stretches of level ground. Never having been cut over, the hillsides were not washed, were covered with a thick carpet of dead leaves. Quail were plentiful. Bluejays screamed at them. Mockingbirds, redbirds, blackbirds, wrens, cardinals fluttered everywhere. Hawks sailed high above the tree tops. In the damp earth near a branch were tracks of rabbit, 'coon, fox, skunk and 'possum.

Clarke went up to the house that day, at noon, when he supposed Fenton would be at home. Seen in the daytime, the house was beautiful, though severely plain and seeming somehow forlorn and wistful in spite of the wide grassy yard and gorgeous flower-beds in front of it. Behind it were barns and a stable, a chicken-run alive with fowls, a pasture. A lazy streamer of smoke hung over a chimney.

Clarke walked rapidly across the yard, mounted the one step to the little porch, lifted the knocker on the neat, white-painted door. As the clang of the gong died away, he thought he heard a rustle as of silk rubbing against silk, and the rumble of a deep, authoritative voice, but he was never sure. No one came. No one answered when he called. At last, his automatic in his hand, he pushed open the door.

The room he entered amazed him, it seemed incongruous here in the middle of this wilderness of trees. The floor was waxed, half-covered by a Chinese rug. The furniture was old, beautifully kept, and, Clarke was sure, immensely valuable. Open book-shelves lined the lower half of the walls—shelves filled with an extraordinary collection of books. Above these were well-chosen pictures, not too many. Above the stone fireplace hung the portrait of a lady in the court dress of a century and a half ago, on either side of her two framed photographs which Clarke recognized—one of his mother, the other of his sister. And on the mantel shelf he saw a snapshot of himself in a silver frame!

Sudden rage mounted in Clarke as he stared at those familiar faces, rage mixed with heart-sickness as he remembered his gentle fragile mother, his gay, thoughtless, lighthearted little sister. They had been so happy, so contented, before John Fenton came! And now his mother lay dying, tortured by uncertainty, by dread, and his sister— Ah, God, what of his sister? What had Fenton done to her through all those dreary years, in the

lost, forsaken regions of the earth? Had he killed her? Or was he keeping her prisoner in this dead end of nowhere?

Clarke squared his shoulders and faced about. He was taking his life in his hands, he knew. But, come what might, he meant to search that house. In two strides he reached a door and opened it.

He found himself in a dining room whose furnishings matched those of the room he had left, and he saw that his coming had interrupted a meal. The table had been set for two. The coffee was still warm. Untouched dishes of sherbet were at either place.

In the kitchen he found the same signs of interruption. The plates used for the first course were stacked on a table, a kettle of water for the dishwashing bubbled on the stove, a door of the ice machine was open. That was a shock—ice in this wilderness! But that was as nothing compared to the shock that followed. The outer kitchen door had been boarded up, and the windows were heavily barred with iron! His mind leaped to the inevitable conclusion. His sister Judith was a prisoner!

Trembling with rage and a sort of vicarious terror, he ran back through the rooms he had already explored, only to find that their windows, too, were barred. So were the windows of the huge, well-stocked pantry behind the kitchen, the music room, the office, the children's playroom, dusty, pathetic, long unused. Upstairs were bedrooms, linen closets, a bath, all beautifully furnished, beautifully kept—and securely barred with iron.

And every room had the look of a place just left, and everywhere lurked a faint, elusive odor, not pleasant, not familiar, hinting, somehow, of danger, of the mystery and terror.

Clarke searched frantically. His reason told him that several persons had left that house immediately before he entered it. Yet the only way out that he could find was the front door. He shook the bars at the windows. He looked for scuttles and secret doors. All to no purpose. Unbelievably, those people had vanished. Why? Judith would never have fled from him of her own will.

BAFFLED, angry, sick to the soul, Clarke went back to Tod and told him what he had found. Tod could make nothing of it, but he was certain of one thing. During his years of hunting over the place during Blackjack's absence, there had been no bars at the windows.

"It looks as if he had made her a prisoner in there," Clarke growled, "or as if he expected a raid of some sort from outside. Wonder if he could be mixed up in a tong war, or wanted for dope running? It might even be—But whatever it is, I've got to find out."

They went cautiously back.

That night Clarke slept uneasily, bothered by dreams of window shades that lashed and whipped in a driving wind. The explanation came when Tod called him in the morning. Just outside their shelter, a huge rattlesnake had been pinned to the ground by a forked stick across its throat. It had strangled and thrashed itself to death.

"That there's a warnin'," Tod Peele asserted with positiveness. "Next time hit'll sure be somethin' wuss."

"I don't doubt it." Clarke looked down at the dead rattler with a thrill of repulsion—but with a distinct tightening of his resolution, too. "I'm going to stick," he grimly declared. "There's no need for you to, though, Tod. You brought me in here and that's all that's really necessary."

Tod spat expressively. "I can stan' hit if you can," he repeated. "Howsumever, we'll have to break camp an' I'll get this carcass away from here. We don't want this varmint's mate comin' here an' lightin' into us for this here thing what we ain't done."

That afternoon Clarke found his way back to the woods opposite the Fenton house. He went alone. His plan was to watch the house and learn something of its occupants, if possible. He found the waiting very tiresome. There was no movement at all around the house till after sunset. Then he suddenly became aware that a man was in the lot behind the house, going in and out of the barns, the stable, the chicken-run, doing the ordinary evening chores of a farm. After a while he lost sight of him—heard a low, harsh, controlled voice just behind him.

"Don't draw," the voice commanded. "I've got you covered."

Clarke turned. Behind him, vague in the tree shadows, Blackjack Fenton stood, a rifle cocked and ready.

"This is the last time I'm going to talk to you, Clarke," Blackjack droned in a voice of deadly calm. "I told you once you couldn't come into my house. And yet you did just that, peeking and prying from the front door to the back. I've told you all I've got to tell you. If you don't want something worse to happen to you than you ever dreamed of in all your life, you get off my land, and be damn' quick about it."

Clarke's fingers itched for the feel of the gun in his pocket. The blood roared in his ears. But he held himself quiet. This was not the time. Blackjack had the drop on him now—but. . . .

"I don't believe Judith's dead," he flung at Blackjack through his teeth. "I told you that my mother's dying. She wants to know— But if nothing else will get under your hide, think of the money. Your wife will inherit plenty when—"

"We don't want it. We've got plenty of our own. And you'll just have to tell your mother that she'll never see her daughter this side of heaven. And you can tell her, too, that I've done my duty by my wife, if it comes to that. But it wasn't duty made me do it. I gave up— I sacrificed—not that I begrudge it any, though. I'll always have the consolation that I did everything I could. So that's that. Now march. My trigger finger's nervous. I'm warning you again that there's worse things can happen to you on this place than a quick bullet."

Clarke went. Smarting with humiliation and rage though he was, he had no chance to retaliate. He found the new camp and a gloomy Tod awaiting him.

"You might look at this here," Tod offered. "I foun' hit under the rattler when I moved hit. Blackjack must've dropped hit accidental like." Clarke took the proffered bit of paper, but he could make little of it. The snake's struggles had whipped it to rags.

" 'One dozen muslin gowns,' " he read aloud. "Magazines as usual. . . . Four dozen new books, Ramón's selection . . . oil, double amount . . . grains, morphine. . . .' That's all that's readable." Clarke finished. "It's not important, anyhow. We already knew he got his stuff from outside. I'm not going back till I know —what there is to know." He stared back along the trail he had followed from Fenton's house. "I've *got* to know."

There was a flash from behind a tree trunk, the crack of a rifle. A bullet spurted gravel over Clarke's shoe.

"Damn you," Clarke shouted. In a sudden excess of fury he jerked out his automatic and emptied it at the spot where the flash had shown. But Blackjack made no answer.

THEY moved again next day, to a camp in a more sheltered spot. And thereafter neither went anywhere alone. With infinite caution—Tod was a master of woodcraft—they reconnoitered the house. But they learned no more than that Blackjack was sticking close at home. He appeared often on the front porch, in the yard or pasture. Plainly, he was uneasy. But no sight did they get of any other person.

Under other circumstances the place would have interested Clarke. A bit of virgin forest, even of no more than a hundred acres, is hard to find in the midst of a settled country. The abundance of wild creatures was unusual, too. From a discreet distance Clarke viewed the den of rattlesnakes Yancey had told him of. It was a low-mouthed cave, with a sunny slope in front of it which was very populous indeed. Clarke wondered how Blackjack found the courage to wade in among those hideous, writhing things and make a capture. Or did he set a trap somewhere for them?

The rattlesnake den was not the only cave they found. Sink holes and miniature caverns were common. It was one of the latter that gave Clarke his idea. Tod found it, in the edge of the woods less than half a mile from the house, an irregular hole in the ground about a yard in diameter. It was Tod, too, who noticed tracks around it.

However, it was Clarke who got the flash of inspiration from the discovery.

"That first time I was watching him," he hazarded. "You know, I told you how I lost sight of him and how he came up behind me in the woods. He might have come this way, don't you think?"

Tod nodded. "He might. There might be another hole near the house there, covered up."

Clarke lighted a match and held it at arm's length down the hole. It burned clear to the end. The air was good, then. He lowered his flashlight next. The drop was all of twenty-five feet, but, more by good luck than by any other means, he found how to negotiate it. Set well back under the rim of the hole the trunk of a tree was fixed upright, its limbs so lopped off as to afford a ladder.

"I'm going down with the flash," Clarke declared. "You stay here, Tod."

"You'd a damsight better take me along," Tod demurred.

"No, I hadn't. Suppose Blackjack came down here and caught us both inside? There'd certainly be a killing then. Best thing is for you to stand guard here. Then if he comes you can warn me. I believe I'll discover something this time."

He let himself down gingerly, turned in the direction of the house, kept the toe of his right boot scraping a line through the gravel of the cave floor.

It was a commonplace cave enough. His flashlight showed him occasional openings on either side, but he followed the main course. And he walked with infinite caution. Below him the trickle of running water came to his ears.

He watched the ceiling narrowly for a way out, yet he was startled when he found it. For it was man-made, a trapdoor at the top of another tree-ladder. Nor was it hard to open. As he pushed up through it, with another start of surprise, he found himself looking into Blackjack's dining room.

The room was empty. But, from somewhere beyond the closed doors, women's voices rose in dirge-like, hopeless lamentation. It made Clarke's flesh creep to listen to it. For it was altogether alien and incomprehensible. Could it be Chinese?

Slowly he lowered the trap, marvelling as he did so at the simplicity of its concealment. For the opening was cut immediately under a corner of the rug, and the rug had been made fast to the trap.

Automatic in hand, he walked to the door of the living room and opened it. This room looked the same as before ex-cept that it was not empty. Blackjack Fenton sat with his arms crossed on the table, his black head lowered to his arms, a weary, beaten figure that paid no heed to the awful sound that came from the room behind him. Something of compassion crept into Clarke's heart.

"Mr. Fenton," he called, a gentleness in his voice he had not meant to use.

BLACKJACK lifted his head slowly. He made no other movement. His eyes looked dazed and sick.

"So. You found the way in here." he said drearily. "It doesn't matter now. I might have known you'd come sometime. But Judith didn't want you to know."

"My mother *had* to know," Clarke told him simply.

"Oh! Well—" Blackjack came stumblingly to his feet. "All right. But maybe you'll be sorry."

He threw open the door into the music room, and Clarke, hard on his heels, looked in.

"Her heart—all of a sudden—" Blackjack groaned.

Clarke scarcely heard him. In the music room the window shades were drawn. On a bier in the middle of the room, tall lighted candles at her head and feet, shrouded in white, a woman lay, a white veil but half concealing her ravaged face and hands. And behind her two wailing Chinese women crouched fearfully in the shadows, yellow women with shiny hair, and—yes, Lazarus had been right. "Motheaten faces," was the only term.

Clarke stumbled backward. He stared at Blackjack Fenton with understanding, almost with reverence.

"That—oil—on your list," he muttered dazedly. "I should have guessed. You say she didn't want us to know—and you —you tried to save us. But we—we— had never dreamed of—leprosy."

THE MAN WHO WOULD NOT DIE!

By Arthur Leo Zagat

(Author of "Thirst of the Living Dead," etc.)

"Not even Death itself can part us," he had sworn that day. Miriam Borisoff had not believed his ugly threat until that grim procession of horrible beings came stalking her, one by one, out of the night—exacting the revenge of Satan's blood-brother!

BLUE flames flickered above the coal on the stone-framed hearth, blue phantoms of fire that threw no light into the vague tunnel of the long room. Even their warmth was cheerless, and their dull mutter ominous, as though

brooding fear had found expression in the low crackle of the fire. There was no other sound, except the whispered rattle of a pulled-down window shade, whispering to the uncontrollable quiver of a slim hand that gripped its edge.

The woman whose white fingers crumpled the hem of the blind, pulling it away from the glass minutely to make a slit for her to peer through fearfully, was a taut, pale blur against the broader, vertical shadow of the window's embrasure. The

man just behind her, shrouded in gloom so that only the glimmer of his white shirt-front and the pallid oval of his blunt-jawed face were visible; ached to take her slender, maturely rounded form in his arms—to cover her lips with kisses—although his scalp was a cap squeezing his skull and his spine was an icy shiver. But instead, his hand tightened on the rough butt of an automatic in the pocket of his dinner jacket; his ears strained for some hint of approaching menace.

Outside, the long slope of the hill was a boundaryless down-sweep of soft luminousness into which great white snowflakes were endlessly falling out of the night. They came down in hushed myriads, silent as Death, implacable as Time, fluttering straight down in slow haste, merging with those that had fallen before till the blanched field seemed to lift visibly, inch by inch—a rising tide of soundless doom.

But it was not the snow of which the two watchers were afraid. Not the chill smooth snow, blanketing the brown earth. The woman whimpered, far back in her throat. The man stirred, laid a hand on her bare, cold arm. "Come, dear, this is foolish. Even if you were right, he won't come tonight. No one could get here from the valley. The snow must be six feet deep by now and. . . ."

She didn't move, but her vibrant contralto voice, tight-cadenced with the fight she was making for control, cut across his speech. "He will come. Tonight. And —and then—God help us."

"Good Lord, Miriam!" the other was suddenly gruff. "That's impossible!" The harshness of his voice rose to shrillness. "You identified his body yourself—what was left of it when they put the fire out and pulled it out of the wrecked train."

She whirled at that, half-crouching with virulence, and her response was staccato, bitter. "Yes, I said it was he. The watch was his, and the scarf-pin. That charred, blackened thing wasn't even human, but I was sure it was his corpse. I . . ."

"There you are. A woman couldn't be mistaken after she had been married to a man for five years. . . ."

"Not if he were an ordinary man, but you know what he could do to himself. The critics called him the greatest artist in make-up ever born. I am not sure that I ever saw him as he really was."

"That's more nonsense. His screen-stuff—"

"Was nothing to what he did at home. I sometimes thought that the parts he played, the monsters and madmen, had warped his soul till he became like them. He used his skill to torture me, to try and drive me insane. He came into my room once, as a bent old man, with eyes sunk in a cadaverous, leprous face—with long-nailed claws with which he tore my night clothes from me and—" She stopped, a shudder ran through her. "He *was* that awful old man, Ned. How do I know that his usual aspect was less of a fraud? How do I know that it wasn't my wild hope of release at last—and the thought of you—that made me certain the corpse they showed me was his?"

"No one escaped from that smoking car. He *must* have been killed." Ned said it defiantly but his eyes slid to the shade, smoky, still half dubious. "It is impossible that he is still alive."

MIRIAM seemed to be listening, listening intently for a sound that did not come. Words dripped slowly from her lips. "Then he *is* dead. But, alive or dead, he has sent me a message that he will be here tonight. And when he does appear—" her voice dropped to a husked whisper, "we shall not know him—until he strikes."

"A message!" Ned jerked out. "You call that a message!" He twisted. A stride of his long legs took him to the center of the room. A lamp switch clicked and light swirled down to lay a cloth of luminousness on a table-top. A tiny object seemed to gather the light into itself, tinting it yellow—a semi-circle of gold, half of a broken ring. The man glowered down at it as if it were something vile, something beyond the pale. "That piece of junk!"

Miriam spoke, startlingly beside him; he had not heard her move: " 'These rings bind us indissolubly together. Even death cannot break their bond.' He said that on our wedding day, putting one ring on my finger and one on his own, and I thrilled to the romantic ring in his voice." She laughed, and the short undertone of that laugh was a curse. "Fool that I was! 'Remember that, my love, *not even death.*' That was just six years ago —tonight!"

"He might have said it," the man growled, "'but his saying it could not make it true. He is dead, and you are rid of him forever."

"Then how did that come here?" the woman questioned. "We found it here when we came in at sunset, right here, and there were no tracks in the snow except our own, no tracks in snow that had just begun to fall and—no one in the house when we searched!"

"Your own ring—?"

"It's in my jewel box, upstairs, locked in. I looked. No. That is half of *his* ring he sent. Living or dead, he sent it on ahead to let us know that he would follow." Her flat, hopeless accents were utterly resigned. "Ned, can a soul be so evil that it cannot die? So vile that even Hell rejects it and it must remain earthbound forever?"

"'No!" He flung the negative at her, swept the half-ring up from the table. "Damn it, no! When a man's dead, he is eternally dead. This was in your clothes, somewhere, in a handkerchief, in your bag. It dropped out on this table when we went out and you didn't notice it."

His hand jerked. A flash of gold streaked through the murk, clinked into the fireplace, vanished between two coals into the white heart of the fire. "That's the end of that, and we'll forget it. We'll forget him too—" He whirled, seizing her, pulling her roughly to him, devouring her lips with burning, avid kisses. "You're my wife now, my wife! He's dead and gone and he cannot come between us."

"Ned! Ned, darling. I . . . *What's that?*"

They clung to each other and the ague of fear shook them. Fear hissed in the slow burning of the coals, gibbered from black shadow-pools beyond the lamp's radiance. Terror was a living presence in the room, brooding in the white silence outside the close-pulled blinds. Fear was a voice calling from that silence—a long-drawn wail, snow-muffled, that rose, died away, and came again—nearer. "He-e-lp! He-e-lp!"

Ned moistened dry lips. "Miriam. It's someone out in the storm, calling for help. Someone in the snow!"

"'Someone in the snow," the woman repeated, shuddering. Then as the man moved, "No! No, Ned!" Her fingers snatched at him feverishly, caught his lapels. "Don't open the door. Don't go out. Maybe . . ."

He hesitated, his mouth tightening. "But dear," he almost groaned. "This is the only house in miles. That snow is death to anyone on foot. I . . ." He checked himself as the cry came once more.

Miriam stiffened; her hands ceased their flutter. "'That sounded like a woman, Ned. A woman." Her whisper was plaintive. "He could not imitate a woman's voice, could he?"

The man pulled her wrists away from his coat. "I don't know and I don't care. I'm going out to see. Woman or ghost or devil, I'll take care of you." Saying it flogged his own courage to belief. "I'm not skulking here like a scared dog any longer." The feel of the gun in his hand was comforting as he thrust out through the portiéres to the entrance hall, his broad shoulders swinging.

THERE was no wind, but the snowfall had redoubled so that the beam of the flashlight he had snatched up in the foyer shone against a white wall only a few feet ahead of him, unrevealingly. He went knee deep into wet softness that clogged his legs; wet lumps settled on his mackinaw and uncovered head. "Hello," he yelled, and the snow-filled air swallowed his shout. "Hell-o-o, where are you?"

Silence again, and the soft hiss of the descending flakes. Ned's skin prickled to the sensation of unseen eyes watching him, inimical eyes somewhere in the snow-filled night. He threw a haunted glance over his shoulder. Nothing was there but the blanketed loom of the house, its windows black, irregular oblongs against the white. "Where are you?" he called again.

A moan answered him, to the right, not far off. It couldn't be far off or he would not have heard it. He plowed a step in that direction, swung his torch, and its ray picked out a curling mound in the snow—a mound that was not yet all white. He heaved to it, saw brown fur, shaggy, framing an incredible face. It was huge, unbelievably large. Beetling eyebrows and the faint down of a mustache were ice-speckled. There was something unmistakably feminine about it; but something evil, too, as only a woman can be evil.

Ned shuddered, but he thrust the gun and flashlight into pockets, bent, and pushed his arms under the great bulk. He could not lift her; he had to drag her, and the snow fought silently, viciously, to keep its prey. Another yard—he thought as he felt stone steps under him —and he might not have made it. "Miriam! It's all right. Open up!"

The knob rattled above him; warm air swept out and around him. Miriam was at his side, helping him with his burden, sobbing a bit. "She's frozen, exhausted. Oh, the poor thing! And I wanted to keep you from helping her."

They had her on the floor, near the fire. Her fur coat was a dark pile near the table, lying in a gathering pool of melted snow. She was tremendous, her lax arms elephantine, the slow heave of her bosom like nothing so much as the swell of the sea. Her face was dough-colored, was like a blob of unshaped dough. Straggly black hair was plastered against the dead-white of her forehead. "I'll give her some whiskey, Ned, and you go up and get the blankets from our bed. We've got to get her warm."

The man stripped off his wet mackinaw as he hurried through the entrance hall, tossed it over the bannister-post of the stairs up which he ran. Pitch blackness greeted him in the upper corridor, but he did not stop to switch on a light. He would be up here only a moment, and he would have his hands full when he returned.

His footfalls thudded on thick carpeting, echoed—*did* they echo? He stopped short, his throat drying, and those other footsteps stopped too. Of course what he had heard had been an echo. Something, the snow perhaps, had made this hall reverberant. Why, his very breathing was unnaturally loud in the quiet up here.

But he could not rid himself of the eerie sensation that he was not alone— that someone, something, was waiting in the dark. Ned's hand stole to his pocket, fumbled in, fumbling for the gun, felt only cloth. He had forgotten it—left it in the thick-fabricked, short coat down below. He bit his lip, shrugged. He'd get the blankets, get down again. And get the automatic out of the mackinaw pocket as he passed.

A little light seeped into the bedroom. Ned stripped blankets from the bed hastily, turned back to the door. What was that thrumming noise? Did it come from within the house or from outside? Just as he heard it, it stopped, and silence swept in again. It had sounded almost like a laboring automobile motor, but no auto could be passing on the hill road, deep as it was in the clogging snow. What then? Could . . . A scream sliced the darkness, "Ned! *Ned!*"

CHAPTER TWO

Wicked, Watching Eyes

"MIRIAM! Coming, Miriam!" Ned hurtled down the hall, flung himself down the long stairs, twisted and jerked aside the curtains hiding the living room. Against the blue glow from the fireplace a heaving mass swayed. Miriam screamed again, and Ned saw that the monstrous woman from the snow towered erect. One hamlike hand was tangled in his wife's long, golden hair, dragging so that Miriam's body was arched backward, her white neck stretched taut. The woman's face was contorted, a clammy gargoyle of mad fury, and a knife gleamed in her other upraised hand even as Miriam's small fists beat unavailingly at her pillowed, shaking breasts.

Ned's legs exploded under him like uncoiled springs. He flung himself across the room, catapulted through the murky air, quivering with horror, hurled himself against the sickeningly soft mass of the woman's frame. His right hand snatched at, clutched the sharp blade of the descending knife; his left fist thudded against her chin. It smacked, rather, for there seemed to be no bone under the fleshy roll. The fat dew-lap seemed to suck his knuckles in—to nullify the force of the blow as putty would have. Ned gasped, twisted at the knife. He did not feel its cut, but his hand was suddenly scarlet, glistening. He pounded at the grayish face, at the beady, reptilian eyes; he might have been flailing at

a statue of undried clay for all the effect his frantic blows had.

He heard sounds, like the plop of a steam bubble in geyser mud; he felt movements like the stirring of primordial slime in the huge body against which he strained—and a clammy hand was on his neck. Cold, moist, formless, the putty-like mass seemed to spread till blobbed fingertips met over his throat, firmed and tightened. They tightened slowly, inevitably, till his breath whistled through his squeezed windpipe, till it was cut off and his lungs were bursting. Tiny lightnings danced before his bulging eyes—vanished in a black swirl of billowing blackness. Agony stabbed mercilessly through his chest, pounded in his temples. The blackness invaded his brain. . . .

Dull sound exploded somewhere finally, and he could breath again. He pulled air into his tortured lungs, went down under a sudden smothering bulk that fell on him and bore him to the floor. His vision cleared; he saw Miriam standing over him, holding in her hand splintered wood that had once been a small end-table. Her mouth was a black circle in her pallid, distorted face. Blood roared in his eyes, through its rumble he heard: "—right? Ned! Are you all right?" He knew that it was her voice that he heard.

"Yes." The monosyllable was a croak that rasped his throat. "Yes, dear. You?"

"I—I think so." Her hair was an aureate cascade over the white round shoulders from which the gossamer frock had been torn. Her eyes were wide, dark pools of terror. Ned heaved; the flaccid mass overlaying him slid off; he realized that it was the woman who had repaid rescue by a murderous attack. He sat up, pain racking him. "Ned! Your hand! Your poor hand!"

He felt dull pain-throb in his right hand, looked down at it dazedly. It was a scarlet mass of blood, dripping from a gash clear to the bone across the palm. "Nothing!" he muttered. "Nothing, dear. Tie—it up. What—what happened?"

"She let go of me—was choking you, killing you. I had to do something. I grabbed this up, hit here over the head. She. . . ."

"Brave—girl." Somehow he was on his feet, clamping his wrist to stop the blood flow. "But—before. How?"

"There are no bandages in the house. I. . . ."

"Handkerchief — my pocket." The room was whirling dizzily. Ned fumbled to a chair, sat heavily down. Miriam was over him, the sweet scent of her around him warm, grateful, as she bound his wound.

HER voice was a murmur in his ears. "I got some whiskey between her lips. She came to, grabbed the bottle from me and half of it was down her throat in a flash. I tried to take it from her and, suddenly, she was a crazed thing. She heaved to her feet, had me by the hair and was pulling that knife from her bosom before I knew what was happening. I screamed for you—her eyes—Ned —hell itself burned in her eyes. She laughed, horribly, the knife was coming down—and then you were there. . . ."

"Good Lord! If I'd been a second slower—She must have wandered in the snow for hours, driven mad by her sufferings. She—"

"Ned." Miriam's fingers trembled as she pulled the improvised bandage tight. "Perhaps he —sent her. Or maybe—" She stopped but the unspoken thought quivered fearsomely between them.

The man forced a laugh. "Silly. She *is* a woman, isn't she?"

"Yes. I loosened her clothing. She is a woman, but—"

"But nothing. Listen, sweet, get that damnable idea out of your head. With all his foul cleverness he couldn't change his body, his sex. Besides, he's dead, six feet under. He's—"

"That's it. That's just it. He's dead, but his hate lives on. And—*Oh God!*"

Sudden pounding reverberated like thunder through the house. It choked off Miriam's speech, pulled Ned's head slowly around tell he stared fearfully at the opening into the entrance hall. The hammering stopped, was renewed—a booming hollow sound like the beating of savage drums. Her hand slid into his unbandaged one, fluttered there—icy.

"It's—at the door," Ned pushed the words through stiffened lips. "Someone —knocking."

"Someone—Who, Ned? Who? In this storm, this snow, who?"

"I—don't know." The sound was a steady thump, implacable, demanding. He pushed himself up out of his chair. "Got —to see."

"Ned! He—" She clung to him, her face gray with terror. "If it is *he—*"

The man put her from him, gently. "There's no danger." His drawn cheeks denied the bravado of his words. "I'll get my gun—" The thought warmed him a bit as he made his legs move through the viscous invisible fluid that seemed to sap the strength from them. Miriam whimpered behind him, he was out in the foyer. The knocking was loud on the other side of the bolted, sturdy door. One hand found the rough cloth of his coat, still hanging on the bannister-post. His bandaged right dipped into its pocket for the automatic.

It wasn't there! The other, then. His fingers felt the cold round of the flashlight—and nothing else! A steel band constricted Ned's forehead. He reeled, pulled himself back against the bannister. *Who—?*

There was an instant's silence, quivering with unutterable fear, a muffled shout reached him and the thumping on the door resumed. He must have lost the gun in the snow outside, dragging the woman in. That was it—it had slipped out of his pocket into the snow. No one had taken it from the coat. No one could have taken it from the coat, there was no one else in the house. But someone was trying to get in!

He managed the few steps to the door, leaned against it. "Who is it?" he called. Then more strongly, "Who's there?"

The knob rattled under his hand. "Let us in!" The voice was far away—no, it was close by. The thick wood made it faint. Ned shook his head, trying to clear it, trying to think. If Miriam were right —but she couldn't be. The dead stayed dead, and Pavel Borisoff was certainly dead.

God but his hand hurt now. "Who's there?" he shouted.

"State-police. Open—door." Relief whistled pent breath through Ned's teeth. His fingers shook as they rattled bolts out of their sockets, clicked the lock over, turned the knob. The big oak portal swung inward, pushing him aside. Two figures surged into the hall, flat caps of fur piled high with snow—snow deep on thick shoulders. Boots were clotted with clinging flakes, but between their tops and the border of the sheepskin shortcoats, the gray-green breeches of the rural constabulary showed.

" 'Bout time," one grunted gruffly. "What's the matter in here, everybody asleep?"

THE big trooper who spoke stamped brawny legs and pulled a furry collar away from his face. It was blue-jowled, brutish. Ned's skin crawled at the heat in his eyes but he contrived a hoarse, "We've had trouble. A woman—"

"Big female, face like a fat cow and arms like elephant's legs?" the officer interrupted eagerly.

"Yes. How did you know? She. . . ."

"Yes, hear that, Dan? She's here. Fat Frieda's here!" Then to Ned. "Where is she? She do any damage?" He saw the blood-stained bandage and his hand went under his coat, came out with a blued, squat revolver. "Gawd, I see she did. Is—"

"She's knocked out."

"Cripes! How'd you do it? I'll be damned if I'd want to meet up with her alone. Wrung a matron's neck and sliced a guard's gullet before she got away from Loomis."

"Loomis?"

"Looney house up at Vinefield. Didn't you—"

"Yes. I remember. Where the penitentiary is, too. So she's insane. No—"

"She dead?" The other officer was shorter than the first. There was a whine in his voice and his face was pinched, somehow wolfish.

"No, she—"

"We'd better get the cuffs on her then before she comes to."

The taller cop turned to a door in the wall to the left, but Ned stopped him. "Not in there, that's the dining room. She's in here." He pointed.

"Oke," crisply. "Come on Dan. Get your cuffs out."

"How're we goin' to get the car started? How're we goin' to find it? How're we goin' to lug her through th' damn snow? She weighs a ton." Dan's words ran together, complainingly, but steel clinked in his hands and he was first through the archway. Miriam was a white flame in the center of the room, her eyes wide. She saw the officers and her hand went up, pulling the shreds of her dress around her shoulders. The taller one grinned at her, but Dan went right past her, knelt at the side of the stertorously breathing flesh-mass they had called Fat Frieda. His hands moved deftly and his cuffs clinked around her wrists. "Gimme yours, guy, for her ankles."

"Oke. Here they are." The other tossed them, holstered his gun. "She won't bother you none with them on, ma'am. Your husband tells me there was a shindig here."

"Yes. Yes, she did make a fuss." Ned wondered why her face didn't lighten, why that little muscle twitched at the corner of her mouth. There was nothing to fear any longer. The two policemen could be persuaded to stay the night. Their guns would protect them against any peril, fancied or otherwise.

Dan got to his feet, stood looking down at his prisoner. "An' they expect me to haul that in to the station by myself? Ain't that like 'em? If I hadn't met up with you—"

"Place looks like she did," the other went on, ignoring his partner's complaints. "But you ain't got nothin' to worry about now. Private Bill Sloane of the State Police will see to that."

Dan half-turned, appeared puzzled about something. "You'll stay till morning?" Ned asked eagerly. "Your friend is right, you couldn't get anywhere in this snow."

"Sure, we'll stay. I wouldn't go out again in that for money." Sloane was gruffly hearty. "I—"

"My orders are to bring her in pronto, Sloane, if I find her. You know the regulations." Dan's voice had lost its whine, there was a new quality in it, vibrant. "You may be on vacation, as you said, but I'm on patrol." His hand moved toward his gun-butt, checked.

The bigger man came around, lazily, but his cheek-muscles hardened. "You said it, Dan Regan. I'm on vacation an' I'm stayin' here." Tenseness had sud-

denly come back into the room, the peculiar tenseness of a thunderstorm just before it breaks. "I can't see how you're goin' to manage it alone."

MIRIAM'S eyes caught Ned's. She was trying to signal something to him, trying to get a silent message across to him. He didn't understand, but the hair at the back of his skull bristled, inexplicably. He seemed to be caught up in an intangible maelstrom of eerie dread. The clash between the uniformed pair was somehow more meaningful than the mere disagreement as to procedure it appeared on the surface. It involved him, obscurely, and Miriam.

"Alone!" Dan's word crackled, and his gun was suddenly in his hand, snouting pointblank at the other trooper. "Reach, damn you! I had a hunch there was something wrong about you when you asked for a lift. *Now I know*—"

Shot-crash pounded to the lance of orange flame from Dan's gat as Sloane dropped to the floor, rolled to the bulking shelter of a heavy sofa. Shot-crash answered from the floor; a red streak whipped across Dan's cheek and stonedust spurted from the mantel behind him. He was down too, sheltered by the mound of the madwoman's massive frame—Ned leaped to Miriam, thrust her against the wall. "Oh, God," she whimpered, "oh dear God!"

There were no more shots as the antagonists lay flat behind their respective shields. No more shots, but the tang of cordite was the perfume of death in the opponents' nostrils, and death poised, grinning, avid, for an incautious move on either's part.

"Alone!" Dan snarled. "No trooper would run out on a pal, snow or no snow. You fooled me for a while, but that crack tipped me. What's your game?"

"That's for me to know, wise guy, and

for you to find out." Sloane growled from the safety of the thick-padded, heavy sofa. Miriam's fingers tightened on Ned's shoulders.

"It's up now anyway," Dan snarled. "You can't stay there forever. Throw your gun out in the middle of the floor and maybe I'll forget one of the charges against you, resisting an officer. That'll take six months off your sentence, whatever else you get."

The one who called himself Sloane laughed grimly. "Guess again, trooper. Mebbe I can't hit yeh without drillin' through Fat Frieda, but the other lady's right over my sights an' I kin burn lead into her without battin' an eyelash."

In the shadows where he lay, across the floor, Ned could see the pseudo trooper's eyes, weird red balls glaring out of the gloom. Something in their uncanny light sent a shiver of sickish dread through him that was distinct from the sharp flare of fear for Miriam. Despite the heat radiating from the burning coals, a feverish chill quivered in the room—a chill that seemed to transmit itself to the woman's body, pressed against him. Ned's heart was a leaden lump in his breast.

"You—yellow-belly!" Dan's curse was a groan. "You wouldn't do that. It's a dog's trick."

"Try me," the other chuckled, evilly. "Just try me, mister. "I'll give you till I count five. *One—*"

The mouthed the count with a sadistic, avid drawl and Ned knew that the man longed to hear the thump of lead into white feminine flesh, to see blood spurt over rounded breasts.

"*Two—*" Even if Dan surrendered there was no safety for Miriam. He who called himself Sloane would have them all his mercy, then *and that was what he had come for!*

"*Three—*" Each tolled syllable retched-

ed Ned's stomach, popped bitter fluid into his throat. His right arm was around Miriam, clutching her to him in a frenzy of despairing farewell, but his left hand crept along the wall, feeling its wood-panelled surface, groping.

"*Four—*" He knew an intaglio plaster cast of Janus was hanging there. He found it, clutched it, ripped it from its fastenings in one convulsive movement and hurled it! It crashed against blued metal of Sloane's gun, smashed to a thousand fragments. Flame spurted, thudded into the floor. Dan was up—the pound of his shot a thunder-clap; its flash, a lightning-bolt. Sloane jerked, screamed once—horribly. His long body twisted out from behind the sofa spasmodically—and was limply still. A dark stain spread on the rug, alongside his breast.

Dan twisted, thrust a gnarled hand at Ned. "Thanks, buddy," he growled. "I was just goin' to give in."

MIRIAM sobbed. Ned went over to her. She was crushed against the wall, her arms outspread, palms flat. But her face was alight. Terror and consuming dread had lifted from it. Her lips moved. Ned bent closer. "I felt that it was he as soon as I saw him. And now he's really dead—at last."

Ned brushed a kiss across her lips, turned to look once more at the corpse over which Dan was bending. Borisoff had been as big as Sloane. It was like his malevolent cunning to have gained entrance to the house disguised as a trooper. How he must have laughed inwardly at his meeting with the veritable officer, making his ruse certain of success. But how had he escaped the train-wreck? The smoking-car into which he had gone had been smashed to splinters by a following locomotive, and then had flared to a fiery pyre. There was no hint even of burn-scars on this dead man.

*And how had he managed to get the half-
ring onto the table, hours before?*

"Jeez!" the State cop looked around,
his nostrils flaring, his voice low, tense.
"What do you know? This guy's Stan
Lindinger—one of the two yeggs who
broke out of the pen day before yesterday. Look!" He pointed. Ned saw that
he had opened the man's shirt, saw a
puckered scar at the base of the corded
neck. "Another con did that with a file
—two years ago." Dan's mouth worked.
"Fifteen grand reward in my pocket—
just like that!"

The words beat dully against Ned's
numbed brain. "Pen—two years." In
those two years Borisoff had stalked
across a million screens, his incredibly
gruesome portrayals distorting light into
blood-chilling horror. This wasn't he,
then. The menace still hung over Miriam,
over him—the menace heralded by the
inexplicable appearance of the half-ring
that was now a lump of molten gold.

Heavily, like a black pall, fear settled
down on him once again, gelid fear that
seemed one with the dark pools of shadow
lurking along the oak-panelled walls and
in the far corners of this room where the
only lights were from the bright cone
beating down on the round central table
and the red glow of the aging fire. And
with it—an obscure premonition of horror
yet to come—there crept over him the
weird feeling that he whom they dreaded
was close by, watching with narrowed,
evil eyes the flutterings of these beleag-
ered humans against the slow closing-in
of inescapable doom.

CHAPTER THREE

The Talisman of Dread

THE jelly-like bulk of the mad-woman
stirred, pulling Ned's glance to her.
Her lewd eyes stared at him from the
formless expanse of gray-white flesh that
was her face. Her incongruously small
mouth was edged by a mirthless, obscene
smile. He knew that she was shackled,
hand and foot, yet a ripple of apprehen-
sion prickled Ned's spine, and he felt
again the smooth yet implacable pressure
of her clammily soft fingers about his
neck. His hands knotted—then he saw
that Dan was watching him queerly. He
forced unmeaning words to his tongue.
"An escaped convict, eh? Had you fooled
nicely!"

"Said he was from Scottsville station,
other end of the state. Busted in a crap-
game and hiking back to his station when
the snowstorm caught him. I was just
startin' to follow Frieda's tracks, draggin'
into your field, an' I was glad o' help.
Didn't ask too many questions. Gawd!
He almost got me!" The cop shrugged
his shoulders. "You never know. . . ."

"How about some hot coffee, trooper?"
Miriam's tone was natural, as it had not
been since they had come in and found
the broken circlet of gold. "You must
be frozen." It was evident she had not
heard Dan's identification of Sloane; still
thought he was Borisoff. Ned started to
speak, tightened his lips. Better that way;
she had endured enough already. From
now on he must watch for her as well as
himself.

"Cripes, lady," Dan was answering her,
"that would be swell. I ain't got the cold
out of my bones yet."

"We'll soon fix that," she threw over
her shoulder, moving lithely toward the
hall.

"Wait!" Ned snapped. "Wait!" Miriam turned, looked inquiring. "I'm going with you, I'll help you." It sounded
lame after the urgency of his exclamation. Miriam didn't notice that, but the
trooper caught the inflection and his
glance flickered to Ned's face again, flick-

ered away. "I'll set the pantry table while you put up the percolator. I couldn't swallow anything in here."

They went through the curtains, across the foyer. Melting snow made a pool on the floor. Ned glanced at his mackinaw. Queer! He had been so certain that he had thrust the automatic deep into his pocket out there, that he had tucked in the flap. But it must have fallen out in spite of that. No other explanation for its disappearance was within reason. Reason! What had reason to do with this mad night—with the fear that still brooded blackly within him?

"I was so happy when he brought me through that door and told me he had built this house for me, that it was mine. I thought it meant that he had changed, that life with him would no longer be hell." Miriam had paused, musingly, with her hand on the knob of the dining-room door. "That was what he wanted me to think. Disillusion would be all the more poignant."

Ned pulled her to him, drank greedily of her lips. "That's all over now, sweetheart. I'll make it all up to you." Brave words, but a bell seemed to clang within his skull, a deep-toned gong of warning, and the kisses could not warm his blood. He held her in his arms. The longer he held her, the longer it would be before she opened that door. *He was afraid of what might be within!*

But she pushed him from her, tenderly, her eyes starry. She turned the knob. Blackness glowered at them. She clicked a switch beside the door frame—Ned blinked to the sudden light. His vision cleared. No one was there. He laughed silently at his fears. The darkly gleaming oval of the big table seemed to fill the room with its broad expanse. A long flat shadow lay across it.

Ned froze, staring. Directly in the centre of the glowing oak, stubby and ominous, was his automatic! Light splintered on it, flashed from it to stab his brain . . .

GLASS crashed from the living room. A shot pounded. A man shrieked in agony, and as Ned snatched up the gun, whirled, shouted, "Stay here, Miriam!" the turmoil was cut off by sudden silence. "Stay here," he repeated and was out in the foyer, across it, lunging against velvet fabric that whipped across his face and blinded him. It held him like something alive, virulent. He ripped the portieres aside, plunged through, stopped just within them. A vicious, bestial snarl—an animal-sound—greeted him from thick darkness. There was the acrid, pungent odor of burning flesh.

What he saw photographed itself on his mind. It was implanted forever like a deep-branded nightmare terror. The lamp was out, red embers were scattered on the hearth. The little trooper lay face down atop the hot coals. The still quivering haft of a knife projected from his back; a dark fluid welled around its buried blade. Frieda's mass was gone from the floor!

A cold wind chilled Ned's cheek. The snarl came again—pulled his aghast eyes from the murdered man to where something loomed against the jagged, pale aperture of a smashed window. The thing moved, growling. A pallid glow from the snow-filled night fell across it. It was a veritable giant of a man, stripped to the waist, bloody gashes netting his torso, blood masking his face so that Ned saw only crazed eyes and long green fangs revealed by pulled-back, black lips.

The intruder bounded forward into a shadow, bounded forward, long arms lifting, curved claws hooking. Ned crouched to the attack, jerked up his gun, pulled the trigger. A click answered him, a mocking click. He had time only to realize that the magazine had been stripped when the sweaty, foetid monster thudded down on him, overwhelmed him with its stink and horror, pounded him down with its blood-slippery weight . . .

His skull crashed violently against wood. Miriam screamed somewhere. Bursting oblivion took him . . .

Ned weltered up, slowly, painfully, through agony-filled blackness—through a gibbering chaos of madness and despair —till drab consciousness tugged at his eyelids and dragged them open. A slaughter-house stench was in his nostrils, the odor of blood and burned flesh— human blood and human flesh! The eerie pale glimmer of a sky from which snow fluttered, sifted into the room, obscuring rather than illuminating it. The pain-wracked man pushed himself to a sitting posture, wondering that he was still alive—that he had not been torn to bits by the half-human monster which he had glimpsed for an appalling second.

He was alive, miraculously. Strength seeped slowly into his muscles and he staggered to his feet, staggered to a wall-switch that no one had thought to use during the swift succession of horrors this room had witnessed. His thumb pressed the white button, and a chandelier, high in the beamed ceiling, spilled yellow light on a shattered shambles that had once been a luxurious living room.

Ned's aching stare fumbled to the fireplace. It held only gray ashes now, and Dan's flaccid form. The madwoman was gone. Only a great clotted stain showed where Sloane's corpse had lain. Blood-stained splinters of glass lay on the floor beside it, on the couch that had been a barricade for the fraudulent trooper. Jagged splinters of glass framed the window above it, and the sill of that window was wet with blood and melted snow.

The shattered threads of his brain began to knit together, slowly, painfully.

The half-nude giant must have smashed that window, surging through it reckless of sharp edges tearing his flesh. He must have plunged his knife into Dan's back so suddenly that the officer had had time for only one shot, one scream. And then—but what had become of Frieda and of Sloane's body?

Ned's burning gaze searched the rest of the floor. They were nowhere. But— his skin crawled—but what was that? That yellow gleam just at the edge of the curtains—just where they closed the archway and hugged the floor?

The tiny thing wiped horror from his mind with greater horror. A tiny thing— a semi-circle of gold—its ends serrated, broken. Half of an old fashioned wedding ring. *The other half of the ring that had brought dread and nameless fear into this house.*

CHAPTER FOUR

This Dreadful House

HE was in the house! Pavel Borisoff! The bloody, green-fanged giant was Borisoff. He had come at last to claim his wife, *Miriam!* Her name, the thought of her, was a red-hot iron searing Ned. Miriam! *He* had her! He had her in his evil clutches—that devil, that fiend whom hell itself had rejected! Ned pushed himself away from the wall, whirled, started through the curtains.

Started through! His legs thumped against something hidden by the dark velvet! He fell forward; his flung-out hand plunged into an oozy, squashy mass, queasily repulsive even in that instant of falling. His other hand felt rounded, cold flesh. He sprawled across a hulking body, rolled away from it. And he lay, shuddering, on the foyer floor, staring at that over which he had fallen.

It was the nude, green-fanged giant!

No longer green-fanged. His head was a pulped, unrecognizable mass into which Ned's hand had squashed. Ned's stomach turned over; nausea retched him. Then the significance of the sight penetrated and he heaved to his feet, his throat rasping to his cry: "Miriam! Miriam! Where are you?"

The squealed, hysterical call sliced silence—was quenched by the same silence. The spasm that had brought Ned erect— that ripped the cry from him, passed— was succeeded by a rigid paralysis holding him immobile, voiceless. Only his eyes were alive and they were focussed on a thick iron bar, a black bar smeared with red and with gray. This was the weapon that had pounded—he understood now—had pounded through the curtains, killed the giant and saved his life. Saved him—*but had it been meant to save?* Whoever had wielded it had struck through the curtains, had crashed it into darkness. Only in that very instant had the giant's head loomed over his own head to take the blow. And in that same instant, Borisoff's half-ring had dropped to where he had found it, *from a pocket of the person who struck that blow!*

That one was Borisoff! But who, in God's name, who? Not Dan, lying inside, murdered. Not Frieda—Miriam said *she* was a woman, truly a woman. Not Sloane—shot dead long ago—*shot dead*— Ned's whirling mind stuck at that. Perhaps those once dead and returned to life can not again be killed!

Blood thumped in his temples, pounded in his ears. Miriam—what had he done to her? Where had he taken her? That pounding was not in his ears. It was a slow thump, thump, thump from somewhere beneath. The floor shook to it. It pounded against the soles of Ned's feet, up his tensed legs, pulsing life back into him — horror-filled, black-brained life, quivering to the obscure, utter terror of

that slow dinning that was so like the leisurely blows of a hammer driving nails into a coffin-lid!

Ned's face was a blood-spattered, stony mask of grim despair. His sunken eyes were dead orbs in which smouldered twin hell-candles of hate and vengeance. He bent jerkily—picked up the brain-smeared bar, straightened. He moved, fancying that he heard the creaking of his pain-stiffened joints. The muffled, significant thumping continued; his body twitched to each dulled impact as if it were a sledge-blow at the base of his spine. Half-crouched, he sidled to a door in the stair-casing, a door that led to the cellar from which that sound must come. He fumbled it open, eased through.

The door closed behind him without noise, and blackness engulfed him. But the pounding was louder, clearer. Each thump was a clink of metal on metal underlaid by a curious, soft thud that rippled inexplicable horror through him.

Someone whimpered below. A husky, sexless voice said: "It's pretty isn't it, my lovely one? But you'll look even better. Ah, yes!"

NED tried to hurry but his terror-bound muscles would move just so fast, and no faster. He curved around the winding steps, and the darkness lightened slightly to dimness. The voice came again: "One more, then it's your turn." The hammer-pound slowed, as if it were reluctant to quit its task.

Ned made the last turn.

A single pendant light spread hazy illumination in a vaulted basement. High stone arches were supported by vertical posts of bark-stripped logs. Directly ahead Miriam lay, bound with strips of her own gown that cut into her white arms, into the firm loveliness of her bared thighs. To one side, somehow fouler by contrast with his wife's sweet curves, loomed the gross mass of the madwoman. Her monstrous countenance was contorted, blood-engorged. Her too-red lips were parted in lewd ecstasy. The ruptured chain of a handcuff dangled from the wrist of one upraised, columnar arm, and its hand clutched a short-handled, heavy-headed hammer. Arm and hammer swept down—to crash on a gleaming spike projecting from a throat, from the encarmined throat of Sloane. His naked, big-thewed frame bristled with spikes that held it to the gory wood of a splintered pillar.

Frieda grinned, stepped back to gloat over her grisly work. "He didn't last long," she lipped sorrowfully. "That bullet took most of the life out of him and spoiled the fun. But you'll be different, dearie. You'll scream sweetly, and beg me to kill you." She half-turned, chuckling. "Well, now, if you haven't gone and fainted. I'll have to go upstairs and get some water for you, so that you won't miss anything." She came fully around—and fury blazed in her face as she saw Ned, immobile with horror. She squealed, lumbered toward him.

Ned jerked awake. The bar he held snapped up, whistled as it flew from his hand, straight at the straggly black of her head. Incredibly agile, she flung her hammer-hand up, parried it. The iron crashed against the tool, both arced through the air. From his light elevation, Ned hurled himself at her. The top of his head thudded between pendulous, pillow-like breasts; his fists flailed into gruesome softness. The madwoman went down before his sudden onslaught; he pounded frantically, blinded by his frenzy, shaken by the red lust to kill that possessed him. The mass under him rolled over, was atop him, crushing him with its loathsome weight. Panic exploded desperate strength in him. He heaved, threw her off momentarily, rolled

away. She squirmed after him, uncannily swift—clamped doughy, irresistible fingers on his ankle, hauled him back to her. He glimpsed her slavering mouth and the lurid laughter in her mad eyes. His other leg jerked up, straightened, its shod foot sank into her belly.

An inhuman screech burst from her, her hold left his ankle—and clamped on his throat! She rolled over atop him again; she flowed, rather, like some unskeletoned, protoplasmic horror from primeval slime. He was flat on his back, his useless arms outstretched to either side, the back of his head grinding into the slimed concrete floor of the cellar. The boneless fingers on his throat tightened. Suddenly they ceased the slow increase of their pressure, but held their lethal squeeze.

Dimly, through the roaring in his ears, he heard viscid words drip from the fish-belly gray of the amorphous face above him. "No! Not so easy, my love. I have spikes enough for you and her too. She shall share my sport with you."

HER meaning penetrated, and obscurely, Ned was glad. He would take long to die—he determined—very long, thus delaying the inevitable torture that must come to Miriam when he was gone. Perhaps—indomitable hope still smouldered within him even now—a miracle would occur to save his wife.

The woman-fiend slightly released her sodden weight. Her other clammy hand gripped his shoulder to lift him—just as a calf might be lifted by the butcher—to the column against which he was to be crucified. She handled him as one would a toy. He felt cold metal press into his hand, the sharp edges of the bar.

His fingers constricted, gripped. His arm-muscles lashed upward. The iron was a live thing in his hand. It seemed to fly up of its own volition. Bone crunched sickeningly; the red-gleaming, pig small eyes above him were suddenly glazed; blood gushed from the tiny, lascivious mouth, spewed its foetid nauseating warmth over him. Jelly-like weight thumped down on him, but his throat was free and he could breathe again.

There was almost no strength left in him. He crawled toward Miriam, lay full length on the floor as he worked at her lashings. But her dear voice, even edged by hysteria, was limpid, musical, in his ears. "I saw you come down the stairs, pretended to faint so that I could close my eyes for fear their expression would betray you. Then I heard the crash of your bar, looked and saw you fighting with her. I saw that the bar had landed here, right here where I could reach it with my tied hands, but I couldn't do anything more—couldn't do anything to help you until just now when she had beaten you. Then I managed to squirm a bit nearer and get it into your hand. I was afraid, my sweet, deathly afraid that I was too late."

"Nothing to be afraid of any more. But we're going to get out of this house, snow or no snow, as soon as I get you loose."

"Out of this dreadful house!" It was a prayer, a prayer of thanksgiving. "And never come back. But even in your arms, Ned, I shall dream of what I saw in that entrance hall."

"I know, I saw it."

"And that bar was at the woman's feet. I screamed. She whirled, had her hands on me before I could move, held me helpless while she tore the rest of my dress from me and tied me up. Then she went in through the curtains, came out with Sloane slung over one shoulder. He was groaning—I was startled to realize that he was still alive—but limp, unconscious. She slung me to her other shoulder—"

"Don't talk about it. Don't think about

it." Ned had Miriam's arms free, started work on the bindings of her legs. His fingers trembled, and weird, impossible thoughts crawled through the aching morass of his mind. "The curtains acted queerly as I went through them, she must have had them folded around her. But I can't understand—" His mouth shut.

"What, Ned? What?"

"Nothing, dear. Nothing important." But it *was* important. If the half-ring had been dropped by Frieda, *she* was Borisoff. But that didn't make sense. Miriam knew her to be a woman. Unless—could an outcast soul find lodging in another form—a form vacated, perhaps, by its own soul and therefore called mad? *Or had Borisoff been other than human?*

Heavy footfalls sounded, descending the spiral stairs.

Oh, God! It was not yet finished!

CHAPTER FIVE

The Pyre Prepared

NED'S neck muscles corded so that it took all the little strength that was left in his spent body to bring his head around—till he could see at last the narrow opening in the basement wall behind which those stairs ended.

The rays of the single small lamp burning down here did not quite reach that wall. It was a misty barrier in the center of which was a vertical rectangle of darker shadow, mysterious, pregnant with dread.

The footfalls came slowly, but unhesitantly. Their very leisureliness bespoke the certainty of the doom they heralded.

Miriam's fingers were icy, death-still on Ned's temple. There was no sound in the dim basement except the implacable *pud, pud, pud* of that which was coming.

Light spread from the straight-sided

aperture, wavering light that slid across the scummed floor and was suddenly still. The sides of the opening cut it off so that it was a glistening bar of uncanny light on that floor.

A shadow jagged the light-bar, the shadow of a clawed hand. It grew, intermittently, with the thudding approach of the threat, grew and crept toward the rigid couple till it was a gigantic hand of blackness, reaching for them.

The hand was suddenly gone. But someone stood in the opening. An oil lamp shielded by his hand threw light up on to his bulking form. It threw unnatural shadows up across his broad-planed face, made his heavy jaw, his thick lips, his heavy nose and dark-browed, abysmal eyes into a countenance of infinite threat.

Breath puffed from Miriam, forming a name. "Pavel!"

Borisoff's smile was a ghastly thing, and Ned knew that he could fight no longer.

"Tableau!" the man in the doorway said. "Enoch Arden returns to find his faithless wife in the arms of another. But this wife did not wait the conventional year to go to the arms of her lover. And this Arden does not intend to slink back into the night from which he came."

"What are you going to do to us?"

"Do?" The booming, sepulchral voice mused. "Do? I wonder. What is there that will give me greater pleasure on the night of my wedding anniversary than that which I have already had, watching your appreciation of the entertainment I staged for you? They played their parts well; the convicts I aided to escape from their cells, the madwoman to whom I supplied the knife with which she made good her evasion. I sent them here, promising them sanctuary. I regret exceedingly," mockery curdled his phrasing, "that circumstances prevented my keep-

ing that promise. I tried to help my guests by knifing the trooper and releasing the feminine member of my trio, but —"

"You—you were here all the time?"

"All evening, watching you and laughing at you. You forgot, my dear wife, that I too might have a key to this house that I built for you, that I might not have gambled it away on the ill-fated smoker as I gambled away my watch and scarf-pin. Nor the ring. Never the ring."

"Then it was not you that . . .?"

"No. The joy that leaped into your face when you looked at the thing you thought was my charred corpse was uncalled for. I saw that, from the bushes where I had been thrown, passing between cars to return to you, and where I lay numbed, unable to move, but fully conscious. If there had been a single twinge of regret in your expression I might have had the farmer to whose home I was carried let you know that I was alive. But you would not have welcomed that news from the mouth of a stranger. I am sure you like it better from mine. Do you not?"

Speech returned to Ned. "Damn your soul, Borisoff! You've done enough to her. If you're human at all you'll stop torturing her with your rotten tongue. It's hell enough for her to know you're still alive."

BORISOFF'S demoniac smile deepened. "Ah, the gigolo is ungrateful, even though I saved his life by spilling the brains of my third guest. All right, my friend, I am a quite complacent husband. I'll stop 'torturing her with my tongue,' as you so aptly put it. On second thought, I'll even go away and leave you two here—*to burn as you hoped I had burned!*" He shouted the last and hurled the lamp far back into the cellar. It crashed, spattered flame; Ned saw a great pile of dried wood there, its chinks stuffed with rags and paper. He saw the blazing oil pour over that pile, saw it roar up into a flare of torrid, whirling flame. He turned back, Borisoff was gone. A door slammed above; the rattle of bolts was quite clear. Running feet thudded overhead, and another door slammed.

Unsupportable heat beat upon them already from the fiery maelstrom. Ned lifted himself from the floor, Miriam came up with him, and they dashed for the stairs, hoping against hope.

Heat surged up to them, enveloped them, and acrid smoke choked them. Cursing, Ned battered at the door—battered till his fists were bleeding, pulped—till he could scarcely breathe and could not see although the black smoke that billowed around him was shot through by scarlet glare. He felt consciousness slipping from him. Sliding down along the immovable door, found Miriam's slumped form, found her lips with his own. And hers moved a little, returning his kiss. . . .

Something crashed, somewhere. The door against which he leaned shook. A pillar must have fallen, burned through, in the raging furnace below. Another fell sounding like the knell of a doom-bell. Voices were shouting somewhere near. How he managed it, Ned could never remember, but he contrived one frantic yell, "Help!" and knew nothing more.

Dimly, through waves of agony, Ned began to sense again. His whole body was one vast ache, inside and out. Someone said, above him, "The woman's all right but we've got to get this one to a doctor damn' quick." Ned got his eyes open and saw a red glare in the sky on a snow field with black silhouetted figures moving phantasmally about him.

"What—what happened?" he gasped. "Where—where—"

A face was bending over him, fur-capped, and under it was a collar with the insignia of the state police. A gruff, kindly voice said: "You come to, eh, guy? Gawd, we thought you'd never talk again."

"Miriam?"

"The lady's fine—didn't even get burned. You fell across her and kept the flames from her."

"How—how—"

"How did we get here? Dan Regan 'phoned the station that he had trace of Fat Frieda. He told us he was going ahead, but to send help. We had a hell of a time getting through, and just as we got to where he said he'd be, we saw a fire blaze out through cellar windows. Took a chance on axing the door and damn' good thing we did. Second later and you'd both been goners. Was there anyone else alive in the house?"

"No. Yes. Big man—think he got out." Borisoff had escaped; there would be no peace for Miriam while he lived. And he—he wasn't her husband—never had been. The thought seared Ned's dizzy brain. He . . .

"Sorry, old man. Your friend got out of the house, but—" The trooper stopped. "Hell," he growled. "I'm forgettin' you're a damn' sick guy. Plenty of time for that later."

Incredulous hope stirred within Ned. "No. Tell me. Tell me now!"

"Sure yuh can take it?"

Ned nodded, emphatically, eagerly

"Well, he must of gotten twisted around in the snow or something. Anyways, there's a well out here, covered with snow. He slipped on some ice, runnin', and tumbled into it. We got him out, but there wasn't no use. His neck's broken."

Ned's lips twitched. Then he said something that made the trooper sure he was delirious. "Can I take it? *Oh boy, can I take that!*"

THE END

DEAD MAN'S SHADOW

By
John H. Knox
Terror Novelette

HE SAT at a desk, writing. A shaded porcelain lamp at his right elbow cast a nimbus of yellow light over his dark hair and broad, pajama-clad shoulders. He was a young man with a square-jawed, intelligent face. His name was Peter Proctor, and he was an investigator for the Lone Star Detective Agency. He was writing a report to his employer, Bill Copeland. The night

In the old country house they sat waiting for death to strike—old Giles Murdock, the sinister, vitriolic owner, and his heirs: Melvina the sorceress and her creaking suitors; Wayne the young weakling; and the orphaned, beautiful Irene. Yet when death thrust its dark shadow over them at last, silent and terrible, they knew not whence it came nor whose tight-clutching hands had moved it. . . .

was hot, windless, sultry. Proctor paused now and then to wipe his brow with a handkerchief. Then his pen scratched on:

". . . have heard plenty of ghost tales, particularly of ghosts of the Murdock family's ancestors. But not a thing has happened. I am beginning to think that our client, young Wayne Murdock, is suffering from a mild case of hysteria.

"There is a queer crew housed here at the old country estate. Old Giles Murdock revises his will each year and the family is forced to gather for inspection. The old man is a sinister looking specimen himself, a gnarled, stooped, vitriolic old devil, who drives his cringing, legacy-hunting relatives with an iron hand. He has a face like a mummy, an eye like a buzzard. Right now he's sitting downstairs in the library, after everyone has gone to bed, coaxing a weird tune from his ancient fiddle.

"I can't quite get what it is that has terrified this boy, Wayne Murdock, and caused him to want protection. Tonight is the night the dreadful thing—whatever it is—is supposed to happen. One reason, I suppose, is that his father died a year ago tonight. It was supposed to be heart-failure, but Wayne persists in describing it as 'sheer heart-stopping terror' that killed his father. Terror of what? I get nothing but evasive answers. Still, if he's willing to pay the fee, I've got no objection. I have nothing to do but carry out my pose of being a friend of the boy's from the agricultural college, interested in the horticultural specimens in his greenhouse, and keep an eye on this parade of freaks. They're all, natuarally, at each other's throats.

"The old man's sister, Melvina, is a tall, witchlike spinster who dabbles in the occult, and who drags her suitor, a creaking dandy by the name of Clinton Abell, at her apron-strings. Abell is a skinny scarecrow, dignified and distant, and he does a lot of talking about devil-cults, familiars, and the strange practices he has witnessed in Paris—all this, I think, to impress his lady love, who dotes on it.

"Professor Clewth, a friend of old Giles', and the old man's pick for Melvina's hand, is a thick-set man with grizzled hair and a face like a lump of red granite. A penniless explorer, it's obvious that he's after the dowry of the fair Melvina.

"That's all, dear patron, except for our spindly-legged, timorous client, and his orphaned cousin, Irene Murdock. I won't say anything about her, Bill; I'll wait and tell you. Maybe I'll . . ."

Proctor lifted his head, stared out across the moon-washed landscape. Wide lawns swept down from the great stone house and terminated in the black line of a hedge which separated the grounds from the sandy beach of Pirate's Point and the vast moon-silvered ocean beyond. Proctor smiled, a picture of Irene Murdock's amber hair and smiling lips floating pleasantly in the tobacco haze before his eyes.

". . . well, maybe I'll bring her along and let you see her."

PROCTOR paused again. Light from the lamp splashed a yellow puddle on the dark carpet of the hall, shone through the half-open door of the opposite room. He could see the foot of young Murdock's bed and the twin peaks where his feet made a hump under the covers. What was wrong with the youth? He recalled the frightened face, the staring eyes, the boy's reluctance to go to bed. What was it he feared? Proctor lowered his head over his letter, a thoughtful furrow creasing his brow.

"Thinking of young Murdock," he wrote, "gives me a new slant on the meaning of fear. Did you ever think, Bill, what a great part *vagueness* plays in fear —I mean real fear, the kind that paralyzes. This boy's really pitiful. He's waiting, waiting for something he can't see or anticipate, something terrible—something he can do nothing about. Get it, Bill?

"I came into his room tonight, surprised him standing in the center of the room jerking his body round and round like a dog chasing his tail. When he saw me he was startled and ashamed. I asked him if he was looking for one of Abell's familiar spirits. But it was no joke to him. At first he said nothing, then he sat down, face pale, hands shaking, and began to talk. He said that it seemed to him that there was something in the room with him, some presence, invisible, malignant. He hadn't heard or seen anything, but he *felt* it. He seemed frantic, tormented because I was smiling at him.

"I talked to him, told him it was silly to be afraid of something he couldn't see.

" 'But Proctor,' he retorted, 'that won't hold. You can't see the wind, but it can knock you down, kill you, demolish towns. And why does a dog howl when somebody dies?'

"I couldn't give him a satisfactory answer, but I tried to get him to be more definite about his fears. He finally talked. It seems that the night his father died, somebody saw something here on the balcony. He didn't know what, he said, but he had heard it spoken of in whispers. He may not have told me all he knows.

"Anyhow, Bill, you see what I'm driving at—the kind of fear I mean, the fear of the unknown, the unexplainable, the sort of fear that shakes the soul, maddens."

Proctor lifted his pen, looked up. The sound of the violin below had ceased. All was silent—almost unnaturally so. He stole a glance at the opposite room, saw that young Murdock's feet had not moved. He lowered his head again.

Then he jerked it up violently, sprang upright on his feet. Goose-flesh prickled his body and an unfamiliar weakness invaded his knees. For the shutter of the bedroom window at his right had closed with a violent slam. Yet there was not a breath of breeze blowing, not even enough to stir the shadows of the oak leaves on the balcony!

For a moment Proctor stood there, staring motionless; then his good sense came to the rescue. He stepped briskly to the window and stared out. Moonlight lay in ragged patches under the heavy trees. There was no one in sight, no movement.

He went back and sat down, frowning, staring straight ahead. Then he laughed. He wouldn't let that upset him. Some mischievous boy prowling about, probably. He took up his pen and began to write:

"Something just happened which might have upset a superstitious person. . . ." He described the incident, and added, "I was startled, but that wasn't real fear either; common sense came to the rescue. Now suppose. . . ."

Again he raised his head, stared vacantly out the French windows before him. Now suppose. . . . He wanted a good illustration.

His eye, idly following a smear of moonlight chalked on one of the pillars of the balcony, wandered vagrantly over the shadow-spattered floor. He leaned forward, blinking. Just where the edge of the French window framed his field of vision he noticed a peculiarly black blot, roughly round and framed in the clear field of light. He poked his head forward—and felt every muscle of his body freeze into rigidity. For the shadow stretched darkly across the moon-bright floor for a good six feet, and it was the shadow of a human body—lying as if in an attitude of death, hands folded on chest, horrid head flung back, mouth agape. And the clearly defined profile was that of Giles Murdock!

FOR what seemed an age, Proctor's frozen eyes hovered in horror on the ghastly sight; then slowly he raised them, searching in terror for the body which must be hanging suspended horizontally in the air. But there was no body. The moon was visible, and the bright air, clear and limpid as spring water, exposed its shimmering, empty depths. . . .

Proctor's tongue was dry and his throat seemed choked with a fine dry dust. Slowly he rose to his feet, leaning on the desk. But his eyes never left the shadow—the black, ghastly thing that lay there defying all the laws of physics.

At last, with an oath, he tore his eyes away, snatched up the revolver that was on the dresser and dashed out upon the balcony.

The shadow was gone. The wide bright square where it had lain was white and empty as a clean sheet of paper.

Proctor stood and stared at it, the gun held loosely in a limp hand. He walked to the edge of the balcony, stared up. Nothing. He assured himself beyond any possibility of doubt that no object could have been held down from the roof in such a way as to cast that shadow, without his being able to see it. It was absolutely impossible. In fact, it was impossible that the shadow could have been there at all!

Proctor went back into the room and sat down at the desk. Sweat covered his entire body, and a damp chill pierced him to the bone. Almost with dread, his eyes sought the patch of moonlight. Had he imagined t? He couldn't have. There were no other shadows nearby to confuse him, and hallucinations were something he had never experienced. Then what in God's name had it been? The question shrieked through his mind like a feverish wail. What in God's name could it mean?

He stared across the hallway, saw that Wayne Murdock's feet had not moved. What if the boy should awaken, find him here, quaking in every joint. How could he explain his fear?

Proctor gripped the gun in his hand, leveled it at the spot of moonlight. His teeth set in a vise, his eyes stared with an almost painful intentness. He heard the clock ticking the seconds. He waited, waited. . . . And suddenly, with a wave of alarm, he realized what an insane picture he made, gun in hand, waiting for a shadow—waiting to shoot at a shadow!

Then something happened which jerked him to his feet, spun him about like a re-

leased top. A voice smote his ears, a voice which seemed to inhabit the empty air above his head. It was hoarse, throaty, and it said in a low tone, unhurried and quite distinct:

"Old Murdock's dead; what'll we do with him?"

And another voice, shrill like the voice of an old woman, answered: "Wrap him in leather."

Proctor dived for the door. Sheer panic drove him, but as he reached the stair-head a definite intention filtered through the confusion of his mind. He took the steps three at a time, turned to his right in the lower hall and dashed into the dimly lighted library. There he jerked to a halt, his head spinning, his unsteady eyes trying to focus on the rocking scene.

On a low divan, near a table on which a smoking lamp still burned, lay the body of old Giles Murdock. The whole attitude of the body, lying stiffly with hands on breast, was the same as that of the dreadful shadow, and there could be no doubt that he was dead. The aged jaw hung down; the eyes were wide, staring at the ceiling with a glassy fixity which seemed to reflect the utmost horror that can wrack a human soul.

Proctor stepped near. There was no visible mark of violence on the body, not a pin-prick. That terrible, rigid face spoke as plainly as words: *"This man was literally scared to death!"*

CHAPTER TWO

The Thing Behind the Veil

PETER PROCTOR straightened, stared about him. The room was empty, silent like the rest of the sleeping house. Great formless shadows, cast by the lamp's licking flame, leaped and gestured on dark paneled walls, and the dreadful chill which seems to accompany the presence of death lay like a dank miasma in the stuffy air. With a steel-willed effort, Proctor got a grip on his jangled nerves, tried to think. Here was death, and here, he was convinced, was murder—though murder of a singularly subtle and hellish sort. He had seen death by sudden strokes, but never a dead man whose tortured face was marked by such utter, abysmal terror.

With an inward shudder of revulsion he stared again at the awful death mask, and the terrible reality of the horror shook him back to an awareness of his mission. The thing which the boy dreaded had happened—might be happening again. And he was the hired protector!

Proctor spun about on his heels, headed for the stairs. As he sprang up the steps, catlike and silent, a dreadful premonition was already forming in his mind. Now he saw that the lamp in his room had gone out. The whole upper floor was in darkness. At the head of the stairs he gripped the revolver in a tight fist and flung himself toward the door of the boy's room.

As he pushed it open a low, strangled moan reached his ears—a forced, choked sound like the mutter of a nightmare victim!

"Wayne!" he whispered harshly. "Wayne!"

Then he saw the boy, and for a moment stood frozen. Moonlight seeped dimly through a curtained window, casting a pale light on the disheveled bed. And there the boy was wallowing, wallowing like a man being strangled, kicking his feet in the air, flailing his arms, while from his throat the rasping sounds sputtered. Yet there was no one else in the room!

With the hair on his scalp bristling, Proctor sprang forward. As he did so the struggling ceased and the boy lay limp. And then—did he imagine it, did he strike

it with his arm in passing?—the filmy curtain fluttered, moved as if to admit the passage of an invisible body escaping through the window!

Proctor's hands gripped the boy's body, lifted him from the bed. Convulsive tremors shook the youth's skinny frame. Carrying him quickly across the hall, Proctor laid him on his own bed, fumbled for matches, struck a light.

Wayne Murdock lay gasping, his eyes rolled grotesquely back, his lips twitching over tightly clenched front teeth. A feverish flush colored the sallow skin of his face; and his hands, jerking spasmodically, rose toward his throat, hovered there, trembling.

Proctor hurried to the bathroom and returned with cold water and a towel. He dug into his suitcase and brought out a flask of brandy. Then he bathed the boy's face, lifted his head and forced a trickle of the brandy between his teeth.

Wayne swallowed, coughed. His eyes rolled back to normal focus, stared wildly about the room, then came to rest with an expression of relief on Proctor's face.

"Proctor! God! I tried to call but couldn't. It was choking me! God! It was choking me, but I couldn't see it!"

"Easy, easy," Proctor's voice soothed. "There, a little more brandy. Gulp it down. Good. That'll help you."

"But my God! What was it?"

"I don't know," Proctor said grimly. "But whatever it was, it's killed your uncle."

"Uncle Giles . . . dead!" The youth sat up abruptly.

"Not so loud," Proctor growled. "Pull yourself together. There's a lot to be done."

"But the others . . . do they know?"

"No," Proctor said, "and I don't intend for them to—yet. Take another drink; get a grip on yourself. You're coming with me. We're going to find out what the rest of this household is doing."

WITH bathrobes over their pajamas, the two crept out into the hall. Proctor led the way with a flashlight ready in his hand. Wayne Murdock followed, his usually sallow face now white as a chalk smear in the darkness, his knees knocking together with each step.

Proctor knocked first at Irene Murdock's door, then gently opened it a few inches and flooded the bed with light. The girl lay peacefully sleeping, her hair like a pile of spun amber framing the rose and ivory oval of her face. Proctor snapped off the light, breathed deeply with relief. Only now did he realize just how anxious he had been.

At the next door, Clinton Abell's, Proctor paused to repeat the process. But when he had opened the door his eyes narrowed with suspicion. The bed was empty, the covers had not even been disturbed!

He hurried to Melvina Murdock's door, and when there was no response to his knock, opened it. Like Abell's room, it was empty and the bed had not been slept in.

"I'm not surprised," Wayne Murdock blurted. "They're up to something, those two!"

"Shhh!" Proctor silenced him. His brows bunched thoughtfully, his jaws snapped like those of a hunting dog who scents the quarry. "Come on," he said, and tiptoed with swift strides to the door of Professor Clewth's room.

He knocked; no answer. He turned the knob, pushed. The door did not yield.

"Locked!" he muttered in an impatient whisper. He turned to face young Murdock with a frown. The frown deepened to a scowl.

Proctor started, leaned forward. "What'n hell?"

A voice, muffled as if by distance, was coming from the darkness toward the end of the hallway.

"*Sint mihi Dei Acherontis!*" the voice intoned. It paused. Wayne Murdock's teeth chattered in the silence.

"What does it say?" Proctor demanded.

"Be propitious to me, Gods of Acheron!" young Murdock translated in a quaking whisper. "It's an incantation!"

Proctor snapped the button of his flash. The beam shot out, plowed through the shadows. Again the voice: "*Valeat numen triplex Jehovae!*"

Then Proctor saw it—the iron grill that covered the air vent from the furnace. He crept toward it. Young Murdock followed, seemed to recover his speech.

"It's coming from the furnace-room," he stammered. "Aunt Melvina's got a sort of a seance room down there in the basement."

"Then show me the way to it—quick!" Proctor growled.

Wayne Murdock faltered. "God! I don't like it. . . ."

"Go on!" Proctor shoved him forward. Then he snapped off the light and followed softly.

From the downstairs hall that led to the kitchen, steep steps dropped through a stair-well, dark and stifling with the musty odors of damp stone. A dim thread of light seeped from beneath the heavy door of the furnace-room. Proctor crept near, stooped, applied his eye to the keyhole.

One corner of the dimly lighted room was visible. It had been draped with some heavy black stuff, like a medium's chamber. At the far end was a sort of cabinet hung with thick drapes on three sides, the front covered with a veil of thin gauze. A brazier of coals glowed weirdly on a dais before the cabinet and furnished the only illumination for the ghostly scene.

Then a figure came into Proctor's field

of vision, a gaunt dark figure whose kimono of black silk blended in with the room's macabre furnishings. It was old Melvina, looking more witchlike than ever with the red reflection from the coals playing on the jet-black surface of her unbound hair and smearing her high cheekbones with streaks of crimson. With long, mechanical strides, she moved to the low dais before the veiled cabinet and knelt above the glowing brazier, from which a whisp of blue smoke was rising.

"Devil worship!" Proctor muttered. He lifted his head, turned to Wayne Murdock, whose breath was whistling in the dark like escaping steam. "I can see only a part of the room," he whispered. "I want to know if Abell is in there with her."

"There's a small window that opens on the ground level," Wayne Murdock sputtered, "but—"

"But nothing!" Proctor hissed. "Go to it! See if Abell's in there! Get along!"

Wayne Murdock hesitated, clenching and unclenching his nervous hands. Then he moved off silently into the darkness.

LOW, eerie mutterings broke out again in the room. Proctor dropped his eye once more to the keyhole. The old woman's hawklike face was lifted in the weird, unnatural light; the thin, cruel lips were moving as she murmured in a tone of suppressed frenzy: *"Ignei, aerii, aquatani, salvete! Orientis princeps Beelzebub, inferni ardentis monarcha, et Demogorgon, propitiamus vos. . . ."*

Now that he had the clue, Proctor, with his half-forgotten Latin, patched up a rough translation of the sacrilegious ritual, and he shuddered. "Spirits of fire, water, air, hail! Beelzebub, prince of the East, monarch of burning hell, and Demogorgon, we propitiate ye. . . ."

There was a pause, a long pause in which the witch-woman's head strained forward with a horrible intentness as she watched the motionless veil, now half obscured by the curling smoke. Then suddenly her gaunt, talon-like hands were out-thrust, began to shake as a hoarse plaint escaped her throat.

"Destroy them! Destroy them! By the secret name of God, I command it! The old viper is dead! Destroy them, the spawn of snakes who stand between me and my dream!"

Violent revulsion shook Proctor. With the memory of the frightful death-shadow which he had seen and the dead face of Giles Murdock, a deep fear—primeval, inherent in the blood of man—flowed over him. For an instant it stripped the veneer of civilization away, left him like the naked caveman, shuddering in hot darkness before the violence of unknown powers.

Silence, heavy and preternatural, now filled the room where the old woman waited with unholy expectancy. The coals glowed brighter, the smoke puffed up in writhing clouds. Melvina was rising slowly to her feet.

"Exsurge! Exsurge!" Her voice rose now almost to a shriek. "Arise! Arise!" One long arm shot out; clawlike fingers dipped in a bronze bowl and arose, dripping. *"Per Jehovam, Gehennam, et consecratum aquam quam nunc spargo, signumque crucis quod nunc facio, et per vota nostra, ipse nunc surgat nobis dicatus Beelzebub!*—By Jehovah, Gehenna, and the holy water which now I sprinkle, the sign of the cross which now I make, and by our prayer, may Beelzebub now summoned by us arise!"

And then, even as the echoes of that dreadful blasphemy died away to silence, Proctor's horrified eyes beheld a stir behind the veil. It shivered as if blown by some unearthly wind. Beyond the confused mists, something dark and formless was projected upward. Proctor's skin crawled. The thing behind the veil rose higher and higher, a black mass without outline that seemed to writhe and flow like the smoke.

"Destroy! Destroy!" the cracked voice of the woman intoned. "Destroy utterly. Leave neither blood nor substance, bones nor dust! By the secret name of God, I command it!"

And then as the black thing leaped suddenly up and hung poised like a flat black shadow behind the gauzy veil, Proctor sprang to his feet, electrified by a sound that drifted down through the darkness from above. It was a scream, a scream of agony and fear, wrenched by sheer terror from a woman's lungs. And there was only one other woman in the house—Irene!

Proctor leaped for the stairs and bounded up, driven by a blind, unthinking frenzy, a sort of madness which made his body a thing of steel propelled by a single impulse—to reach her, to reach her before. . . .

The stairs shook under his tread. Another cry came from above. At the head of the stairs he whirled and plunged down the dark hallway to the girl's room.

On the threshold he paused, fear and despair clawing at his heart. For in the moonlight from the open window beside her bed, he could see her figure lying motionless as a statue among the tumbled covers.

"Irene!" Terror forced the hoarse whisper from his throat. He stumbled forward, snapping on the flashlight. "Irene!" He thrust an arm under her head, lifted it gently—saw with a surge of relief that she was breathing.

HER eyelids fluttered faintly, opened wide. "I must have fainted," she murmured.

"Thank God you're all right!" Proctor breathed. "What was it?"

Small shapely fingers lifted, touched her throat where reddish marks still showed against the ivory skin. "Hands . . . they were choking me . . ." she said breathlessly. "It was like a dream—a dreadful nightmare. I awakened feeling those awful fingers digging into my throat, choking the breath from me. . . ."

"But what was it? Did you see?"

She blinked, dazedly. "Why no, I couldn't see a thing. Whatever it was, it must have climbed up those vines. The hands could have reached me from the window-sill. That must have been how it was."

An ashy pallor overspread Proctor's face. "Yes," he said in a curiously hollow tone, "that must have been it." But he was thinking of something else, of a shadow that had lain motionless in the moonlight on the balcony; and of another shadow, a dreadful, formless thing that had stirred behind the veil in that chamber of sacrilege and blasphemy beneath the house.

Footsteps pounding in the hallway broke in upon his thoughts. He looked up to see Wayne Murdock's haggard face framed in the doorway. "What is it?" the youth gasped. "You, Irene . . . are you hurt?"

He came into the room, seemed to breathe more easily when he saw that she was not.

"Was Abell in the room down there?" Proctor demanded quickly.

Young Murdock shook his head. "No," he said, "nobody in there but Aunt Melvina, and—" His features tautened. "Proctor, did you see it . . . the thing . . . behind the veil?"

Proctor tried to keep his voice calm when he answered. "I saw a shadow," he said.

"God!" Wayne Murdock cried. "God! There's a curse on this house. If there's one of us alive by morning it'll be a miracle!"

"What does he mean, Peter?" the girl asked.

Proctor turned to her, the muscles of his jaw set grimly.

"He means," he said, "that your uncle has been murdered, and that there's some malignant power loose in this house that seems bent on destroying us all. But slip a robe on and come with us. We can't leave you here, and I've got to get back down there at once." He picked up a satin robe and threw it over her shoulders.

A moment later the three of them were moving down the hallway toward the stairhead, preceded by an exploring finger of light from Proctor's torch.

"Anything happen in the basement after I left?" Proctor asked.

"Nothing," Wayne said, "except that that damned shadow-like thing rose up behind the curtain, then seemed to fade out as it moved toward the window behind the cabinet."

They had reached the stairs and now they stopped. The beam of light plowing down through the gloom revealed the figure of a man standing on the stairs. He wore a dressing-gown and slippers, and a revolver was gripped in one big fist. It was Professor Clewth. He stared up at them, blinking against the light. "What's all the disturbance?" he demanded gruffly.

"Maybe you know." Proctor answered. The man's tone nettled him.

"What do you mean?"

"I mean," said Proctor, "that Giles Murdock is dead—and his murderer is still prowling about this house."

"Murdered? Giles! Where is he?"

"Lying on a divan in the library," Proctor said.

The squat, grizzled professor stared at Proctor with a strange expression. "Are you seriously trying to tell me . . .?" he began.

The others had now reached his level.

"I'm not trying to tell you anything," Proctor said. "You can see for yourself."

Something that was like a laugh, but unpleasantaly cold and hard, escaped the professor's lips. "Why you damned fool!" he sputtered. He sprang down the remaining steps and pushed into the library ahead of the others.

A match sputtered as they reached the doorway; the flame of the lamp surged up out of the dark. Professor Clewth stood beside it, hands on hips, sharp eyes fixed challengingly on Proctor.

"Now what was it you were telling me?"

Proctor stared, too utterly bewildered to speak. There was the divan, just as he had seen it; but there was no Giles Murdock in the room, either dead or alive, no trace to show that his body had been there!

CHAPTER THREE

Hell Collects

"WELL?" Clewth demanded. He seemed to take a cold pleasure in Proctor's bewilderment. "What sort of stunt is this—a joke, or some new kidnaping racket?"

Proctor's face clouded; his eyes snapped to the man's face. "Maybe you'd like to answer a few questions yourself," he countered.

Clewth ignored his words. He turned to the others. "Did either of you see this purported body?" he asked.

The girl shook her head. Young Murdock hesitated, looking at Proctor. "No," he said, "I didn't see it—but I've seen some other things. . . ."

In a choked, faltering voice, he described the night's events and the scene in the basement.

"So!" the professor exclaimed then. "Melvina is playing the devil, eh? And you say Abell wasn't in the room?" His eyes narrowed and he shook a finger at the girl. "Look here, you probably know that this rascally scoundrel, Abell, has persuaded Melvina to make him her heir, that he's playing on her nerves with this devil stuff. He's got her thoroughly in his clutches. . . !"

"She's devil enough herself," Wayne Murdock put in sourly.

"Hadn't we better call the police?" Irene asked.

"Police!" Clewth sputtered. "What would you tell them when they get here?" His gesture toward the empty divan was eloquent of his meaning.

Wayne Murdock interrupted him by whirling abruptly toward the hallway. "Hear that?"

"What?" Their eyes followed the direction of his gaze.

"Something like a—"

Then it came. Out of the black silence of the hallway, apparently from the empty air very near them, the same throaty voice Proctor had heard in his room: "Old Melvina's dead. What'll we do with her?"

And again the dreadful, mysterious answer, in the screeching voice of a woman: "Wrap her in leather!"

Wayne Murdock's voice was shrill with terror as he spun about, facing Irene. "Remember—that story," he stammered, "that story Uncle Giles told us—our ancestors, the corpses they wrapped in leather?"

Irene nodded, too horrified to speak. Proctor broke the spell which held them by plunging into the darkness of the hall. Round and round he went, the beam of his flashlight crossing and crisscrossing the shadows. But there was nothing there —nothing!

Professor Clewth was now at his side. "The basement!" he rapped out. The two men dived for the basement stairs with Wayne and the girl following at their heels.

Clewth was the first to reach the door from beneath which the faint light still seeped. He shoved at the door, which held fast, then dropped to his knees. A moment he crouched there, his eyes glued to the keyhole. Then he drew back.

"God Almighty!" he gasped.

"What?" Proctor grated. "What!"

Clewth seemed to find speech difficult. "Look!" he said weakly.

Proctor bent, peered in. His breath hissed between his clenched teeth.

There, as he expected, was the woman, lying stiff and rigid across the dais, the same expression of indescribable horror on her bony, staring face. But it was not this which held Proctor's eye. It was the black shape that lay against the curtain— a shadow, thick and impenetrable—the shadow of Melvina Murdock's body, lying in that strained and terrible attitude of death. Yet the real shadow of the body lay beside it, a black smudge upon the floor!

Proctor jerked upright, grasped Wayne Murdock's shoulder.

"Quick!" he snapped. "The window— get in if you can, but see that no one escapes. We'll break the door down!"

AS WAYNE MURDOCK sprinted away, Proctor stared about for some tool with which to attack the heavy door. He saw a lawn-mower in a corner, dragged it out, lifted it. "Here," he said to Clewth, "grab hold. We'll use it for a battering ram."

With all their might they rammed the heavy mower against a panel of the door. It crashed, leaving a splintered hole. As they drew back for another blow, they saw, through the hole, Wayne Murdock springing into the basement through a shattered window. He stumbled as he landed and his body struck the bowl of water on the dais, overturning it and the brazier of coals which sizzled and went out in smoke.

Another heavy blow; the door yielded with a crash and they were groping in the thick dark while Proctor fumbled for his flashlight button.

Wayne Murdock's scream shrilled through the gloom just as the beam of light shot out! It revealed him lying on his back upon the floor, his pale, thin fingers fumbling at his throat.

Proctor was at his side, lifting him. "Hurt?"

Wayne scrambled shakily to his feet. "It was the same thing," he stammered. His terrified eyes rolled over the group. "Bony, powerful hands in the darkness . . . nothing I could see . . . God!"

Instinctively Proctor's eyes lifted toward the curtain at the front of the cabinet. Clewth stared too. But where the dreadful shadow had hung like a black body suspended in mid-air, there was nothing; the shimmering surface of the veil was bare and clean of any blot!

For a moment Proctor and Clewth stared at each other; then Clewth's eyes turned toward Melvina Murdock's body, lying rigid and ghastly at their feet. A rush of blood surged to his granite face and he looked up scowling.

"It's Abell!" his harsh voice rumbled. "That devil! First he gets her crazed with his devil-cult talk and conjuring tricks, and now he's murdered her." His big hands knotted into compact bludgeons. "Wait till I get my hands on that fiend. I'll—"

"You'll what, Professor?"

The voice, suave and unruffled, seemed to slither through the dark from the direction of the doorway. As one body, the group spun around. The flashlight's beam described an arc in the blackness and came to rest upon a figure in the doorway. It was Clinton Abell, his lean,

emaciated body faultlessly attired in evening clothes, his thin, skeleton-like face creased by a faint, sarcastic smile, his pale eyes glinting cold as cracked ice. In each hand he held a squat black automatic, pointed toward the astonished group with unmistakable menace.

"Kindly elevate your hands," said Abell smoothly. "I'm not a particularly good shot, but I could scarcely miss all of you."

Their hands went up, Proctor's still holding the light on Abell's figure. An impulse to switch it off and make a dive for Abell in the dark was quickly checked. He could feel Irene's body close against his, her shoulder touching his breast. No, it would mean shooting and he couldn't risk Irene's life.

Professor Clewth stood at his other side, his breath wheezing with choked rage. "I knew it!" he bellowed. "I knew it was you, Abell! You damned bloodthirsty devil! You'll kill us all, eh?"

"On the contrary," Abell said evenly, "I'll save my own life and the lives of the others of you who are innocent. For one of you is a monster, and I think I know which one it is. . . ."

"A fine bluff!" Clewth growled. "Why mince words, Abell? Where did you get the stuff—the Owl's-eye bulbs?"

"Owl's-eye bulbs?" Abell inquired with a slight lifting of his eyebrows. "I don't know what you mean. I do know that there's only one way to avoid any more murders—and that is to hold you all prisoners until I can get the police here. For one of you, I repeat, is a fiend. These killings are not the work of devils or spirits, but of a depraved human."

"No doubt of that," Clewth said with a bitter laugh. "And you're the fiend, Abell. I suppose your pious talk is to make us docile so that you can kill us all. But you won't kill me!"

The words were scarcely out of his

mouth when his hand, fist knotted, abruptly flew to one side, knocking the flashlight from Proctor's hand. It smashed to the floor. Darkness submerged them, and Proctor felt Clewth brush past him in a mad charge.

SWIFTLY Proctor shoved Irene to the floor. On the instant two jets of flame roared from Abell's guns. Proctor ducked to one side, went zigzagging toward the door where Abell was standing.

But Clewth's heavy body had already collided with Abell's. The automatics belched flame toward the ceiling as the two men fell, threshing, to the floor. Proctor plunged into the fight. In a few seconds the panting body of Abell was pinned to the floor with Clewth and Proctor holding him down.

"A light!" Clewth called. Wayne Murdock came running with matches.

A ruddy flush of triumph lit the stout professor's face as he rose to his feet and stared down at his helpless enemy. Abell had ceased to struggle; his pale eyes returned Clewth's glare with cold malice.

"You are all fools," he said darkly. "I could have saved the innocent; now you may all die."

Clewth laughed mockingly. "You can save your wind now," he said. "You can't take us in with that talk. The jig's up, Abell, and it'll be the chair for you. Here, somebody, get a rope."

Wayne Murdock found a coil of trunk rope. Clewth and Proctor trussed Abell up neatly. But there was a puzzled, uncertain frown on Proctor's face as he got to his feet. Something in the look on Abell's face, the quiet assurance of his words, troubled him. He shot a glance at the thick-set professor, a glance in which there was a questioning uncertainty.

"Now," Clewth said, "we'll just leave him tied here until the police arrive. Suppose you stay here and guard him, Proctor."

"No," Proctor said, "I'll go along." He didn't like the brisk way in which the professor had taken charge. "He won't likely get loose before we get back."

Clewth shrugged, started for the steps. The others followed. The professor went straight to the telephone in the upper hallway. The others waited while he spun the crank, spun it again and again, muttering angrily. Finally he slammed the receiver back and turned to the others. "Might have known it," he growled. "He's cut the wires. I'll have to go in my own car."

"I can go," Wayne Murdock volunteered.

"No," Clewth said, "my car's already in front." He started for the door without pausing to argue the question further.

The front door slammed behind him. Wayne Murdock turned to Proctor, a frown wrinkling his wide brow. "I wonder," he said, "if he was really so anxious for the phone to work?"

Proctor gave him a sharp glance. He said nothing, but the same question had crossed his mind.

"Well." Proctor said, "the thing to do now is to search the house and grounds. I'm not completely satisfied with our solution. . . . There are several things I want to look into. Wayne, suppose you go out and wake the servants up. We may need their help."

Young Murdock nodded, stalked toward the kitchen and out the back way toward the garage, above which old Perkins and his wife the housekeeper lived. Proctor turned to the girl, laid a hand on her arm.

"It's not over yet, Irene," he said. "I'm afraid we're far from the end of the tangle. I imagine there'll be something startlingly hellish when we get to the bottom of it. I want you to stay close to me."

She smiled bravely, but here eyes were fearful as she probed the shadows massed ominously in the corners and doorways of the long hall.

"You mean," she asked, "that you don't think Abell. . . ?"

"He was up to something," Proctor said, "and there's no doubt that he put your aunt up to this devil-worship stuff. But—"

He never finished the sentence. A scream of agony and fear rose from the depths of the dark house, rasped against their eardrums with maddening volume!

"Abell!" Proctor gasped. He seized the girl's arm. "Come on!" And half dragging her, he started in a run for the basement stairs.

HE HAD no flashlight. The dark pit from which the frightful scream had risen, seemed to close around them like the black arms of death as they stumbled down the stairs and groped toward the battered door of the furnace-room.

On the threshold Proctor paused. A match scraped on the wall, spattered into flame, and the pale light leaped out to reveal the pitiful and terrible thing that lay upon the floor. The limbs of Abell's body, twisted grotesquely, told how the man had struggled against his bonds; and the horrible face, with eyes staring and swollen tongue lolling from his mouth, spoke clearly of the horrible agony of his death.

With a suppressed cry, the girl turned her head away. The match burned out between Proctor's fingers, and he dropped it.

He struck another match, found a lamp on a stand near the wall and lit it.

As he straightened above the smoking flame, a sound like the scrape of creeping feet on gravel reached his ears. He stared toward the shattered window. The shadow of a pair of legs moved in the moonlight. Proctor swung about toward Irene, shoved his revolver into her hand. "Stay here," he ordered, pushing her back against the wall, "and keep this gun in your hand."

Then he snatched up one of the automatics which had fallen from Abell's hand during the struggle. He ran to the window. Again he heard the scrape of feet. He vaulted out, scrambled up and stared about. He saw nothing.

Again he heard the sound. He started toward the front of the house. A shadow moved. He ran toward it.

The lamp still burned in the front hallway, throwing a yellow square of light through the glass of the front door. He stopped, listened. There was no sound; the fleeing shadow had vanished. He went inside, picked up the lamp in the hallway, and carried it into the library. Something had been nagging at his mind since he had heard the strange words of Professor Clewth, addressed to Abell in the basement: "Where did you get the stuff—the Owl's-eye bulbs?"

Proctor carried the lamp to the table on which rested the lamp that had burned above old Giles Murdock's head. He removed the globe and bent to squint at the rim surrounding the wick. Suddenly he straightened, staring at his finger. An exclamation escaped his lips as he peered at the faint smudge of whitish powder that clung to his fingertip. He lifted his eyes frowning, gazed a moment abstractedly at the shadows. "The Owl's-eye bulbs. . . ." Where had he heard that before?

Then, with a sudden tingling of his nerves that was his sixth sense warning him of danger, he remembered that he had left Irene alone in the murder chamber. He took up the lamp quickly and hurried down the hall.

"Irene!" he called from the top of the stairwell. "Irene!"

There was no answer. . . .

Perhaps she had not heard him. "Irene!" he called as his feet clattered down the steps. "My God! Irene, are you all right?"

But before the echoes of his voice had died out in the velvet darkness, he seemed to know the awful truth. A mad panic of alarm tugged at his straining heart as he dashed across the basement toward the furnace door.

At the door he checked himself, panting, staring wildly about the black-draped room. The corpses of Abell and Melvina Murdock still lay upon the floor; but Irene had vanished! . . .

"Irene!" he called at the top of his lungs. Still no answer. He rested the lamp on the stand and ran to the window. Perhaps, perhaps she had simply gone to look for him. He stared out into the moon-bathed night, called again.

Then, faintly it seemed, and coming from the direction of the greenhouse, he heard a faint cry. He vaulted over the window-sill, scrambled to his feet and pounded across the garden. The faint cry, ringing in his ears, drove him on like a burning whiplash.

But as he neared the greenhouse, the door swung abruptly open. A figure darted out, a figure which Proctor recognized with a startled shock. It was Professor Clewth, and doubled up, he was running toward the shelter of a nearby hedge.

"Clewth!" Proctor called and started after him.

At that moment the weak cry was repeated. This time—Proctor was certain of it—it came from the greenhouse. He jerked to a halt. Let Clewth go; he could get him later. Now he must find the girl! He turned and plunged into the building.

Inside, the air was hot, sultry. The crisscross of shadow and light, falling through the glass roof on terraced shelves of flowers and plants, confused his eyes. "Irene!" he called.

There was no answer. Had his ears tricked him? He listened, holding his breath, probing the shadows with his eyes.

Abruptly he sucked in his breath, started forward, craning toward something which lay black against the slanting glass roof of the greenhouse. It was a shadow, like the others a shadow of a body, lying on its back with hands folded as in death —but this shadow was different, different from all the others, and the difference was horribly significant.

For as Proctor crept nearer, staring in weird fascination, he saw that the profile of the recumbent corpse was a likeness of his own features!

With a muttered oath, Proctor raised the automatic, aimed at the black blot and pulled the trigger.

Simultaneous with the gun's report and the crash of shattering glass, there was another explosion in Proctor's brain. Lights flared crazily before his eyes, then faded away into whirling darkness. He felt himself sinking, sinking. . . .

CHAPTER FOUR

Horror Hole

PROCTOR stirred, opened his eyes. His head ached dully; he could feel the swelling bump on the back of his skull. He tried to move his hands; but they were tied behind his back. His ankles, too, were bound together. His eyes blinked against the feeble candlelight which faintly illuminated the dirt-walled pit in which he lay.

He jerked his head to one side, squinted. Something like a trickle of icy brine crawled through his veins. Very near him lay another body, trussed up in a sort of strait-jacket of leather. It was old Giles

Murdock, his face still frozen in its death mask of terror. This was the murderer's lair! But where was Irene?

He turned his head the other way, jerked his body upright. The girl lay a few yards on the other side of him, her amber-gold hair a tumbled mass on the dirt floor, her eyes closed as in death. A coil of rope was bound tightly about her motionless body.

For a terrible instant the syllables of her name hung frozen on Proctor's lips as if his brain and nerves were shrinking before the task of discovering the awful truth. And then a glow of light appeared behind the thick curtain which hung over a tunnel-like aperture in the earth wall, and he swung his face toward it.

The curtain moved. A figure appeared —and Proctor's breath caught in his throat like a hard lump. For the figure whose long, white fingers held a lamp and whose pallid face was thrust between the curtains, was Wayne Murdock!

Now he stepped softly into the chamber, a twisted, insane smile on his weak lips, an inhuman glitter in his shifty eyes. A long-bladed butcher knife was in his right hand.

With his glittering eyes glued on Proctor's scowling face, the youth set the lamp down on a stand and stood in a half crouch, staring warily at his captives.

Proctor studied him, studied him with the frantic intentness of a man who knows that he faces a maniac, knows that his only chance is to see clearly the peculiar and particular twist of the mad brain.

The boy's first words gave him his clue.

"Heh." An unpleasant grunt, half laugh, half sneer. "Thought I was just a coward—a fool! So did the rest of them. They treated me like a weakling."

Bitterness twisted the weak, cruel mouth. A paranoiac of the most dangerous type, Proctor decided. *Paranoi perse-cutoria,* delusions of grandeur, sadism . . .

Proctor took a grip on his jittery nerves. He must humor him, play up to his vanity, spar for time. He said nothing, allowing the other to talk.

"You want to know why I did it—how I did it? I don't mind telling you, because I'm going to kill you too. That's the best thing—kill all of you. I didn't mean to at first, but I decided to later."

Worms of yellow light crawled in the youth's small eyes, a certain zest for bloodshed was evident in the way he spoke of killing. Weak, cowardly, he was one of those introverted neurotics whose apparent weakness, cowardice, makes them seem harmless. But Proctor shuddered inwardly. Better the clutches of a gorilla than one of these cringing, cruel halfmen.

One question forced itself to Proctor's lips.

"Irene?" he asked, trying to keep his voice steady. "Is she dead?"

A light of evil pleasure shone in the youth's neurasthenic face. "You'll wish so, before I get through with the two of you." He chuckled insanely, and Proctor's skin crawled. "It serves you all right for treating me like a weak coward. They—they've persecuted me. Old Giles —he killed my father. Melvina and Abell —they were going to get rid of me for the money. They treated me like dirt, all of them. It serves them right. . . . I enjoy it too. . . . " He squatted down on his haunches now, and toyed with the knife as he spoke.

"Ever since I made up my mind that old Giles killed my father to get the whole estate, I've been planning it. A man in a carnival taught me ventriloquism, so I could throw my voice." He chuckled. "That fitted in with the rest of it—the shadows.

"You wonder how I did that? It was simple. Life-size silhouettes cut out of black paper, all prepared ahead of time.

I even made one of you, when I decided that to have a detective here at my request would throw all suspicion off me. I'd have let you live, too, if it hadn't been for Clewth. He's traveled, he's heard of the Owl's-eye bulb. See there, I raise them. . . ."

He pointed toward a box of damp earth near Proctor's head. Tall, blade-leafed lilies of a strange purple color were growing there. "The root is a queer-colored bulb, like an owl's eye. The llamas of Tibet use them to stupefy and madden. The powder, when burnt, is scentless, but it brings visions that literally frighten men to death."

He jerked his head toward the body of Giles Murdock. "I gave him too much. I was going to bring him here, torture him and make him change his will, leaving the estate to me—then kill him. But the first dose was too much, so I knew I'd have to kill the rest of them. Then I'd get the whole estate just the same."

"That was simple enough," Proctor said. "But look here, how are you going to get by with it? There's Clewth—he'll bring the police."

WAYNE MURDOCK shrugged. "Not till he's done some prowling first. He's already been nosing around in the greenhouse. This pit is just underneath it, and it's soundproof. By having the greenhouse I was able to do the digging and get rid of the dirt without anybody's noticing it. Oh, I'll catch Clewth in there all right. Then I'll manage to lay the murders on old Perkins, make out he was crazy. I'm a good actor—you know that."

"Yes," Proctor agreed, "you're a good actor—clever too. I don't see how you managed to keep me fooled."

"It wasn't so hard," the psychopath said, leering with pleasure at the flattery. "I planned it all carefully. While you were writing, I stuck my shoes under the covers to make you think I was still in bed after I'd slipped out. I'd already planted the powder in the old man's lamp, and that did its own work. I slipped out and put the paper shadow on the balcony and then snatched it away from below, before you got out there. Gosh, it scared you, didn't it? I got back into bed then, threw my voice into your room. Then when you came back after finding the old man, I was in bed pulling my little show about being strangled." He paused to laugh and lick his lips.

"The others must have been harder than that," Proctor prompted.

"Expert timing," Wayne Murdock resumed with evident relish. "I knew the old woman was down there playing the devil-stuff, and I knew Abell was behind the curtain with a hood over him, fooling her so he could swindle her out of her money. When I left you down there I crawled up the vines and grabbed Irene by the throat—just to get her to scream so you and Abell would leave. Then I rushed back down, saw Abell slipping out the window.

"I crawled in, got behind the veil and threw the powders on the coals. She was right close, and on the hot coals the stuff worked fast. She was out in a jiffy. I pinned the paper shadow on the curtain. Then I rushed to the library and dragged the old man's body out here before coming up to where you were in Irene's room. Then, you remember, I was the first one in the room when you and Clewth were battering the door down. That gave me a chance to kick the coals over and snatch the paper shadow from the curtain.

"The rest of it was easy. When you sent me to wake up the servants, it was no trick at all to go to the basement and strangle Abell while he was tied. I was afraid he really suspected me instead of Clewth. Then I waited around for my chance to get Irene. I led you off and came back.

"I hit Irene with a sandbag. It didn't knock her completely out though, so I had to hit her again to stop her yelling when I was dragging her in here. You'll have to admit it was smart—and I fooled you too. You'll have to admit it."

"I admit it," Proctor said. "But you're liable to overplay your hand."

"You think so?" the other snapped. His eyes gleamed with a hostile light; he fingered the knife. "You won't think so when I go off and leave you in here with the Owl's-eye stuff burning in the lamp. It chokes you. You can't even yell. And I'll be up there fooling the police while you and Irene are dying!"

Proctor stared at him, trying to fight back the horror that was creeping over him like a slow paralysis. Out of the corner of his eye he saw that Irene was stirring. He didn't look at her; he wanted to hold the fiend's attention. He prayed that she wouldn't cry out or say anything to throw the crazed boy into a rage.

"Look here, Wayne," he said, struggling to suppress the sheer desperation of his tone, "you're biting off more than you can chew. That's how all murderers get caught. Suppose you turn us loose, let us help you. We'd be willing to do that to save our lives. You'll need us to help fool the police." He felt that any sort of lie would be justified if he could only win the confidence of that warped mind. "We'd make up a story, we'll swear never to tell. . . ."

He broke off. For instead of the reaction he wished to arouse, he saw that a dark scowl was spreading over the maniac's face, saw that he had hopelessly underestimated the other's cunning. Abruptly the mad youth leaped to his feet, stood crouching like a monkey while he brandished the blade of the murderous knife under Proctor's eyes.

"Still think I'm a fool, eh?" he grated in a tone of hoarse fury. "Still think you can pull such childish stuff on me? I'll show you! I'll . . . I've got a notion to cut your throats right now—hers first, so you can see it. . . ."

HE PAUSED, while his crazed eyes roved from one to the other.

"No, I won't do that. I want to see you die slowly, with horror tearing the insides from you. . . ."

He jerked about with a quick gesture, snatched a leather pouch from his pocket and began to sprinkle the fine white powder around the wick of the lamp. His brain reeling with panic, Proctor stared, saw the maniac whirl about, holding his nose, then bound away toward the curtained exit. There was a mad cackle of laughter as the black drapes closed about him.

"God," Proctor muttered between clenched teeth. "God!"

Then his eye fell on the box in which the poison flowers were blooming. Near the box lay the end of a garden hose which had been used to water the plants. The other end ran out beneath the curtains. If the other end is only loose, he thought, there's a chance. . . .

He threw his body about, pushed his head toward the hose, closed his mouth over the end of it and sucked. Thank God, it was disconnected! He could suck air through it.

He seized the hose in his teeth and began to snake his body toward the girl. He lifted the end of the hose to her face and dropped it. "Get your mouth on it quick!" he ordered. "Breathe through it. Try not to breathe through your nose. If you can hold out until I get myself loose. . . ."

He rolled over, began to tug at the bonds that bound his wrists. The rope bit into the flesh, held tight. His eyes were on the lamp from which the horrible fumes were coming. He could turn the lamp over, but it might explode. . . .

A glass, in a corner near his head, caught his eye. He rolled toward it, twisted his hands around. He managed to seize the glass, slammed it against a rock in the dirt wall. It shattered.

With one of the sharp fragments, he began to saw at the ropes that bound his wrists. It wasn't easy.

Another strand, another. . . . Something was fogging his brain, choking his lungs. The room reeled wildly around his head. The light seemed to surge out until it filled the room, then fade to darkness. And in the darkness black shapes were moving, monstrous, formless things that hovered over him, pressed in upon him, crushing the life from his body. . . .

And then, the last strand gave! His straining wrists flew apart. Swiftly he freed his ankles.

In a blind, tortured daze, Proctor scrambled to his feet, groped for Irene's body. He grasped the rope that bound her and staggered madly through the curtains, dragging her with him.

The air was fresher, flowing into his burning lungs like a cleansing bath. Now he could see—stairs leading up.

But on the stairs something moved, leaped toward him. It was Wayne Murdock, a savage leer on his face, the knife clutched in a tense hand.

Proctor dropped the girl, ducked as the maniac's body hurtled toward him like a winged thing. He seized the flying arms. The knife swished near his throat, then fell from distended fingers. Proctor's strong arms had closed about the squirming body like the coils of a snake.

There was a moment of struggle. Then, with a choked gasp, the body went limp in his arms. Proctor lifted it, hurled it to the floor.

He did not look down. Snatching up the girl he stepped over the inert body and began to climb the steps. From the greenhouse above came the sound of smashing glass.

It was Clewth with the police. Proctor collapsed as they carried him to the house.

AN HOUR later, Proctor was sitting in a chair in the library, a bandage on his head and a weak feeling in the pit of his stomach, but otherwise quite sound. Irene lay on a divan beside him, and their conversation was unquestionably important, for both looked up with annoyance when Professor Clewth came into the room.

"He just died," Clewth said quietly. "He was still alive when you left him, but when he saw us coming he gulped down some of the poison powder he carried in that pouch." He drew up a chair near them. "And now," he said, "please finish with your explanation."

"May I write a telegram first?" Proctor asked, smiling.

"Certainly," said Clewth. He proffered his pen.

Proctor put an envelope on his knee and began to write:

Mr. William Copeland,
Lone Star Detective Agency,
San Antonio, Texas.
    Case concluded stop will arrive tomorrow with brand new

He paused, looked at Irene who was watching over his shoulder. She nodded, and Proctor finished the message:

                wife.
                        Peter.

"That's that," Peter Proctor said. He handed the pen back to Clewth. "And now, Professor, if you'll pour me a drink, I'll finish the story."

THE END

KINSMAN'S CURSE

By G. T. Fleming~Roberts

(Author of "Madman's Mate," etc.)

Margie Tremont didn't know that murder lust and red madness was a part of her family heritage—till that ghastly night when she first met her next of kin. . . .

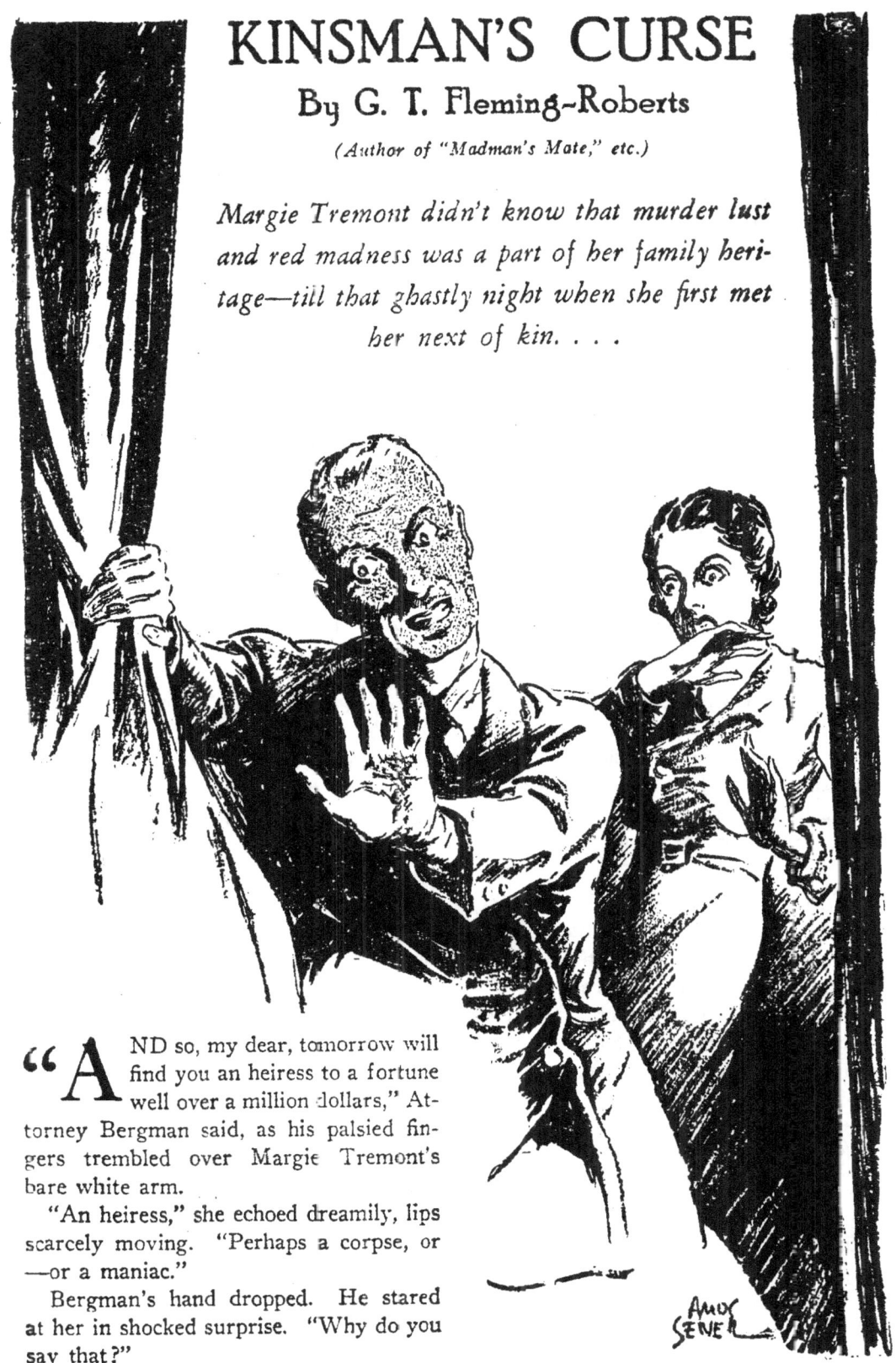

"AND so, my dear, tomorrow will find you an heiress to a fortune well over a million dollars," Attorney Bergman said, as his palsied fingers trembled over Margie Tremont's bare white arm.

"An heiress," she echoed dreamily, lips scarcely moving. "Perhaps a corpse, or —or a maniac."

Bergman's hand dropped. He stared at her in shocked surprise. "Why do you say that?"

She shrugged pettishly. "The terms of Uncle's will. Look at *them*." She nodded toward the group of people gathered about the smoking fireplace. They were her relatives; yet what strange, strange, strangers! There was her cousin, Gerald Cragg with his close-clipped cottony hair, his pedantic gold pince-nez astride his narrow nose, the livid scar that was like a second mouth across his chin. There was her aunt, Mrs. Case, a sort of animated obelisk, so utterly unmotherly! The bulbous-nosed, bald-headed man who had once prospered as a bootlegger was James Tremont, brother of the dead man and her uncle. Dr. Martin Arrow, step-son of James Tremont, was a young man of Mephistophelian appearance. His fingers made her think of some sort of flexible icicle, they were so cold looking. She knew that if Dr. Arrow ever touched her she would scream!

Bergman frowned disapprovingly at his beautiful new client. He buttoned his ulster. "Nonsense, my child. I admit that the terms of your uncle's will are unusual. But your own people—you must make an effort to know them better. Blood is thicker than water, you know."

"Blood is sometimes the culture of the germs of hate," Margie Tremont replied. "They hate me, oh, I know they do! I'm not a neurotic, Mr. Bergman. Really, I'm not. But here I am, a perfect stranger. I've come to take all that is theirs away from them—even this very roof!"

"The estate," Bergman said sternly, "belonged to Perry Tremont, your uncle. It was his to do with as he pleased. As to taking this house from them—why, who would want the old place? It's been empty for years." Bergman jammed his derby on his head. His hand found the doorknob. "Er—goodnight, Miss Tremont," he muttered hurriedly. "Don't be afraid. I've left a watch-dog . . .

ahem! My taxi has the meter running. . . . Firm will be bankrupt. . . ." He opened the door.

Outside, the cold night wind was driving a rattling, dry rain of pine needles to the ground. Margie's spirits sank as she watched the attorney's great bulky shadow move farther and farther from the door. She was alone with these—her relatives. How they must hate her!

"But who would want the old place?" she breathed. Even if there had been any pretension of cleanness about it, the room would nevertheless have been a cheerless one. The ceiling was crossed with black oak beams so low-hung as to make one entering the room fearful of their impending weight. Chimney-damp defied the efforts of even the best firemaker to coax anything more caloric than a hissing smolder from the most seasoned logs. Doorways, windows, even pictures were enshrouded with sombre velvet curtains, dusty as the wings of a miller moth, tied with phantasmal gray threads of cobwebs. There was not a chair in the place that had not played host to a family of mice; upholstery, where it was not worn bald, was tufted with dirty gray stuffing plucked from the cushions. The venerable clock in the corner, stern preceptor of Time that it was, had long ceased ticking and seemed content with the ominous inscription about its face: "It is later than you think."

SHE found her womanly instincts speculating as to what might be done with the place. Bright chintz curtains would help some—electric lights to replace the ancient candelabras. . . .

Mrs. Case—Margie couldn't think of the woman as "Aunt Agnes"—sailed across the room, voluminous skirts hiding all muscular effort. Her tiny eyes snapped venomously. "I suppose you've no objection to our staying all night,

Niece, even though this is *your* house?"

Margie tried to smile; she just couldn't do it! "You are welcome to stay just as long as you like, Mrs. Case. Please consider this house as much yours as mine. When I have opened the town house, I hope to be able to offer you something better in the way of entertainment."

Mrs. Case snorted through thin nostrils. "That's looking a long way ahead, young woman. You're not sure of your sanity yet." She sailed to the hall doorway, parted the curtains, and called: "Wickton! Wickton, show me to my room." Another snort. "That servant is as deaf as a post!" And off she sailed, bent on giving Wickton a piece of her mind, no doubt.

Gerald Cragg got up from the hearth where he had been diligently plying the bellows. He approached Margie, smiling. The pink scar on his chin smiled, too. He extended his hand to her, palm down. Was she supposed to kiss it?

"My congratulations, cousin—er, I suppose congratulations are the order of the day? Though I must say I shouldn't care to have that insanity clause hanging over my head!"

Margie laughed, light-headedly she knew. She said, "Surely you're not leaving us tonight?" She wished he would!

"Well, I should say not. Fancy walking twenty miles on a night like this! But that reminds me, I always enjoy a stroll before retiring. Good for my nerves, you know. I probably won't see you again tonight." He went into the hall, and she could hear the door slam behind him.

She turned to find her uncle, James Tremont, standing with hands on his broad hips, staring up at the full-length portrait of his brother, Perry Tremont. It was the first time Margie had seen the portrait. It was a remarkable likeness— she had seen her uncle just once in life—

wearing, as Perry always had worn, a black frockcoat. He had been a man of stern aspect, this Perry Tremont. Cross, mutton-chop whiskers hadn't helped his face any. In the eyes of the portrait, the artist had done a fine job; there was fire in them, a sort of mad eloquence.

James Tremont laughed insolently up at the white face gleaming ghoulishly from the canvas. "Dirty old sinner," he muttered. "You damned old crook. Guess I'll have a drink to your hell-roasting, damn you!"

Tremont's step-son, Dr. Arrow, yawned behind his cold white hand. "I wouldn't talk that way, Dad," he said. "Have you ever read that little book called 'The Dead Alive'?"

James Tremont shook his head. Arrow smiled evilly. "Your brother wrote it."

"Zat so?" absently from Tremont. "Well, me for a drink anyway." He turned, faced Margie, leered: "Ever think of marrying an heiress, Martin?"

Margie sent Dr. Arrow a glance that shuddered. Arrow shook his head slightly, his thin-lipped smile splitting across his narrow face. "Don't mind him, Miss Tremont. Dad's always that way when he's drunk."

"Drunk, hell!" James Tremont growled as he entered the dining room.

Dr. Arrow went on glibly: "Your Uncle Perry—speaking of drink—used to go off on a spree every time he condemned a man to hang. Did you ever hear why Uncle Perry was forced to resign from the bench?"

SHE shook her head. She really didn't care. When a man's dead, he's dead, she thought. But Dr. Arrow was speaking again:

"Perhaps the examination of some of these pictures on the wall will explain his madness better than I can," he said.

He stepped to the wall, jerked aside a black curtain. Beneath the glass of the picture frame rested a piece of hemp rope stained brownish with blood. "This piece of rope," explained Arrow, "bound the hands of a French revolutionist until the guillotine made them hands of clay. The Iron Judge, as Perry was called, was an advocate of the guillotine. This—" he stepped to another picture frame and took hold of the black curtain that covered it, "illustrates his somewhat sadistic tendencies—"

"Oh, don't, please!" A cold qualm of fear passed over Margie. She didn't want to see anything more. There! She had whimpered when she had resolved to be so brave.

But the covering was off the picture. It was an enlarged photograph, the nude body of a woman, brutally, horribly mutilated! Margie felt herself wavering. She had never fainted. She couldn't account for the misty red curtain that swam before her eyes. And through the mist gleamed a face, a frown of displeasure like the shadow of a bat's wing flitting across it. It was the face of Dr. Arrow. Given horns, she would have known it for the face of Satan! Hands of ice touched her, shocked her to her senses. She jerked from his grasp, flattened against the wall, breast palpitant. "Your hands," she whispered. "So cold."

Dr. Arrow looked deeply injured, yet she knew in his mind he smiled. "Forgive me," he said. "We medical men become so calloused, you know. Please believe me when I say I want to be your friend. You will need friends!" His hand went to the pocket of his black coat and came out again holding something that caught the gleam of the candle flames and fairly dazzled her. It was a silver-mounted revolver!

"Wh-what are you doing?" she questioned in a murmur.

Arrow did not answer. He broke the revolver and methodically loaded it with round-nosed thirty-two cartridges. He then handed it to her. "I sincerely hope you won't need this. Can you shoot?"

She accepted the gun without a word of thanks. "Rather well," she replied. "I've not lived on a ranch all my life for nothing!" This was as much of a warning to Dr. Arrow as anything else. He must have known as much, for he shrugged mockingly. He turned towards the door.

Inside the dining room, the steady churn of the cocktail-shaker suddenly stopped. A glass clinked. A voice boomed, "Oh, my God!" The clash of shivering glass; the slop of splashing liquid. The curtains of the doorway suddenly swished apart as James Tremont pitched backwards into the room.

Margie's hands went up, locking a scream in her throat. Arrow turned in the doorway, his narrow head twisted sideways, right eyebrow slightly raised as he looked askance at his step-father. Margie's eyes hurried back to Tremont and locked on his ghastly blue face. *Blue face!* As blue as billiard chalk! But that was not where horror lay. Rather it was the expression on Tremont's face —a sort of deathly animation, paradoxical as that may seem. A man may die smiling, Margie had heard; apparently Tremont had died laughing! His bulbous nose was crinkled, his lips wide apart and twisted at the corners as if he were muttering one of his peculiar guffaws. Death had frozen his merriment with icy breath!

Arrow knelt, took Tremont's wrist. He shook his head despondently. He looked up at Margie and pointed silently at three feathers that bristled from Tremont's coat front. "A dart," he explained. "Poisoned. Every symptom of aconite poisoning."

"Perhaps he killed himself." Margie spoke woodenly.

"Quite impossible. He was murdered by *something* in this house." Dr. Arrow stood up, yanked down one of the velvet portieres, and flapped it over the body. "Go to bed, Miss Tremont," he said sharply.

"Why, what do you mean?" her voice was brittle as her foot stamped once, sharply.

Dr. Arrow attempted to seize her hands. She uttered a little cry, clasped her hands behind her. "If you touch me, I'll—I'll—" she threatened feebly.

"Then go to bed!"

"All right," she consented. "I'll go. Don't forget I have your pistol."

He laughed harshly. "Don't flatter yourself, young lady!"

MARGIE almost ran across the living room, her right hand clenched over the butt of the revolver. Passing into the hall, she ran straight into someone. She choked a scream, looked up into a white, pinched face relieved by a gray thatchy mustache. "Wickton!" she gasped. Then, regaining composure: "Show me to my room at once."

The servant's mouth sagged open. His gnarled right hand caught at a pad of paper that hung from a string on his belt. "Write it down, Miss. I'm deaf." His words were halting, poorly formed things. She took the pad and pencil and scribbled her order. He bobbed his head, took up a candlestick, lighted the wick from one of the flaming candelabras in the hall. Margie followed him up the stairs, stumbling, sometimes, because she could not take her eyes off the shadows that crawled along the wall, keeping pace with them.

The labyrinthian hall ended abruptly in the door of her room. Wickton opened the door, wished her a good night mechanically. Through the opening, rosy beams of cheerful fire-light came to welcome her. Several candles were burning. This was something like home! She stepped in, carefully closed and bolted the door. For a moment, she stood before the fireplace, arms stretched above her head. She indulged herself in a pleasureful yawn that caught in her throat before it was completed. Something rustled behind her. She pivoted.

Curtains were drawn around a high-canopied bed. Cold air from a half-open window billowed them slightly. She sighed her relief and crossed to the window. "Wickton must be trying to heat all outdoors," she muttered.

"Nope, I did that. Got to have air when I snooze."

Margie's hand froze on the window-pull. She had heard a voice, a decidedly masculine voice. Assuredly, she must be dreaming! She turned from the window. Then her eyes widened. Her hand cupped over her mouth. A long-fingered bronzed hand parted the curtains of the bed. A face appeared—a very pleasant, though somewhat drowsy-looking face, with blue eyes windowed by shell-rimmed glasses. The man swung tweed-trousered legs over the edge of the bed, stood up, rumpling sleepy, straw-colored hair. "Morning!" His broad smile yawned. "Or is it morning? Dog my cats if I know!" He straightened his tie. "Breakfast ready?"

"Who are you?" Margie asked, wondering at the steadiness of her voice.

"Your own watch-dog, Miss Tremont. Standard Bell is the name. Ambled in through your window."

"You'd better go. I've a gun."

"No. Why should you have a gun? I'm a detective, but I don't carry 'em. They go off sometimes at half-cock. Fists don't."

"What are you doing here?" she insisted.

"Didn't old Bergman tell you? I'm to keep an eye on you. That crazy will fairly begs for trouble. If you were to be proved insane, or if you should die, the estate would go to Dr. Arrow, whom Judge Tremont admired greatly. If Dr. Arrow goes balmy or dies, the estate goes to the next in line, and so forth. So you see, there's trouble afoot. Pardon my saying so, but you've got the funniest bunch of relatives! James Tremont, for instance: one-time bootlegger and gang boss."

She nodded. "He's downstairs now. He's dead. Murdered!"

Eyes behind the horn-rimmed spectacles bulged. "While I've been sleeping? Lord! Let's—"

Standard Bell's teeth clamped shut. A sound like the snap of a bass fiddle string huddered throughout the house. It seemed to penetrate Margie's body, racking her very soul. It was the most inexplicable, agonizing sound she had ever heard. It *pained* her!

MOMENTS later, she found herself staring up into Bell's face. Somehow, his arm had gone about her shoulders. She didn't mind.

"Lord, what a toot!" he muttered. "Gotta find out what that was. Sort of went through me. Come along. Not leavin' you alone!"

The next moment, Margie felt herself being hurried down the hall and down the winding stair. There was self confidence in this man's stride; it brought her a comforting sense of security.

The lower part of the house seemed deserted. Standard Bell's owl-eyes compassed the living room and came to rest on the black mound that was the curtain-shrouded body of James Tremont. Margie, too, stared like one fascinated at the covered body. "His face was all blue," she muttered, reliving the minutes of horror. "And he was laughing—dead, laughing!"

"Yeah? What killed him?"

"A dart poisoned with something—aco—something."

"Aconite?" he asked sharply. "Say, that couldn't be. Why the blood then?" Stan pointed at the covered mound. Margie saw it now—a crooked line of blood that crawled from beneath the velvet.

Bell strode to the body and jerked aside the covering. Perhaps he said something; Margie couldn't have heard him above the scream that ripped from her own throat. "The picture, the picture!" she sobbed. For beneath the curtain she had glimpsed not the body of James Tremont, but the nude, statuesque form of Mrs. Agnes Case! Her body had been horribly mutilated. Arms had been severed. Gory gouts bubbled from shoulder stumps. White limbs were furrowed with red-seeping slashes. Her head was twisted half off her angular shoulders, for the knife-gash at her throat had nearly decapitated her!

The black curtain rippled over the bleeding form. Bell sprang towards Margie, strong arms closing about her. "Margie," he breathed, "can you ever forgive me? I'm a damned ass. But you see, I didn't know it was like that! You said James Tremont. . . ."

Margie clung to him. Her throat ached with sobs. God, dear God, was she going mad? Mrs. Case like the woman in the picture!

Suddenly, she felt the pressure of Stan's arms relax. He had twisted around and stood staring at the door. A deep-chested laugh boomed throughout the room. She stepped over his shielding shoulder and saw in the door a strange figure—a tall, oldish gentleman in a rusty black frockcoat. His square, angry jowls were gray-whiskered. His eyes seemed to lash out at them.

Tense muscles in Margie's throat seemed to break. She knew she was laughing, giggling idiotically. She swayed drunkenly. The man in the doorway, the man in the frock-coat, was her Uncle Perry! Old Judge Perry Tremont returned from the grave! Old Iron Judge with a gore-dripping knife in his hand!

Stan turned. His square chest blotted out the doorway and the specter it framed. His eyes were fastening hers, fiercely serious. "Get a grip on yourself, dear! Remember, it's some sort of a fraud—got to be!" Was he trying to convince himself? "I've got to go after that devil. Got to leave you a moment. Use your gun if you have to." He swung her from her feet and carried her to a chair. "Remember . . . all a fake! Shoot!" And he was gone, running through the hall where the specter had disappeared.

Margie's lips formed his name; they couldn't utter a sound. She was frightened beyond speech. Her lips pressed firmly together, drawing a tight, crimson line across her face. She brought out the revolver from her pocket. Its cool grip gave her strength. She broke the gun, saw the six copper eyes that were the caps of the cartridges. Then she remembered that Dr. Arrow had loaded the gun. She didn't trust Arrow. You couldn't trust a man with a face like Satan! She picked out one of the cartridges just to make sure it wasn't blank. Satisfied, she replaced it and leaned easily back in her chair. Fraud, she repeated. It's all fraud. Trying to drive her crazy! She hoped they were watching her now so that they might see how completely she had mastered her nerves.

"My charming niece in a pensive mood!"

THE words held a world of score and hate. She looked up swiftly, resolving to master fear. Not ten feet from her stood the man in the frock-coat—the mutton-chop whiskered ghost of the Iron Judge. Blood daubed his sleeves like a butcher fresh from the shambles!

She did not scream. Instead, she heard herself whispering: "You're a fake, an ugly fraud." The revolver in her hand snapped up. She knew without looking that it was beaded on the *thing's* heart. "I am going to shoot," she said tonelessly.

The Iron Judge bowed low. "You have my consent. But you should be more kindly inclined towards a corpse. You really can't kill a corpse, you know." He came nearer, raised his hands with fingers distended.

"One step nearer," she said icily, "and you're a dead man."

"Of course I'm a dead man!" His laugh boomed. "And I take another step —so. Now what?"

Her teeth grated. Her finger suddenly constricted on the trigger. She heard the shot, felt the recoil, heard the bass laugh again. She was screaming now. She tugged the trigger once more, saw the mad face close to hers, smiling. She felt hands on her throat—fingers that caressed her flesh. The cold waves of blackness dashed roaring over her head.

She clung to unconsciousness, fearful of the sensation that now came over her. It was like the touch of ice on her forehead. She thought of cold, cold fingers.

But the impulse was not to be denied: eyelids must pop open. She stared straight into the small, black eyes of Dr. Arrow. She shrank against the floor, avoiding the touch of his white fingers.

"You fainted, Miss Tremont?" he asked mockingly. "What could have happened?"

"The ghost came here—the ghost of

Uncle Perry. It's a mad ghost. A knife—"

"Now, now, Miss Tremont," Dr. Arrow smiled. "I'm afraid you're very ill. You have a fever. Perhaps it is only a temporary disorder of the mind."

Her hands clenched. Her arms beat out wildly, small fists striking his chest. "Go away!" she sobbed. "I know. You're trying to drive me mad. Telling me I didn't see a ghost!"

A laugh that started from Arrow's throat was never finished. Big bronzed hands closed over his shoulders, lifted him to his feet, shoved him against the wall. Standard Bell grinned broadly. Eyes glittering, he looked down at her. "Is this man annoying you, lady?" he asked. He lifted her to her feet. Then his good humor vanished. His voice snapped at Arrow. "Go upstairs, look in my suitcase, and bring down that bottle of brandy. Miss Tremont needs a pick-me-up."

Arrow's eyebrows raised. "Who the devil are you?"

"I don't tell," Stan growled, "but I sometimes leave my trademark on mugs like yours. Get!"

Dr. Arrow shrugged, left the room stealthily.

" 'Magine how annoyed his Satanic Majesty will be when he finds I didn't bring a suitcase," Stan whispered. "Now, tell me what happened to you."

She recalled every detail, and when she had concluded, Stan's brows knit in a puzzled frown. "I suppose Arrow's entrance scared your ghostly uncle away, proving that he's afraid of something, even if it's not guns. 'S funny."

"It isn't!" she insisted. "Don't try to make light of it. We're all in terrible danger. I know!"

Stan nodded. "You're right. This blood-thirsty shade gave me the slip, but I picked up something enlightening. How's

this for sleuthing?" He dug into his pocket and brought out a large, blue powder puff.

"That's Mrs. Case's!" Margie exclaimed. "What does it mean?"

Stan took her shoulders in his hands, gazed earnestly into her face. "We don't care whose puff it is. Baby, it tells me that one of the most dangerous criminals in the country is in this house tonight. This isn't his first job, by any means. But for the first time he's left a clue to work on. He is—"

"But I shot him—shot at him—*it*. It wasn't five feet from me and I'm a good shot!" she insisted. "He—it just couldn't be human!"

He said, "Perhaps he isn't human. I've often wondered—"

A HARSH, strident cry of terror knifed the air, died in a wail of pain. It was followed by a thump—a rumbling, tumbling series of jolts that shook the house and echoed from room to room. Then sudden silence unbroken save for quick-drawn, rasping breaths.

Bell leaped through the hall doorway. For a second, Margie watched the swirling curtains that had swallowed him. Then she followed. At the foot of the stairs lay Wickton, the servant. The hilt of a knife protruded from his coat front. His thatchy mustache was blood-flecked; his lips were working slowly, trying to form words.

Stan Bell knelt beside the old servant. "Can't you make it plainer, old man?" he urged. Then he glanced over his shoulder at Margie. "He's trying to say something."

Margie dropped to her knees, took the servant's gnarled hand in hers, and stroked it gently. "He's deaf," she explained. "Write on the pad—"

A light shone from the old man's eyes. "Miss, I saw—" he choked, "saw him kill

Mrs. Case and cut her to pieces. I knew he'd come for me 'cause I saw. I hid. But you can't hide from a ghost. It— it was the old master, him that's dead— dead and buried—"

Suddenly Wickton's eyes became fixed. They mirrored stark terror. Margie turned her head. A sharp cry shrilled from her throat. "Look out, Stan!"

Bell twisted around; knees unbuckled, and he was half way to his feet. But the man in the frockcoat moved quicker. The heavy brass candlestick that he held in his hand slashed down. Margie saw Stan suddenly become limp, sag to the floor, groaning. Beneath his mop of straw-colored hair, a thin stream of blood was crawling.

"Stan! Oh, Stan!" But the agony of her cry only provoked a diabolical laugh from the man in the frockcoat. He dropped his candlestick, seized the girl by the shoulders, held her in vise-like grip. She struggled fiercely, got the revolver from her pocket, leveled it at the noxious, whiskered face. She heard the gun blast, saw the black wound that suddenly appeared on his high, white forehead. The Iron Judge laughed hollowly. "You think to kill me?" His arms crushed about her. Gray whiskers brushed her cheek. She seemed falling, falling through a vast expanse of empty air. Then, blackness. . . .

As her sense gradually returned, Margie thought that she was confined in some narrow box. She thought of the tomb, wondered vaguely if this was death. She tried to move, couldn't. Then she realized that she was securely bound. She could feel cruel, thin rope, cutting like knife edges about body, limbs and forehead. Her eyes snapped open. She was in a stone-walled room—probably some hidden cellar of the house. Directly in front of her stood the Iron Judge. She

could still see the black wound in his head. It was absolutely bloodless!

"Stan!" she called helplessly.

The specter chuckled. "He's dead, my dear. Don't you see him lying over in that corner?" He stood aside. Beyond, in the shadows, she could see a stiff, stretched form. Light from the room's single candle reflected on the crooked circle of crimson that surrounded the body. She uttered a piteous cry.

"Save that!" the Iron Judge snapped. "You will have something to cry about in a minute!" He moved to the end of the room. Margie's terrified gaze followed him. Resting on a pair of trestles was a long wooden cylinder with skin drum-heads bound over each end. A wooden slide arrangement at the top served to tighten the heads. She wondered what this long drum could have to do with her.

"This, my dear," the Iron Judge explained, "is the only specimen of a Tibetan torture drum on this side of the world. As you probably know, everything has its keynote. Now, this drum is particularly adapted to the keynote of the human organism. It is adjustable, you perceive. If I can manage to tune the drum exactly to your particular keynote, the result beggars description. Since you are not free to move around and thus break up the sound waves, you will very probably disintegrate! However, that would be too fast a death to offer me any amount of entertainment. I am going to bring the drum so close to your keynote that you will suffer exquisite agony. The very pain will kill you—eventually! But let me experiment."

THE Iron Judge began to sway in a grotesque, barbaric dance without moving his feet. In his hand, he waved a padded drum-stick. His swaying body picked up rhythm. Down swung the stick, bashing against the drum-head. The sound, if it was a sound, was like the snapping of a bass viol string; yet it seemed to Margie that she did not hear with her ears. The sound knifed through her entire body, setting up converging waves within her that sickened, racking every organ in her body. She knew that her mouth was open, knew that shrill screams ripped from her throat. Yet she sensed only the painful, rippling vibrations of her own body. Sweat, mingled with tears, bathed her eyes, blinded her. As the final vibrations died away, her tormentor struck again, this time harder. She felt that her body was swelling, lungs distending to the bursting point. In her screaming mouth was the flat taste of blood.

But the vibrations died way; the pain abated. Her eyes cleared. Why didn't he strike again—hard enough to finish her this time? God, why didn't he kill her?

She turned her eyes on the man in the frockcoat. He was standing perfectly still, hands clutching his chest, eyes bulging with terror, skin as gray as his whiskers. Margie's eyes darted to the door of the room. Now, now she *knew* she was mad—worse than dead—stark, raving mad! For in the doorway stood another man—another ghost with the pale, bewhiskered face of Perry Tremont. Two ghosts—two identical ghosts of the Iron Judge staring at each other!

The specter in the doorway spoke: "So you have dared to impersonate me—me, a dead man!" He advanced slowly towards his trembling counterpart. Suddenly, he leaped—this second Perry Tremont—seized the other by the throat, twisted him half off his feet, threw him to the floor. Then he dropped to his knees, still clutching at his opponent's throat, drew back the man's head and

dashed it against the floor. The fiend lay very still.

Margie watched her rescuer, this valiant ghost. A big bronzed hand passed over the ghastly features, crumpled them, and came away holding a bit of painted canvas. And beneath was the eager, boyish face of Standard Bell!

"Grit, baby, you've got it!" he cried through teeth still rage-clenched. He sprang towards her, an open pocket-knife in his hand. "I had to mutilate your uncle's portrait," he explained as he began ripping away the bonds. "I cut out the painted face just after we found Mrs. Case's body. Knew that if I confronted that fiendish fraud with the real thing he'd scare. Lucky the light of the room was so dim he couldn't tell what I was using for a mask."

"But he said you were dead, lying over there in the corner." She pointed.

Stan's grin returned. "'I'm not so easy to kill. That man in the corner is Gerald Cragg. The killer got hold of Cragg some time before he began his slaughter. Dr. Arrow told me that the killer was trying to get Cragg to sign a confession to all the killings to come—the entire family. About the time you and I bumped into each other, this fiend was torturing Cragg with the drum. When I first heard that hellish sound, I should have remembered the torture drum that Perry Tremont brought from the Orient. Guess Cragg had more nerve than you'd think, refused to sign, and had to be killed to keep quiet." Stan's teeth gritted. "He might have killed you, darlin'!" He took out his handkerchief and gently wiped her face.

"Arrow's plot was to scare you into madness, darlin'. That gun he gave you was loaded with compressed graphite that disintegrated as soon as the charge was fired. That's why you couldn't kill the 'ghost'."

"But—but who is *he*? *What* is he?"

"Oh, didn't the blue powder puff tell you that? But of course not. You're just one brave girl, not a detective. That, too, was part of Arrow's plot. James Tremont was to feign death by sticking those feathers in his coat and dusting his face with blue powder. That's why the puff was blue. Blue skin and a ghastly grin are the symptoms of aconite poisoning. James Tremont was then free to run around the house disguised as his dead brother—all to drive you mad so that Arrow could take over the estate.

"But Arrow made his mistake in taking James Tremont into his plan. James Tremont is the insane member of the family —not Perry. What's more, James was a criminal, as I told you before. He was criminally insane. While playing ghost for Arrow, James saw an excellent opportunity to gratify his blood lust and at the same time get rid of the entire family. In that way, he hoped to get the estate for himself. Up until the last, James Tremont was afraid of Dr. Arrow. But he did manage to stick a knife into the doctor, and Arrow died in my arms not ten minutes ago."

STANDARD BELL lifted Margie in his arms, held her for minutes, gazing into her eyes. "Now, little lady, it's all yours, the whole estate. God knows you've earned it!"

Margie shook her head. "The insanity clause is going to cut me out, I'm afraid."

Stan looked puzzled. "I don't understand. You'll be all right after you have had a rest."

"I mean," she explained, "that I think I'm becoming a little mad. It's the old, old madness, yet an entirely new and thrilling sort of madness to me."

THE BLACK CHAPEL

I T WAS a very long time ago, before TERROR TALES was even a thought in the editor's brain, that we first read *Dracula;* but the memory of that story, vivid and terrifying, stays with us still. Especially do we remember those first chapters, describing the trip of the young hero to Dracula's moulding castle.

It was a night of storm, a dark, weird night when witches might have sailed the sky and warlocks plied their trade. The young man, arriving in the little European mountain village, found the natives strangely furtive and afraid. They warned him of the dread fate in store for him if he went to the castle on the mountain where lived Dracula.

And despite their warnings, the young man went—in the coach that came to meet him. The face of the old driver was a hideous, leering mask that seemed afire with an evil nimbus. The young man did not know that the evil coachman was Dracula himself, Dracula who prowled the night in strange forms, seeking his sustenance of human blood. Yet without knowing it, he knew terror. He knew, as surely as if it were written in letters of blood upon the evil face before him, that a fearful doom awaited him. Yet he did not turn back. . . .

Reading these chapters, we too felt fear and terror. We lived those scenes so vividly that we have never forgotten them. We knew then the stimulus that terror alone can give to modern man. And it is not too much to say that from this knowledge, years later, the idea of TERROR TALES, the magazine that gives you the stimulus of fear, was born. . . .

A few weeks ago we had a similar experience—one that surpassed even the reading of *Dracula.* We had gone to a cabin in the Catskills for the weekend, taking with us a sheaf of manuscripts to read for TERROR TALES. Among these was *The Unholy Goddess,* a novelette by Wyatt Blassingame. . . .

We were alone in the cabin that evening when we sat down to read. Outside, the last winds of autumn howled, and thunder rolled on the distant mountain-tops. Before us was a blazing log fire, and an oil lamp shed its flickering glow upon the pages of the manuscript.

We read the first few pages, of young Nate who, like ourselves, sat alone in a mountain cabin, striving to finish the work he had set himself to do. We read of the strange consciousness that seized him of a presence out there in the moonlight, of a thing that menaced him. We shuddered.

We threw more wood upon the fire, and read on. Outside, the storm swept closer, seemed to be speaking with the thousand shrieking tongues of hell. The fire burned low. From out the corners of the cabin, living shadows crept and crawled. . . .

We reached the end of the tale. Sweat was on our foreheads, and an iciness along our spine that the wind had not caused. We built the fire to a blazing furnace. We turned the lamp high, striving fearfully to drive away those creeping shadows. . . .

You too, by now, have trembled with young Nate through the menacing horrors of that tale. You have felt the stimulus of terror—and liked that which you felt. It was a strong dose indeed—but it is the policy of TERROR TALES to provide stimulus only for the strong!

There will be more nerve-wracking, bloodchilling tales by Wyatt Blassingame in future issues. There will be a host of equally spine-tingling stories by other masters of the terror tale. For we cater not to the weak but to the strong! . . .

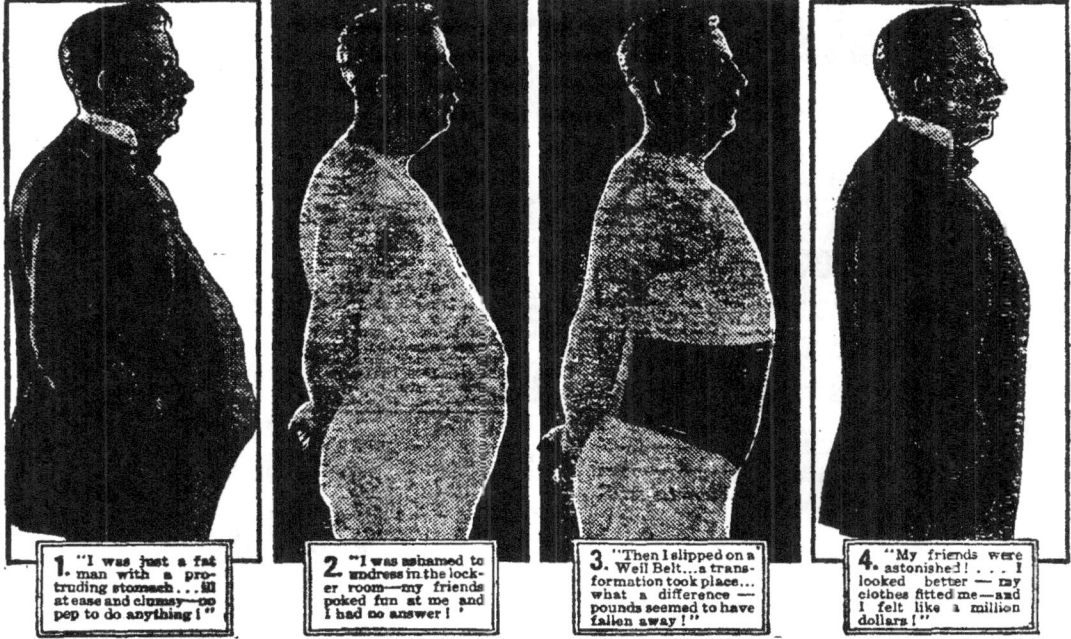
125

STOP YOUR Rupture Worries!

Learn About My Perfected Unique Rupture Invention!

Why worry and suffer with that rupture any longer? *Learn now about my perfected rupture invention.* It has brought ease, comfort, and happiness to thousands by assisting Nature in relieving and curing many cases of reducible hernia! *You can imagine how happy* these thousands of rupture sufferers were when they wrote me to report relief, comfort and cures! How would YOU like to be able to *feel* that *same* happiness—to sit down and write me such a message—a few months *from today?* Hurry — send coupon quick for Free Rupture Book, PROOF of results and invention revelation!

Mysterious-Acting Device Binds and Draws the Broken Parts Together as You Would a Broken Limb!

Surprisingly — continually — my perfected *Automatic* Air Cushions draw the broken parts together allowing Nature, the Great Healer, to swing into action! All the while you should experience the most *heavenly* comfort and security. *Look!* No obnoxious springs or pads or metal girdles! No salves or plasters! My *complete* appliance is feather-lite, durable, invisible, sanitary and CHEAP IN PRICE! Wouldn't YOU like to say "good-bye" to rupture worries and "hello" to NEW freedom . . . NEW glory in living . . . NEW happiness—with the help of Mother Nature and my *mysterious-acting* Air Cushion Appliances?

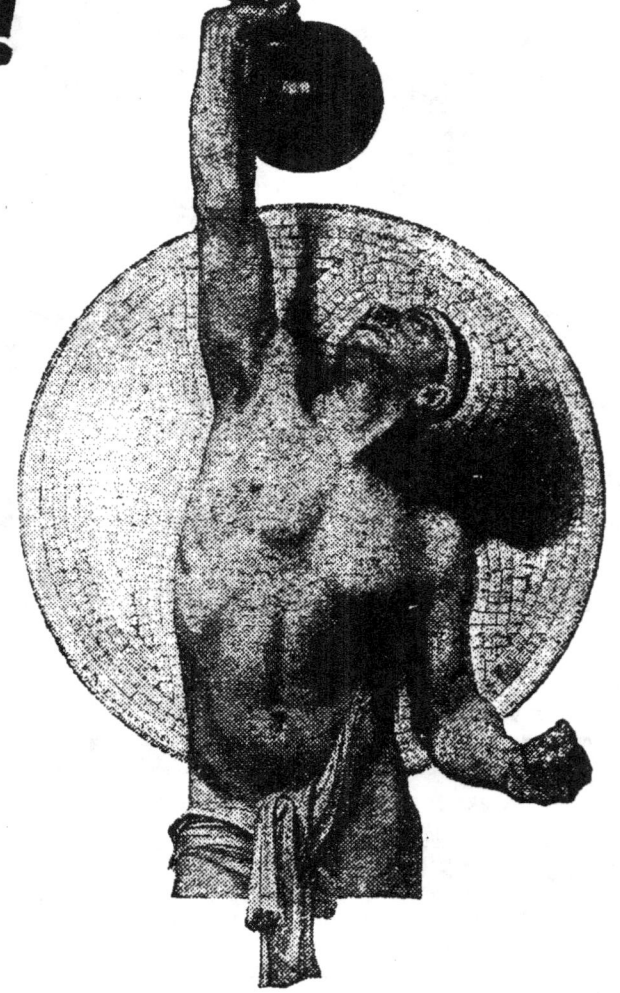

Rupture Book FREE!

PROOF!
Reports on Reducible Rupture Cases

"LIFTS 400 LBS.!"

"Have no further use for your Appliance as I'm O. K. Wore it a year. I now can lift 400 lbs., without any fear."—John L. Heiges, 635 W. Locust St., York, Pa

"CAN RUN UP HILL"

"I had a rupture about 14 years, then wore your Appliance for 8. It is about a year since I threw it away. I feel fine, gaining weight nicely. I can run up and down hill which I never could before." — Mr. J. Soederstrom, 1909 Trowbridge Ave., Cleveland, O.

Sent On Trial!

My invention is never sold in stores nor by agents. Beware of imitations! You can get it only from my U. S. factories or from my 33 foreign offices! And I'll *send it to you on trial.* If you don't like it — if it doesn't "work"—it costs you NOTHING. But don't buy now. Get the facts about it FIRST! Write me today. I'll answer in plain, sealed envelope with amazing information *free.* Stop Your Rupture Worries; *send coupon!*

BROOKS APPLIANCE CO.
173 State St.   Marshall, Mich.

www.ingramcontent.com/pod-product-compliance
Lightning Source LLC
Chambersburg PA
CBHW080913020726
47502CB00008B/2442